Gemini God

GEMINI GOD

GARRY KILWORTH

FABER AND FABER
LONDON ● BOSTON

First published in 1981
by Faber and Faber Limited
3 Queen Square London WC1N 3AU
Printed in Great Britain by
Willmer Brothers Limited, Rock Ferry, Merseyside

© 1981 by Garry Kilworth

British Library Cataloguing in Publication Data

Kilworth, Garry
Gemini God.
I. Title
823'.914[F]

ISBN 0-571-11661-2

For Robert Holdstock
    J. C. Meredith Scott
    June Hall
    Ken Bulmer
    and my godson, Luke Robert George Hall

Acknowledgements

Essex Worthies by William Addison (Phillimore and Company Limited)

Twins and Twin Relations by H. Koch (Chicago Press)

Twins and Supertwins by A. Scheinfeld (Chatto and Windus)

Town Fox, Country Fox by Brian Vesey-Fitzgerald (André Deutsch Limited)

The Book of Lists by David Wallechinsky, Irvine Wallace and Amy Wallace (Corgi)

Prologue

On 23 September 2096, the media informed its news-thirsty public that Captain Miro Alexander, commander of Earth's first starship, had discovered an inhabitable planet circling the star Wolf 359.

Petral Craven listened with only limited interest, since most of his attention was focused on his wife whom he could see on the other side of a glass screen. He could hear her too, through the communicator. She was giving birth to their first child.

"Relax now—don't strain. Let the rhythmonitor do its work," said an attendant.

"Using the transmission medium *fast light*," whispered Petral's wristband, "or, to give it the correct term, *accelerated photonstream*, we were informed this morning that a module from the starship *Dido* entered the oxygenated atmosphere of New Carthage and touched down successfully. First pictures show an extraordinary world . . ."

"Oh, ohhhhhhh!"

A head and pair of shoulders had appeared. One of the doctors moved in the way, obscuring Petral's view.

". . . New Carthage is a planet comparable in size to Mercury. It appears to be inhabited by an intelligent race of creatures that are, by necessity, nomadic. The side of New Carthage which is in daylight is unfortunately too hot for habitation. However, the planet has an extremely slow equatorial solar motion of, we are informed, one kilometre every six Earth days. Thus it is possible to stay on the dark side of the planet by periodically walking a few metres towards the night . . ."

Petral wiped the sweat from his brow as the baby dangled by its legs from the doctor's fist. What was it? A boy or a girl?

Why was he holding it the wrong way round? *Petral wanted to see his child.*

"The natives cultivate the dawn area and harvest the crops before their farm-strips creep out into the deadly sunlight. Thus they have been called *People of The Dawn Country* by Captain Alexander and his crew."

A boy! It was a boy! Praise God! Elaine was smiling at him. What was that?

"A name, darling? We still haven't chosen a name," she said.

She looked weak. Completely washed out. He thought quickly, searching his mind for the nearest name to his memory.

"Alexander!" he blurted out. "How do you like that?"

She lay back with a happy smile on her face.

"Alexander," she said. "Yes, I do like that."

PART ONE
People of the Angles

—having vertigo, you lie spread-eagled, face-upwards towards
   the pit of the sky
envying the safe trees with their roots roped to rocks
and the casual hawks pressing their backs against the wind,
the stone-still bats hanging blind in the caverns like
   stalactites
and the mole boring itself to sub-zero heights.

—having vertigo, you wonder not at the length and breadth,
   the span of space,
but how deep? how deep is the fall of the black shaft
   of the universe?
and you cling to the flat green meadow grass of the
   balled world
afraid to close your eyes in case the floor becomes
   a ceiling.

From 'The Long Drop Upwards' by Mathew Tse
   (Born: 2013 Died: 2060)

1   The Island

He felt unprotected, vulnerable. It was difficult to adjust to the sharp definition of the stars. Seeing them like this, with no translucent canopy between his eyes and their brightness, gave Alex some insight to Nicole's letters. He had found the tapes strange, difficult to analyse—possibly because he had been searching the words for half-hidden references concerning her feelings for him. They were, in fact, just descriptive accounts of her new life in the Outer Angles. Then the letters had stopped arriving. That would have been shortly after she had begun her work in earnest, whatever that work might be.

"Where are we?" Alex asked.

"Nearly there. . ."

Peter was driving the hummer very slowly. Alex had the impression Peter was a little afraid now that they had left London's boundaries, although there was no need to be. Possibly Peter felt the same way about the Angles as Alex did. There was a trace of latent malevolence in the way the mist hung above the marshes. They had both been outside the City into the country before, but this was different. This was not a Sunday jaunt to a picnic spot between Regions but a night drive into the flatlands of the east coast, an area of sparsely inhabited salt marshes. Alex could not understand the reasoning behind Nicole's desire to work in such dreary environs.

"There's a light," said Peter, his tone failing to hide the relief he felt. They had just passed Marker Post Five and were nearing their destination.

Peter slowed the hummer almost to a stop and both men peered through the windscreen into the darkness ahead. A dim yellowness, as fuzzy as a moon seen through a poorly focused lens, shone steadily from within the mist from about two kilometres away.

"That'll be the farmhouse, I'm sure," Alex said.

"I'll just drop you there, Alex, then return to the City. I have to be up early tomorrow . . ."

Alex turned to him in surprise.

"You said you'd stay the night. What's the matter?"

"Nothing, nothing. I just . . . well, I feel uncomfortable. It was all right back there, in the City, talking about it. But I hadn't considered the atmosphere out here. . ."

"The dampness?"

"Yes. Yes, the mist. It's not at all healthy—are you positive you want to stay? They don't even have mains power out here you know."

"Okay, have it your way. Abandon me," Alex replied, with just a trace of drama.

Peter said nothing. He really did seem worried.

They reached a single-storey sprawling farmhouse a few moments later and it seemed that Peter would have turned around and gone away before Alex had met the owners, if Alex hadn't stopped him.

"Wait a second, Peter. I won't be long."

After knocking on the door of the house, Alex waited as the damp air began to penetrate his oversuit. A small hatch in the door suddenly snapped open, startling him.

"What's this?" asked someone from the other side. It was a male voice, and a pair of eyes regarded him steadily.

"Alex Craven," he replied, feeling rather foolish. He felt he should be shaking a hand or something while the introductions took place. "I sent you a written letter—about a month ago. You said you could put me up."

"It's him," said the voice again. The eyes stayed on his face although he was obviously speaking to someone in the room behind him.

There was the sound of a bolt sliding and then the door swung open. Alex was confronted by a bearded man about two-thirds his height—and Alex was not particularly tall—wearing a robe of some peculiar patchwork design. The eyes seemed to glare rather than merely appraise.

"Have you got luggage?"

Peter had placed Alex's cases quietly behind him and as

Alex turned Peter said, "See you soon, Alex. Shall I tell Lila where you are—if I'm asked, that is?"

Alex ignored this question. Peter knew the answer to it anyway.

"You're not staying then?"

"No, no. I'd better be getting back. Alice would prefer me to get back tonight."

"Well, don't surprise her." Alex grinned in an attempt to lighten the mood of their parting.

Peter merely frowned. "No, of course not. I'll call her when I reach the limits. Take care—and give my love to Nicole."

"I'll do that, Peter—and thanks. For bringing me here, I mean."

"Okay."

Peter climbed back into the hummer, which still had the motor running, and slid out of the yard. Alex had not realized before tonight what a coward Peter was. He watched the vehicle's lights drift over the fields towards one of the tall illuminated marker posts that had been their guides.

The man Alex believed to be his host had already picked up his cases and carried them into the house. Alex followed him into the first room and closed the door behind him.

"Pleased to meet you."

Another man, much taller than the first but no less bearded, held out a thick red hand for him to shake. Alex did so.

"Mr Polgrove?" said Alex, realizing his first assumption had been a mistake. The man before him had the air of an owner about him.

"S'right. This is Jamie, my uncle. He lives with us." He indicated the other man who seemed as young, or rather as old (since they were both white-haired), as his nephew.

"My wife, Rita." He spoke her name as if he rarely used it.

A small, muscular woman with cropped hair bobbed a smile from behind Polgrove.

"You found us then?" she said.

"I don't think we would have done if your lights had not been on. Unfortunately we started out late and by the time we reached Marker Post Five, it was dark."

She nodded. "Sit down then, sit down. Jamie will take your

things to your room. We don't have many visitors here—not any more. One or two nature people—for birds and things—two summers ago. But nobody in the autumn before."

"But you are a recognized guest house?" Alex said, a little alarmed.

"Oh yes. We're that all right," replied Polgrove. "It's just that people don't seem to want to come any more. Out this way, I mean. Not just to Mrs Polgrove's." Not Rita. *Mrs Polgrove.*

They stood looking at one another while Jamie dealt with the luggage. Finally he returned.

"Cases in your room," he said.

"Where does your power come from?" Alex pointed to the glow-lamp.

Jamie answered. "There's a power station out past the Nose." He pointed vaguely towards the window. "We run a cable from her. The waves do it—moving those floats up and down."

"Ocean power?"

"That's it," said Polgrove. "S'there for the ships to recharge from. Several houses round here use it."

Without thinking, Alex said, "Isn't that illegal?"

There followed a terrible silence while they stared at him, their faces inscrutable. His heart pounded in his chest. He was dealing with primitive people. He realized he would have to choose his words with care in future.

Finally, Mrs Polgrove asked if Alex would like some food. *Real food,* she emphasized. Being used to factory-farmed synthetics Alex knew he would have to be careful about the local home-grown produce. His doctor had warned him that the richness of it might upset his digestion, so he declined, having eaten before setting out, hoping to put off the moment of truth for as long as possible. Making his excuses, Alex said he would like a short walk before retiring. Polgrove nodded and opened the hinged door for him.

"We shan't be long before bedding down," Polgrove said.

Alex nodded.

"Is there—am I likely to encounter anything dangerous?"

he asked, stepping outside. In all truthfulness all he wanted to do was get a few breaths of air and recover his composure a little. He also had a headache, which refused to be ignored, just above his right eye.

"No, but don't go too far. Some of 'em get lost in the marshes." Then he closed the door.

By "them" Alex supposed he meant the tourists that stayed at the house. Alex had no intention of doing a cross-country walk in the middle of the evening, so there was little fear of that happening.

Looking around him there was nothing but blackness, with one or two more small lights in the distance. Smells wafted around him, thick and heavy. Some of them were even recognizable, especially that of the ozone. They had an atmosphere like that in the City—artificial, of course, but who could tell the difference? There was a salty taste to the air and the night seemed to be alive with sounds. Birds in the reeds? All his senses, bar that of touch, were finding it difficult to tune into the new surroundings. The rhythms of the country, though not unpleasant, were out of harmony with those of the man from the City.

He looked upwards, and immediately felt giddy. The stars were up there, swimming around their courses, and he had to clutch the side of the house for support. The cool brickwork was solidly comforting. All his twenty-seven years of life until then had been spent in one or other of the self-governing city states into which civilized Britain was divided. The enclosed cities were loosely connected, in a political sense, by a Federal Council which met annually at York. Physically, the states each controlled a region of countryside which ringed their city boundaries and were connected by an enclosed network of railways. The shrinking population of Britain, like most countries, withdrew from sprawling suburban and country areas into its main bodies, the cities. The human race had lost interest in itself. One day its numbers would drop below the critical level.

One or two day trips to the "outside" had satisfied his curiosity at a very early age and, from fourteen onwards until now, Alex had used the tubeways to cross from Region to Region. It was going to be hard to adjust to the openness, the depth of the sky.

There was a poem written by Mathew Tse which Nicole used to recite to him called "The Long Drop Upwards". He knew the last few lines by heart, she had read it so often.

—having vertigo, you wonder not at the length and breadth,
    the span of space,
but how deep? how deep is the fall of the black shaft
    of the universe ...

In his closet flatlet, protected and held safe by layer upon layer of metal and plastic, the lines had meant nothing to Alex. Out here, dizzy with the nothingness that fell away above him, he knew exactly what Tse had meant. Some of Alex's friends had trained to be astronauts—others had emigrated to colonies located on planets of the solar system. One had even been to New Carthage. Alex's narrow upbringing had, to a certain extent, helped to define the limits of his desire to travel. The Outer Angles was foreign enough for most tastes.

Something barked nearby. The sound was cold and harsh, making his skin prickle with apprehension. He went inside straight away and Jamie showed him to his room: a stone cell with white-washed walls. However, the bed was soft and comfortable and he soon fell asleep, dreaming of the metamorphosis of townships into a strange wilderness men had once called East Anglia.

Alex woke the following morning with Mrs Polgrove looming over his face. She offered him a hot drink.

"And I've eggs for your breakfast—fresh from the run. They're still warm."

"I'll have some bread and . . . an egg," he replied. She left him to dress.

Looking out of the window, he saw Polgrove and Jamie moving around a muddy yard, apparently engaged in farming tasks. The land below the yard sloped away very gradually to some creeks in the distance. There was little water in them but the mud gleamed wet and grey. Alex guessed the tide was on the ebb. Several river mouths fanned out to cut the area of the coast into a network of tidal backwaters. It was difficult terrain to cross longitudinally.

Mrs Polgrove called him and he went to face the egg. In fact, it was not at all bad, having been scrambled into a yellow aerated mess, but he found the bread soft, pulpy and barely digestible.

After eating Alex thanked her and said that would be fine until the evening. She shrugged and left him alone. Possibly she had chores to complete.

The objective in coming to the Angles was to find Nicole. Alex decided it was best he accomplished that as soon as possible. Going out into the yard he found it had rained during the night and everywhere was wet. Underfoot, the ground was soft and slippery.

"Mr Polgrove," he said, as he approached his host.

"Mornin'." Polgrove was hammering a stake into the ground and Alex could see the power behind each swing was considerable. The beard on his cheeks and chin glittered with droplets of perspiration.

"Mr Polgrove, do you know how I can get to Feerness? It's an island around here somewhere—but I'm told you can walk out to it at low tide."

"The broomway."

"What? I'm sorry. . ."

"The broomway. There's poles topped with brushwood alongside a 'hard' going out the island. See that bank?" He pointed towards the creeks. There was a mound of grass-covered earth winding away from them.

"Yes."

"Well that's the sea wall. You walk along 'top and you'll come to the broomway. The tide's not long out so if you want to go today, you'd best do it now. Mind," he said in a warning tone, "if you take too long you'll be in trouble. The tide comes in faster than you can run across mud—hard or no."

He looked quizzically at Alex and then asked the question Alex had been expecting.

"Why d'you want to go there? If you don't mind me askin'."

There was no reason to keep the truth from him.

"I'm looking for my . . . for a girlfriend. She works there—a place called Manston House."

"Ah!" Polgrove continued to stare at him.

"Do you know anything about it?" Alex asked casually.

"She a teacher is she? Of school or some such?"

"I think that's what she said she was doing, yes."

This was a direct lie but it appeared to suit the farmer because he merely nodded and gave Alex another "Ah!"

Then he added, "Lots of children there—in that place. Used to be a hotel of sorts, many years ago, when Jamie was a lad. Then it closed and they only just opened it for these people. Orphanage, I suspect. *Twins* though."

"Twins? What do you mean?"

"All twins—the children. Every damned one of 'em's half a set. Every damned one." He shook his head as if he doubted the truth of his own statement. "Funny kind of thing to do. Open an orphanage for twins, out here amongst us stems."

"Yes. I suppose it is," Alex replied. Then, to change the subject, he asked the farmer, "What was that word? Us what?"

"What d'you mean; stems? That's us. That's what the tourists call us." He looked Alex directly in the eye. "I suspect it's because we *stem* from real farming people."

"I expect it is. Well, I'll see if I can cross to the island. I'll see you later." Alex hesitated then asked, "There's no transport, is there? Out to the island?"

Polgrove didn't take the hint. Instead, he shook his head, and added, "Not any that you could use, coming from the City."

Alex wasn't sure what was meant by that but decided not to pursue it. He left the farmer pinning some netting to the posts and grumbling about foxes. Alex wondered which of those noises he had heard the previous night was a fox, and he shuddered. It was a reminder that the countryside around the farm was a wilderness and he hurried over turf-sprung fields to the sea wall.

On top of the earth wall the sea air hit him hard in the chest. It was cold, damp and very pungent. Two metres below him was the mud—a grey shining monster that disappeared beyond a vaguely—near horizon swallowed by mist. There were shallow pools of water out on the flat, which lay black and oily now that the early morning sun had retreated behind clouds. Alex walked along the watershed of the man-made ridge until he came to a stone-and-earth ramp.

Two lines of poles stretched out into the mud, forming a channel approximately three metres wide. Hatting each pole was a bunch of tied twigs. This was obviously Polgrove's "broomway hard". A path of witches' brooms. He shuddered. This particular part of the coast had once been the haunt of witches—mostly male witches that had once lived in the now abandoned villages in and around the marshes.

Alex began walking but found that, despite the hard surface beneath the broomway, his feet still sank several centimetres into the covering silt and the going was slow. There was a large, long-necked bird that periodically let out a guttural, croaking "rronk" before disappearing into the mist ahead of him. Every so often it reappeared, saw that Alex was still approaching, and sounded off again before leaving. It was almost as if it were leading him in some way, rather than Alex coincidentally following in its footsteps.

His thoughts left the bird after a while and he began pondering on those events which had led him to the wilds of the Angles on a day when he should have been comfortably installed in his small office awaiting calls upon his services.

Exactly two months previously, Alex's father, Petral Craven, had died at the age of seventy-five years. It had been shortly after his father's cremation that Alex met Nicole.

Nicole Toupe was tall with very black shoulder-length hair and a tanned skin. Alex had invited her to lunch and was told over the meal that she had been born of Panamanian parents. He felt at the time that her voice might irritate him if he spent too long with her: it had an underlying note of dissatisfaction, though he had no idea why. It was her large, damp brown eyes that attracted him, however, and though she was not at all encouraging, Alex had asked her to meet him again. She had agreed, somewhat reluctantly, and over the next two weeks Alex had pressed his company on her until finally he had asked her to live with him.

"You're married," she had said, flatly.

"You don't have to marry me. Look, I'm twenty-seven—you're thirty-one. We're not children. Most people don't even *want* to get married these days."

"My background is old-fashioned. We still believe in marriage in Panama."

"If you loved me enough, Panama wouldn't matter."

Her lips had drawn together in a thin, dark line. "I haven't said I love you at all."

Not long afterwards she had quit her job in Head Office and the next time he had heard from her, it had been by mail. The tape had been delivered by hand to one of the boundary Mail Transfer Offices. She had taken a position outside the City, at Feerness in the Outer Angles. It was a job with Government Communications Research and she had no wish to return to London.

Then followed a series of letters containing information about the Angles, though not about her job. Alex's questions concerning her feelings for him went unanswered. In the meantime he had applied for a divorce from Lila. Unfortunately his wife saw no reason to let him go since it was very fashionable to be married to a Government Official. His dull existence gave her an anchor during those times she became depressed and needed a temporary rest from promiscuity. Foolishly he had continued to let her use him as her confidant (Alex was lonely too) and nearly always on those occasions, they made love. Alex was the one stable influence in Lila's life and he knew she would not let him go easily. A couple had to remain apart for three months to obtain a divorce and Lila had always managed to persuade Alex to see her before that period elapsed. Well, that was over. Even Lila would not follow him to the Outer Angles, he thought.

"Rronk! Rronk!"

Damn that bird. It was still there, somewhere, in the mist. The mud seemed to stretch endlessly ahead.

Suddenly he heard a small noise behind him and turned just in time to see a shape bearing down on him which made him step backwards in fright. It was a man riding a large creature, which, once his panic had subsided, Alex recognized as a horse. Protruding from the man's head was a silver cross.

The horse itself was splattered with mud along its black flanks and its nostrils were wet and streaming. It snorted, shying when Alex made a sharp movement, and took one or two steps backwards.

"I'm sorry," Alex started to say.

The rider merely glared at him. He was a youth with short, unevenly cut hair. His shoulders were broad and a dark red cloak hung from them and flowed over the horse's rump. The top half of his body was clothed in a tunic and below he wore leggings, criss-crossed with leather thongs.

Alex stepped aside as the youth quietly urged his mount forward. There was no saddle of any kind and his heels kicked into the bare ribs of the giant animal. This was obviously Polgrove's "transport". As they passed, man and beast, Alex saw that the cross belonged not to the youth's head but to a weapon—a huge sheathed sword—that was strapped to the youth's back. Soon they were gone, swallowed up in the mist that had muffled the sound of their approach.

Annoyed with himself for being afraid but at the same time intrigued with the reason for the youth's strange clothes, Alex pressed on towards the island. Some of the brooms were missing their brushwood tops at this point but they still showed the path very clearly. By this time his legs were aching quite seriously. Alex was not used to walking and had overestimated his own capabilities. There was no choice, though. Presumably the tide would be coming in soon and he would find himself wading the last few metres. When Alex had looked at the chart in his office, Feerness had been three kilometres from the mainland. He felt he had walked twice that distance already.

The long-necked bird returned to annoy him. However, the distraction was probably good for him in that it did to some extent take his mind away from his aching limbs.

"Thank God we don't have birds in the City," Alex said aloud.

His feet suddenly felt cold and he looked down at them. Water! While the day-dreaming had taken his mind away from his complaining muscles, it had also taken the sting out of his urgency. The tide was flooding in from the left of the broomway in long, sweeping rays. Soon he would be cut off from the island. The pull around his feet of the incoming tide was strong enough to hinder his progress and panic began running loose in his chest.

"Help!" he shouted. "Somebody help!"

All he received by way of reply was a distant *"rronk"*. Grasping one of the brooms Alex attempted to climb it but his hands merely slid down the algae-covered wood. Then he saw that the green slime on the poles reached to at least half a metre above his head. The water would be deep enough to drown him!

Alex could not swim and anyway he had no illusions about staying alive in such cold conditions. He would die of exposure very quickly.

"Oh God!" he cried. "Please, somebody!"

The water had reached his knees and underfoot the silt was being swept away. He stumbled forward, crying out for aid that might be too far distant to hear. Falling, he swallowed some of the foul water and had to splash to his feet to prevent being swept away between the brooms.

"Help!" he screamed.

His eyes were stinging with the salt water and he heard the sound of someone splashing towards him.

"Here! Here!" Alex cried, wiping his eyes on his sleeve.

He had hardly let out the second "here" when he felt himself wrenched from the water and swung bodily over the warm back of a sweating beast. He was in the humiliating position of being draped over the rump of a horse. Nevertheless, Alex clung to the animal as it jolted him up and down. It cracked his chin on its belly several times while trying to keep its balance on the shifting mud that covered the broomway hard. Finally they reached the shore and Alex slid panting and groaning to the stony beach below.

"Didn't think you'd make it", said a calm voice from above him, "when I saw you before. Too slow, you was."

Looking up he saw the youth who had passed him earlier.

"Then why", Alex remonstrated ungraciously, "didn't you come back for me sooner? I nearly drowned out there."

"No, you didn't do that. You just got wet—and it were deserved. Ambling along as if you was on a stroll. Even stems have a respect for the broomway. See *you* get a little before you go back."

"Who the hell . . . ?" Alex was about to protest in full when the youth suddenly rode away leaving him feeling very foolish and not a little angry.

2 The Institution

Nicole was teaching her particular charges, the Lo twins, in the yellow room. It was John Strecker's idea of a joke that the yellow room should be allocated to the Chinese twins.

Rather than bother with numbers, John Strecker had had the doors to the rooms painted in different plain colours. He believed this would enable the infant inmates to recognize their location more easily in the large house.

Strecker was the Project Leader in the Manston House experiments, and the only adult male. He might have been labelled a chauvinist by his female subordinates, except that he was not. He was simply an old-fashioned autocrat. Had there been any male members on the team, he would have treated them no differently. The rest of the team at Manston tolerated his dictatorial attitude because he was also straight-forward, sincere and very hard-working.

"This is a blue ball," read Nicole to the two four-year-old girls. She was giving them some early-evening lessons before they went to bed. They sat cross-legged in front of her, their faces expressionless. She passed the card to On Lo. "Can you read it for me, On? Show me the words with your finger."

On Lo took the word-picture card and her pretty face frowned in concentration.

"This is a *blue* ball," she said slowly, pointing to each word as she pronounced it. Ti Lo looked over her shoulder. They were really very pretty, thought Nicole. Both girls had short black hair and small pouting mouths, but their dark eyes were large and shone like sea-wet pebbles.

Nicole recovered the card and took out a new one.

"The child-ren like to play ball," she recited.

There was a buzz from behind and the door slid into its

recess. Looking round, Nicole saw John Strecker in the doorway.

"Sorry to disturb you during lessons, Nicole. You have a visitor—I left him in my office. You can talk there if you wish."

"Who is it?" she asked, her mind running over the names of half a dozen close friends.

"Says his name is Alex Craven. Anyway, he's down there. I'll look after the children."

Nicole was taken aback and for a second the name did not register. When it did, she tried to read John's face, looking for the annoyance that she knew must lie beneath his unruffled expression. The project, while not officially a secret, was better kept at a low profile. The media would make a great fuss over experiments involving children. It was one of the reasons for their remote location.

"I'll speak to him . . . John?"

"Never mind." There was a trace of irritation evident in his features now. "We'll talk about it later," he said.

She left him with the twins and used the stairs to the floor below. John Strecker's office was next to the common-room and she entered without pausing in her stride. The door slid shut behind her.

"Just what do you want, Alex?" she said in a voice loaded with suppressed fury. She knew her anger plainly showed despite her previous intentions to keep herself under control. She had wanted to appear calm and in full command of herself.

He stood up and put out his hands towards her.

"Nicole? I just . . . I wanted to see how you were. You stopped answering my letters."

His hair was lank and his oversuit wet and creased. Her anger disappeared almost immediately.

"What happened to you?" she asked. This time she felt concern.

"I fell in the sea," he said simply, looking down at himself. "Like a fool I misjudged the tide on the broomway. . ."

"You *walked* across the broomway?" she said, incredulously.

"Yes, and I was saved from drowning by a strange youth

riding a horse. John Strecker has just explained that the boy must have been on his way back from a pageant. I understand a local hero called Sweyn of Essex has an annual festival in his honour. . ."

"I'm not sure. Yes, I do remember some of the stems saying something about it recently . . . Anyway, he saved you? The boy, I mean."

"Lifted me off my feet by the scruff of my neck and dumped me on the beach. I've never been so humiliated . . ."

She laughed at this and, despite her previous resolve, she began relaxing.

Alex said, "I'll have to ask Polgrove—he's my landlord—about this Sweyn thing. Anyway, how are you? You look well enough."

Nicole smiled.

"I am. Never felt more healthy in my life. You City people don't know what you're missing." Then she paused. "Look, Alex, you shouldn't have come you know. John, my boss, won't like it at all . . ."

The door slid open and a voice said, "John, I . . . oh, I'm sorry, Nicole. I'll come back later."

"John's with the Lo twins in the yellow room, Judy," replied Nicole, half turning.

"Okay. Thanks." The woman left immediately.

Nicole continued. "As I was saying, Alex, this is a Government project and although it's not supposed to be a closed box without windows, it's sensitive. . ."

"I don't intend running off at the mouth, Nicole. I merely wanted to see you. I . . . I've left for good. She won't follow me out here."

"Seeing me is one thing. I don't want you to stay, Alex."

He looked crestfallen at these words and again Nicole hated herself for being so blunt.

"Perhaps", she said, "it would be easier if I explained why I'm here. Then you might understand. You will keep it to yourself though?"

"Of course. I could find out anyway—through official channels."

The words came out too quickly. She smiled. "You've already tried that, haven't you? Anyway, as you know, we're experimenting with a new kind of communication. . ."

He interrupted. "What about these twins? Why all the children?"

"They're part of it. In fact they *are* the experiment. We need a very fast means of communication, and the twins. . ."

Alex groaned.

"Don't tell me," he said. "Telepathy. They're not trying that *again*?"

Nicole narrowed her eyes in annoyance. Alex could be so stupid at times. He always thought he had the answer before she had even formed the question. There were those unpleasant arguments (which he called "debates") over the relevance of Mathew Tse's poetry.

"Not telepathy, Alex. Just listen, don't be so all-knowing. You're not, you know—you're a plain, simple man."

He stared at her for a moment, then nodded slowly.

Nicole continued. "Not telepathy. Empathy. The empathic relationship that exists between twins. This is empathy in the popular sense of the word. *Closeness*."

"I don't understand. How can you transmit and receive messages using . . . empathy?"

He made the word sound distasteful.

"It's not necessary, for our purposes, to receive messages. All we need is an indication—a *feeling*—that registers within the second twin. The child herself can tell us what emotions her twin is undergoing."

"But what good will that do?"

"It'll be a signal that an event has occurred. Look, what would happen if a fire started in a building? What would you do?"

"Personally? I would operate the manual extinguishing equipment—if it hadn't already begun to function automatically."

"Then what? How would you warn the inmates of the building?" she pressed.

"By setting off the alarm?"

"Right. But you haven't sent a message—in the sense you mean. All you've done is alert the occupants by sending out a signal which they will recognize as a warning that something is happening."

"I see," he said. "No, no. I *do* see. This is some kind of telemetry system you're working on. Is that it? What's it for?"

"New Carthage," Nicole replied with some pride in her voice.

At that moment the door slid open and John Strecker entered.

"Sorry to disturb you folks," he said in the bland way he had with visitors. "Class is over for the day, Nicole. Judy has taken your twins to the dining hall. Perhaps you'd like to transport Mr Craven back across the broomway in the hummer. We don't want him caught a second time."

"The tide will be in by now," said Nicole.

"Well, across the water then—if it's not too rough that is." He nodded sharply at Alex. "Nice to have met you. You will keep this to yourself, won't you?" He failed to keep the anxious tone out of his voice and Nicole winced inwardly. She was in for a nasty time with John later.

Alex smiled at him. "Of course. I'm a communications man myself. Nicole and I used to work for the same department."

Strecker, about to leave, paused in the doorway.

"Oh, what's your discipline?" he asked, the concern having been replaced by interest. God, no, thought Nicole, *this can't be happening.*

"I'm a monitoring expert. Non-executive of course. Advisory."

"I see. And what are you doing at present? You on a job in the vicinity, or what?"

Alex made a casual gesture with his hands.

"I'm on leave-of-absence for an indefinite period. My own choice—I haven't been a naughty boy or anything like that. Truth is," he said, "I came looking for Nicole. We were close at one time."

It *is* happening, thought Nicole. She blurted out, "But we're just good friends . . ." and then realized how inane that sounded. Looking at John Strecker's face, she could see he was not really interested in what she had to say. It was Alex who held his attention.

30

"So you're free at the moment?"

Alex made another depreciating gesture.

John Strecker stepped back inside his office and the door closed behind him. He walked across to the window and looked out.

"I expect Nicole's told you what we're doing here?"

Nicole desperately tried to signal to Alex but either he failed to understand or he was deliberately ignoring her.

"A little. You're working on a telemetry system for New Carthage—which involves using twins."

"The empathy—the closeness—that exists between identical twins," breathed John Strecker.

He turned to face Alex and Nicole once more.

"You understand the set-up on New Carthage? No? Well, basically it's this. New Carthage has a *day* equivalent to two and a half centuries on Earth. Its orbit time around its sun is almost synchronous with a single revolution on its axis—but not quite. Thus, if you stood on one spot your evening on New Carthage would last approximately sixty of our years. Martinis on the balcony at sunset could turn out to be a lifetime's debauch. More to the point, our own colony there, Stingray Raft, has to keep on the move to stay out of direct sunlight. So it's shaped like a huge wing and it hovers in the dawn, just above the planet's surface, trailing a long tail back into the day to obtain power. The natives are primitives—somewhere between man and ape. We had hoped, I know, to find an equal in the galaxy. An equal or a race more advanced than our own. . ."

"Technologically," said Alex.

"And philosophically. Still, we didn't and our method of travel has limits. We've been beyond Wolf 359 but . . . What I'm really getting at is the fact that both natives and the colony share a common way of life—a nomadic existence. So far they have been sufficiently uninterested in one another not to come into conflict. The gin, as you know, are sleek creatures—a little like cheetahs in their build except that they occasionally stand on their hind legs. Should there be trouble, however, it would be extremely difficult for Earth to send timely help to the colony. Even using fast light it takes a message four months real time to reach Earth. Then there's the return journey of the ship to consider—another four months. What we really need is instant communication—or rather, in the absence of that, an instantaneous warning."

"And you think the twins will provide you with that?" interrupted Alex.

Nicole could tell by his expression that he was as fascinated as she had been, when John had first approached her with the idea.

"There are many case histories", replied Strecker, "that provide us with evidence of instant communication between twins. Twin children are conceived in the womb at the same time. They share the same bloodstream and exactly the same pre-birth environment. This may seem like stating the obvious but what I'm trying to put across is that I believe twins to be one person—a single spirit, if you like—continued in two bodies.

"Take the case of the Bellini twins. The children were separated at birth by a tragedy in the family and went to live in different parts of the world—one in Italy, the other in the USA. At twenty-seven years of age Marco Bellini was admitted into an American mental hospital. He was suffering from schizophrenia. Although there had been no contact between the twins for some years, the authorities thought Frederico Bellini might be able to help his brother and set about tracing him. . ."

John Strecker paused, Nicole knew, to allow the significance of what he was about to say to have its full effect.

"They found Frederico in a Swiss institution. He'd been admitted just one month before his brother and was a victim of the same mental disorder. It's not a coincidence. There is a name for it—'folie à deux'."

Alex nodded.

"And there are lots of similar cases?"

"Dozens," said Strecker, his eyes bright with enthusiasm. "The libraries are full of them. There are those who knew the instant their brother or sister had died—that's pretty common. Or have been involved in an accident, tragedy or some deep emotional stress. Those are the sort of things we are working on."

"You see, *telepathy*, as you're probably aware, involves point-to-point communication with a physical path between. Mind waves. Waves have to *travel* and travel involves *time*. New Carthage is a long way away—we can't afford to take time. We need *instant* communication. . ."

"You've already used those words several times. You've convinced me. Now what? Why are you telling me all this?"

Nicole said drily, "As if you didn't know. He's going to offer you a job, of course."

John Strecker sat back on his desk and folded his arms.

"She's right. I think I am. I could arrange it with your boss . . ."

"I don't have a *boss* as such. If I want to do it, I merely have to submit a recommendation to the Minister. He decides whether it is worth my while."

"We've *all* got bosses," Strecker said. "Think about it. We're going to do some tests soon. What I would like you to do is monitor the path between the twins—we have six test pairs—to see whether there is any sort of, let's say *physical path* for want of a better phrase, that's set up between them. Myself, I very much doubt it. I would prefer it to be an experience simultaneously *shared* between them rather than a transmission from one to the other. Maybe you can't do it, though?"

"If there's a field or transmission of any kind, I can find it. It'll depend on the strength of the power. My instruments will measure electrical brain waves—we've investigated genuine telepathy and registered a response—but this may be entirely different. Entirely new—if anything at all."

Nicole interrupted them, saying she had a lot of work to do before the day was over. Could she give Alex a quick tour of the institute then drive him home? She knew she had spoken tartly and both men looked at her in surprise. Then John Strecker nodded and Alex followed her through the door.

"What's the matter?" he asked, as they climbed the stairs.

Without thinking, she rounded on him.

"You know very well what's the matter. I suppose you had all this worked out?"

Her face felt hot as she waited for his answer.

"I haven't said I'll take the job yet, Nicole," he said coolly. "I'm not even sure I want it—and anyway the Minister has a say in what I do. I may be in love with you but I wouldn't make a recommendation on the strength of *that*. I have some integrity left."

She stared at him dumbly for a few moments and then managed to mumble an apology. Strangely enough, she believed him. A man who desired a woman's body might be willing to lie and possibly put his reputation at risk—she had known that to happen—but a man in love retained a certain starchy code of honour. She was well aware that sexually there was little about her which would infatuate a man: her breasts were too small and her hips too large. She had been secretly a little glad of that because it meant that any prolonged advances were genuine. But genuinely what? Did she expect them to fall in love with her mind? Her face had been described as "beautiful and aristocratic", but how long would that last? She was almost thirty-one years old.

"This is the yellow room," she said. "My room—and the twins'. Their names are On Lo and Ti Lo, and, to all intents and purposes, I am their mother."

He looked at her sharply.

"Where's their real mother?"

"They don't have one. That is, they were 'genetically engineered' as I believe it's termed, and produced in an artificial uterus. The sperm and ovum came from donors, of course, so they do have real parents of a sort, though they'll never know them."

"Isn't all this a little cruel?" His eyes were expressionless as he asked the question.

"Possibly—no, not really. I'm a good mother to them, and it's best they don't have a father. Optimum closeness between twins is produced with a single parent in her early thirties—it's supposed to be the age at which a woman has the most affinity with her children—and monozygotic girl twins."

"Monozygotic?"

"One ovum fertilized by two spermatoza. Identical twins. We do have some fraternal twins in the test and control groups but no one expects too much of them. The male-female and male-male sets provide healthy playmates for the girl sets if nothing else."

Alex frowned, looking around the small classroom.

"It all sounds a bit cold-blooded to me. I suppose you know what you're doing, though?"

"No, I don't suppose we really do," she replied, surprising herself as much as him with the reply. "But if I wasn't here, someone else would be and I think I can do as well, if not better, than most. I've always wanted children. And I do love them both."

He studied her face for a few moments and then said, "I'm sure of that."

Nicole showed him the twins next. They were tucked up in bed and looked, as they always did, like two small painted dolls. She kissed them goodnight, taking away their drawing books. These she gave to Alex and asked him to look through them later.

"You'll see what level they're at. They're really quite bright, you know."

He nodded, smiling.

"Don't they have a visiphone out here?" he asked.

She told him they did, but reading, writing and drawing were encouraged as much as watching. The old arts were considered as necessary as the new.

"But they can draw on the screen," he said, obviously puzzled.

"We like to see everything that they've drawn—or written. They can wipe a visiphone screen. It's necessary we have a record of their development through the conceptual stages."

Alex nodded but was plainly a little mystified by the teaching methods. It wasn't surprising, she thought, since both she and Alex had been taught by remotely situated teachers using "state of art" equipment and methods ranging from ultrasonic mind penetration to the brain-moulding techniques of Delacroen. One could be taught to write and draw without having to practise these arts. She knew the institute looked antiquated to Alex, but then he didn't have to stay after all. She hoped he wouldn't, in fact; it would complicate her life too much if he did decide to remain.

35

"Are you going to show me the rest of the building?"

"There are two hundred rooms in all. I don't think you want to see every one, do you?"

"No, of course not, but what about some of the staff? Do I get to meet any of them?"

She took him along to the common-room and introduced him to several of the other teacher-mothers resident at the establishment. Alex flirted with Odell, a blonde Nordic woman, but Nicole knew he was paying attention to Odell because she was exactly the opposite to herself in looks: large breasted with a milky complexion. It was a compliment in a way.

Afterwards she collected the hummer to drive him back to his lodgings.

As they followed the water-covered broomway back to the mainland, Alex reflected upon the day's events. He had set out intending to contact Nicole only to try to persuade her that his presence was not a threat to her new way of life. He merely wished to re-establish their correspondence through the medium of letter tapes. However, it now looked as if there was a chance of working beside her. The thought frightened him as much as it pleased him. It was a make-or-break situation. There would be no gradual courtship by mail as he had previously planned. She would either fall in love with him or grow sick to death with his persistence.

The mainland was a black grimace against the swiftly dying sky as they skimmed over the small waves. Occasionally a flock of birds would take to the air, their long necks reaching before them. He recognized them as belonging to the same family as the mocking spirit of the mists he had encountered earlier that day.

"Brent geese," explained Nicole, when he asked her if she knew what they were. He was silenced by her knowledge, not wanting to appear any more ignorant than he felt. However, as they neared the shore, flocks of smaller, black-and-white birds exploded from the salt creeks, and Nicole said, "Oyster catchers", without him even asking. He was ashamed to say he didn't know what oysters were, until a vague remembrance of a type of shellfish entered his mind. That made him feel a little happier with himself.

They arrived at the farm just as the darkness was about to complete its descent upon the Angles. A light was showing in a window of the house but there was no anxious face watching for Alex's return. Perhaps they were not concerned about the safety of a City dweller, a tourist?

"Okay, Nicole. I'll say goodnight here—see you later. Perhaps tomorrow?"

"Perhaps. Alex. . ."

"Yes?"

Her voice had an unusual softness to it.

"Don't let my presence at Manston influence your decision —one way *or* the other."

He smiled. "I'll try not to."

"I mean it, Alex. I . . . don't love you, you know."

"It doesn't matter," he replied, feeling a pang in his chest. It damn well did matter. It mattered a lot.

He waited until the hummer was out of sight before trying the door to the house. It was locked again.

"Hey! Polgrove?" he shouted. He knocked lightly.

The hatch slid back and Jamie's face appeared. Then the door was unlocked and Alex stepped inside. Polgrove's hand was poised over a steaming plate of food and Alex remembered he had not eaten all day.

Polgrove said, "So you nearly got yourself drowned, eh?"

Alex felt his heart sink. His foolhardiness was probably known all over the Angles by now.

"Yes. Silly of me. Who was the boy that saved me?"

"T'ant no boy. He's a man going on eighteen or more. Pagey's his name. Real stem that one. Lives in the thick of the marshes." It was Jamie who had answered him.

"What's this about a festival or pageant or whatever?" asked Alex, determined to change the subject.

Jamie said, "Sweyn's Day. He were a knight in the days of the kings. Long time ago that, but he were a farmer like us. A sheepman—biggest one ever." There was no mistaking the fervour in the voice of the little white-haired man standing before him and Alex realized that either these people had manufactured a local hero, or one of the clever ones had reached back into history and pulled one from the pack. The strange thing was that they needed a figurehead. They seemed such self-sufficient individuals; it was a wonder they even needed each other.

"Sweyn of Essex," said Polgrove through a mouthful of food. "You should've stayed with us today. We all visited the castle over at Hadley. Mrs Polgrove too. There was wrestling and such."

"Castle?"

"Was a ruin but my father and some of the others—Jamie's one—they built it up again, right as a tree."

Alex said, "You mean they received a restoration grant from the Government?"

Polgrove and Jamie both looked puzzled and Jamie replied, "Don't know about that. We just cut new stone and put it back as it was once. Kind of a market place see? We use it for gathering and to meet and think on what to do about the land, month on month. First Thursday of all the months'll find us there—and Sweyn's Day of course. No one missing on Sweyn's Day."

These people were deeper than Alex had first given them credit for and he began to reassess his earlier judgements. They were not just uneducated dirt-grubbers; it seemed they had a system which they talked over amongst themselves. They planned their way through the year.

Mrs Polgrove came into the room from the back of the house and said he looked terrible. She had hot water waiting so he could wash before his meal. He went into the kitchen and did as he was told, combed his hair, took off his oversuit and returned to the living-room tolerably clean. There was a meal of potatoes and bean hash waiting for him which he had to let cool before tasting. Surprisingly, it was not as bad as he had expected it to be.

Throughout the meal, he maintained a flow of light chatter with his landlord, telling him that he might stay for some time since he had been offered a job at Manston House.

"Of course," Alex said, "I might need to stay at the House

itself some of the time, but I'll still come here for the odd night—if that's all right with you."

"All right with us," replied Polgrove, swilling back some beer with obvious relish. "Though I can't see why you should want to."

Alex replied, "Because I want to know you all better. You're different from any people I've ever known."

Jamie laughed. "They all say that—the tourists. They think we're wild folk."

Alex nodded, smiling faintly. He accepted a glass of beer, found it bitter-tasting but finished it in order not to offend his hosts, then excused himself and went to his room.

As he undressed himself, he realized his whole body ached with fatigue. He had overeaten too, for which he would suffer during the night. While he was pulling down his shorts, Mrs Polgrove opened the door and without batting an eyelid, calmly handed him his oversuit. Luckily she left before confusion blossomed on his face.

Sticking out of the knee pocket of the suit were the drawing books of the Lo twins and he slid under the huge feather-filled bedcover, clutching the two notepads.

There were lots of crudely drawn pictures of people—some of them probably supposed to be Nicole and one obviously John Strecker, the nose being excessively long. Other sketches were of boats, toys, birds and all the things one might have expected a bright four-year-old to draw. It was in the middle of On Lo's book that Alex came across a drawing that made him sit up in bed with a jolt. It was not that the sketch was good, for, although there was some evidence of an adult's guiding hand, overall it was essentially childish. It was the repulsive way in which the creature was represented that sent chills crawling through his mind.

Despite the exaggerated length of the rolled ears, making them look like horns, and the unkempt fur which holograms usually showed as being sleek and well kept, Alex recognized the drawing as being a picture of a New Carthaginian native. A gin, as they were normally called.

It was the words beneath the portrait that made his mind prickle with the unpleasant feeling of having stumbled on something ugly, something out of synchronization with life as it should be. In thick, snaking letters, they read simply: BOGEY MAN.

From somewhere in the house, Alex's light was extinguished and his mind was left with an indelible image printed upon it for a restless hour or two. One of Tse's lines came to him at the point he met sleep:

> In the night, the magical foxes paused and passed
> like pieces of darkness looking for their slots.

3 A Professional Nuisance

Over the next few days, Alex helped Polgrove and Jamie around the farm. He needed time to think before confronting Nicole and he also wanted to consider carefully the post offered him by John Strecker. He had no doubt the Minister would approve his recommendation, especially if it were couched in the right terms.

The type of help he could give to the two stems, however, was obviously limited by his physical strength and his lack of knowledge. It seemed to afford the two farmers some amusement to answer what must have been to them very basic questions. Alex was careful to ask only essential queries: he was afraid they might tire of his curiosity very quickly.

On the fourth day after the visit to Feerness Island, Alex was leading a large bay horse to a meadow a kilometre from the farm. He still had not the courage to attempt to ride it, although Jamie had said the mare was very gentle.

As Alex threaded his way through paths marked by bouncing reeds, a strong wind funnelled its way between the gaps. An oversuit made for the City was only just proof enough against an early October wind. He would need to obtain some warmer clothes if he intended to stay until, or through, the winter.

The ducks were busy migrating in purposeful arrowheads, flying low over the marshes and rippling over any object in their path with the perfection of a single body. Alex never failed to be affected by the desolation of the flatlands of the Outer Angles. Not a tree, not a hill interrupted the hinterland within his line of sight.

Farther inland he knew there were two exceptions; the first was the rounded swelling known as Canewdon, and around to the south was Hadley Ridge, which shouldered the castle built by Jamie and his contemporaries. Alex was determined to visit this landmark as soon as possible.

Hot breath on Alex's neck reminded him he had a duty to carry out and he made his way along the bottom of the sea wall coaxing the mare to stay with him. In the pasture he chained the horse on a long length to a post Jamie had told him he would find there.

When he had finished his task he looked up and was surprised to see a man standing above him on the earthen wall. The visitor was obviously a city dweller: a pallid complexion was set with pale but intense eyes above a large hooked nose. For a second Alex felt strangely menaced. The man was absolutely still, as if waiting for Alex to do or say something which would release him from immobility. A key word? A magical gesture?

"Who are you?" asked Alex.

Still there was no movement. Just the short hair on the narrow head fluttering in the wind.

"Did you hear what I said? I asked you who you were. What are you doing here? This is Polgrove land."

"This land belongs to no one." The voice was as colourless as the apparition. "Common land."

Was this a ghost? Alex had heard the marshes were haunted. A week ago he would have laughed, but not now. Not after listening to the nocturnal sounds of the Angles for several nights.

"You *are* Alexander Craven?"

Alex cleared his throat. "Yes."

"Thank you," said the man, and began to walk away.

Alex's apprehension suddenly turned to anger. What the hell was the man doing, asking his name then walking away? It was plain rudeness.

"Hi! You. What's your name?"

The man paused.

"Pointless. You don't know me." Then he continued along the wall until he was just a black mark against the cloud-laden sky.

Alex was breathing heavily by the time he reached the farm. His annoyance with the stranger had made him step up his usual pace. He found Jamie turning over Mrs Polgrove's winter cabbage plot with a spade.

"Do you know of any other people from the City?" he asked the old stem. "Are there any visitors staying at neighbouring farms?"

Jamie looked as though he was thinking very hard. "Nope. An't heard of any."

"Hmm. Well, I've just seen someone—on the sea wall. He must be staying somewhere."

"Maybe he's from Feerness—at that orphanage place?"

Alex smiled and nodded. "Of course. That *must* be it. One of Nicole's people. Ill-mannered bastard if he was—unless he's put out because I'm here." A sudden thought occurred to him and a pang of jealousy followed close on its heels. Would Nicole take a lover without telling him? Of course, why not? He had no claim on her. Absolutely none at all. She could sleep with whom she pleased. *Except.* Except that Nicole was so damned moral. Hers had been a very narrow upbringing, by religious parents who instilled in their daughter a very real fear of Hell. She hadn't told him as much but it had not been difficult to read between the lines when she spoke of them.

No, Nicole was pure. Had to be. He *wanted* her to be, dammit, badly. But why, for godsakes? Why did he want a thirty-one-year-old virgin for a wife? She would hate him for deflowering her so late in life. Would despise his nightly insistence and believe him unstable and over-sexed. They would no doubt settle for a very strained relationship which would make their lovemaking a mixture of pretence, frustration and god-when's-this-going-to-end? They had their rewards, those unions. She would never entirely deny him and there would always be a childlike fondness, an affection on both sides. A clinging together for security. Holding hands beneath the sheets, forgiving one another for incompatible sins. To err is human and harmlessly exciting, thought Alex, provided you both did so in the same direction.

Still, he loved her and would take her despite his fears. It was *impossible* that Nicole had a lover. Those deep brown eyes were incapable of hiding a lie. Was he going to *ask* her?

He thought not. She would tear strips from him with her fingernails.

"What are you a-dreaming of, boy?" asked Jamie, staring intently into his eyes.

Alex snapped his attention back to the present.

"Nothing. Nothing really."

"Well, if that's nothing, don't let me think on it 'cause I like to feel happy in my last days."

Alex was surprised. "Why, where're you going?"

Jamie smiled through several missing teeth. "I'm going to die, boy, soon enough. That's where I'm going to. It's no' but a heartbeat's distance."

"You? You're a young man. Relatively."

"I'm old for a stem. We're not City people. We don't spend the last twenty-odd years in bed, soaked to the eyeballs with trash."

Alex knew he meant drugs. It was true. Recently most people were sustained beyond their normal span by the skilful use of narcotics. His own parents had been exceptional. They had rejected drugs.

> —having vertigo . . . you cling to the flat green meadow grass
>   of the balled world
> afraid to close your eyes in case the floor becomes
>   a ceiling.

Mathew Tse again. Damn the man. He was becoming part of life amongst the stems. It was not so much that he disliked Mathew Tse but that Nicole should be right *once again*. Or was it Nicole's self-satisfied attitude that annoyed him? In the main, he disagreed with the worship. Poets were men, like him. Alex preferred to remain with the old religions like straight Christianity, albeit a jaded—no, *faded*—religion. He could not, *would not*, deify an ordinary man just because that man had the gift of producing fine, philosophical words. Earth was ready for a new religion, he thought, when its occupants were reduced to reaching God through poets. He considered the choosing of a mortal—a dead poet, through whom all individual worship should be channelled to God—a cold-blooded method of prayer. Alex felt closer to God out here, in the fields and open countryside, than he ever had in a poet's house. God's hand was in a bird or a bush, not a symmetrical pile of bricks.

Alex assisted Jamie for an hour, raking where Jamie had dug, until the exercise made him feel quite hungry. He had become so used to stem food in the short time he had lived with them that he now looked forward to the meals. Except that potatoes were almost always on the menu and that particular vegetable was rather tasteless and textureless.

As the pair of them worked quietly together, Polgrove himself appeared, leading the mare Alex had tethered on the common land by the sea wall.

Polgrove's brow was ridged.

"Can't you do a job right, Mr Craven? I found her wandering all over the marshes. Thought I said to chain her?"

Alex replied, "I did tie her up. She must have pulled loose."

"She's never pulled loose afore."

Alex was puzzled. "Well, I certainly ... wait a minute." He turned to Jamie. "That man I mentioned. On the sea wall. Maybe he came back and released the horse?"

"Why would he do that?" asked Jamie.

A light was beginning to break through Alex's clouded thoughts.

"To annoy me. I've an idea he's someone sent by my wife— I've separated from her. She's done this once before. I wonder. . . ?"

Polgrove asked, "She hired a man to annoy you? Seems a bit silly."

"Not really," said Alex. "She's trying to chase me back to the City again. The man's a professional nuisance. He'll call himself a private detective, but his prime purpose is to make life uncomfortable for the victims of his clients. He'll make himself thoroughly obnoxious in an attempt to force me back to the City and my loving wife."

"If he starts letting my animals free, he'll have me to work with!" thundered Polgrove, showing Alex a huge, hairy fist.

"Then he'll just call the police and accuse us of assault," replied Alex, feeling uneasy since the situation had been caused by his presence. He wondered when Polgrove and Jamie were going to recognize that fact, and whether they would indeed begin to blame him.

Jamie shook his white head.

"Police don't mean too much out here," he said.

There was a sinister note of truth in his voice and Alex realized, not for the first time, that the law did not stretch far beyond the limits of the City. It was not that police would condone crime in the Angles, or even shrug it off. It was the cold fact that if individual stems wished to evade the police, or obstruct them, they could do so relatively easily.

Alex could not help but feel gleeful at the thought.

"Perhaps she's bitten off more than she can chew this time? She's obviously too frightened to come here herself—other—wise she wouldn't have sent a man. I expect he intends to drive out here each day and return to the City at night? Might be an an idea to find his hummer and throw a spanner in the engine. A night in the open, under the stars of the Outer Angles, might sate his curiosity of nature, eh Jamie?"

Jamie stared hard at him.

"Not everyone's as frightened as you are, Mr Craven. Could be he's been out of the City before and doesn't care too much?"

Alex felt deflated. Was he so transparent to these people?

"Well, I don't care too much for the adders and things," he said.

" 'And things' is right," replied Polgrove quietly. "*All things*. But Jamie an't a-mocking you, Mr Craven. He says what he says, blunt. It don't mean he thinks less of you. Our ways an't your ways. Daresay we'd be feared in the City at night, eh Jamie? I hear tell of gangs of girls that would slit your nose, and maybe also. . ."

Alex nodded miserably. He hated being a fish out of water but it was all true. The open spaces and the nights outside the well-lit City did frighten him. He could not get used to the sounds: the slithering, snuffling, hissing, rustling, whispering blackness. He would never get used to it. Owls crooning at the moon, swooping on small running shadows. Hedgehogs masticating noisily on live worms. It was all so *weird*, so *uncitylike*.

The three of them went into the house to eat and a little

while later a hummer appeared in the yard. Polgrove went out first because they all thought it might be the professional nuisance, but it turned out to be Nicole. She had come to find out why Alex had not been to Manston and if he had decided on whether or not to stay.

Nicole was bewildered by his anger.

They faced each other in Alex's small bedroom: the only place, apart from outdoors, which was private.

"What the hell is this?" asked Alex. "What are you teaching these children of yours?" He confronted her with the drawing of the gin. "This has been distorted—*deliberately* distorted, it seems to me—in order to instil fear in small minds."

She looked down at the sketch in his hand, wondering why he was so upset.

"I'm afraid that's how it works, Alex. I didn't like the idea any more than you do, but I'm afraid you're going to have to accept it. . ."

"Idea? What idea?"

"The twins—they need a common fear to transmit to one another. No, that's the wrong word, *transmit*. They need a common feeling which we can recognize."

"It seems I still don't understand this telemetry system of yours. Look, has it got anything to do with State Five brain patterns? I've done some work in that direction." He let the drawing book fall on to the bed. "Faith healers use State Five," he added, by way of an explanation.

She frowned almost to the point of a scowl.

"No, no. State Five is a form of brain-wave transmission, isn't it? Where both halves of the brain are transmitting simultaneously?"

Alex nodded. "Normally we use only one side."

"Alex, our experiments have nothing to do with conscious signals—we're dealing with subconcious communication. It's important that the twins are unaware that they are in any way unusual."

"And what about that?" He pointed to the book on the bed.

"That's the trigger. We're all afraid of something—spiders, snakes. We all have a phobia."

"Like vulpephobia?" asked Alex, in a peculiar tone.

She was puzzled, but let it pass.

"If there are people with a primal fear of foxes, yes. Anyway, the phobia which has been indoctrinated into the twins is a fear of the gin. That way, if one twin is ever confronted by a gin—her nightmare—her fear will be felt by the other twin. Or we hope it will. . ."

She looked at the man before her with some concern. In a way he was right, this angular, excitable man who would not stay out of her life. It was immoral to use the twins as signalling devices, pieces of equipment. But still she felt that it was a necessary thing to do.

She knew Alex was a man who came down hard on things that he felt directly affected him. Gaunt, somewhat hatchet-faced, he was in no way handsome but, he had that indefinable air of enthusiasm which attracted women. A boyishness that she knew would be with him well into his middle age and possibly beyond.

"You do see that we're not harming the children in any way?"

"I'd need to be a psychologist to agree with that. I don't know. I reserve judgement. The drawing shocked me, that was all." He laughed humourlessly. "I'm easy to shock you know. A naïve city boy. Show me a prejudice and I'll suck in my cheeks in distaste and back away. Incidentally, you do realize this smacks heavily of racism."

She shook her head. "It's not meant to. We don't wish to interfere with the natives. There's no reason why we should. But we need the system just in *case*. We know very little about the gin, although I understand there are people on New Carthage with the time and expertise to study the natives . . ."

"Anthropologists?"

"Something of that nature, though the gin aren't men, strictly speaking. They are aliens—and aliens think in unhuman terms. For all we know, they may be smiling and nodding their own brand of hate and fear in the direction of Stingray Raft. The colony probably wouldn't recognize the symptoms of an organized attack building up . . ."

"So we have to protect ourselves. The old story, but . . ."

48

He held up his hand. "I take the point. We need to be warned. Okay. As I said, on the issue of the twins, I'm undecided, but I see the need for some sort of fast signalling device."

Nicole relaxed and then they both sat on the bed and they talked of more mundane matters.

"Why did you come here, Alex? Not to see me—that's no answer."

He smiled wryly. "Maybe to escape from Lila. Anyway, I'm here and I'm beginning to like it. The Polgroves look after me well and the food is beginning to behave itself once it's inside me. It's a good feeling—knowing that you're not dead after all."

She squeezed his hand quickly, and then stood up.

"Well, how about a drive out somewhere? Where would you like to go?"

"Hadley Castle," he replied without hesitation.

They took the old coast road around the corner of the bleak estuary of the Thames. On the way, they passed the ruins of towns whose names had almost been forgotten. There had been a scheme at one time to revive the sprawling leg of London's East Side almost to the sea itself, but that would have meant extending the City's canopy, an expensive and unjustified extravagance since the population implosion had limited numbers to the point where London no longer needed to expand.

One or two fishermen still remained at Leigh, their boats like black limpets stuck to the smooth mud. They were probably men without families, since the sale of fish could surely not support more than a lone Spartan man. Possibly the stems would purchase in kind, but not many city people would be so adventurous as to attempt once-living table fare. The market for fresh food was almost non-existent in the City.

The western cliffs behind them, they approached Hadley Down and Nicole heard Alex pull in his breath sharply.

"Is that it?" he said, and she knew from his tone he was impressed. She was not surprised. The castle was a magnificent structure that reached upwards with tall, grey towers towards the weak October sun.

In the centre of the castle, the keep stood solid and formidable. Nicole had never failed to be fascinated by the perfection for which the builders had striven and gained. The castle was perfect, even to the arrow loops—vertically aligned eyes in the turrets—and the allures marking a path behind the crenellation. These had been builders with supposedly no education, working from reinforced memories and small pieces of the original building.

"Do they have a problem with foxes in there?" asked Alex.

Nicole laughed. "Good heavens, no. What makes you say that?"

Alex fingered his chin. "I was bitten by one as a child—on the face. Vicious creatures. You know London is full of them? The scars have gone now," he added, and she realized she was staring at his face. "I had them surgically erased."

"You're a fully grown man now, Alex. Surely those small creatures don't worry you?"

"A little . . . they worry me a little. You've no idea what it's like to experience the sudden snapping of steel-sprung jaws around your face. I had nightmares long afterwards. The eyes, the teeth. . ."

Nicole's hummer passed beneath the portcullis, over which were incised the words: SWEYN CASTLE—KEEP IT HOLY. The outer bailey was bustling with market traders behind their stalls.

Alex was obviously fascinated by the scene: the chanting traders, the noisy pens full of domestic beasts and birds of all varieties, the flowers, the fruits, the grain. There was even an illegal trade in drugs which Strecker had discovered, having been offered some topsy quite openly. Topsy—or rather *Ceratopsiae*, named after the dinosaur for its *heavy* withdrawal symptoms—was a synthetic drug and therefore manufactured in the City. Apparently, even the stems were not out of reach of City crime. It was bewildering and a little nerve-racking—but *fascinating*.

"Where do they all *come* from?" said Alex in wonderment.

"The marshes. The farms. It's good cattle country, the grass grows quickly, and alluvium is excellent for agriculture. A lost art, if not for these people."

Alex looked into her eyes.

"You like *these people*, don't you?"

She nodded.

"I find them . . . honest. They may be primitive but they're not shallow. Oh, I know, there're bad ones. There are always bad ones. But on the whole I prefer them to my own kind."

"Does the Government—does *anyone* in the City—know about this place?"

"Somebody must—they don't hide it from the tourists—but I'll admit officially it doesn't exist. Does it matter?"

"No, not really," replied Alex absently as they alighted from their vehicle.

He wandered over to a nearby stall and Nicole heard him saying to the owner, "These are wild flowers, aren't they? What are they for? Decoration?"

"They're herbs—for sickness and such," replied the trader, a formidable-looking elderly woman. Nicole could see she was suspicious of the two autumn tourists.

Nicole said, "Is this a daisy?"

The woman nodded. "Like a daisy, only bigger. It's called feverfew—for headaches. You got a headache?"

"No, but I'll have some. Only I haven't anything . . . oh yes, would you like this red kerchief in exchange?" She unclipped a small scarf from around her neck.

"I'll take it," said the woman shortly and handed Nicole a small bouquet of feverfew.

"And what's this?" asked Alex, as Nicole was about to return to the hummer, having handed over her scarf.

"Yarrow."

"What's it for?" he presisted.

A youth standing near them answered for the stall woman.

"It's for healing wounds."

Alex turned and stared at the young man and Nicole saw that they had recognized one another.

"Who is it?" she whispered to Alex.

He ignored her, asking the youth instead, "Is it ever necessary?"

A silence ensued and Nicole gripped Alex's arm, applying pressure, gently urging him towards the hummer. Alex allowed himself to be moved but just as he and Nicole were climbing into the vehicle, the youth replied, "Necessary. Sometimes people get hurt through foolishness. Like the clod I lifted from the mud t'other day."

Alex paused halfway between standing and sitting, and Nicole felt the tenseness in his arm as she gripped his wrist again. Then she saw that the youth wore a grin, and she felt relief flooding through her body.

Trembling, she started the hummer and drove through the gateway.

Alex said nothing. They drove back to the farm in silence. On the way they passed the nuisance, who stared—and then waved. They ignored him.

4   The City

Childhood had been the indulgence of middle-aged, comfortably placed parents. However, he had, on occasions, escaped their gentle but firm hold and had run the streets for several hours.

Why had they worried? What harm could come to a youth in a city closed to the elements? Encapsulated, dry, warm, safe. In a city which was never dark?

While Alex had not yet accepted the job at Manston House, he had at least promised Strecker that he would put the proposal before the Minister. However, given time to reflect, he now felt he could not subscribe to the indoctrination of the twins. Strecker had been more enthusiastic than ever at their second meeting and said he was certain Alex was now on his way back to his lodgings to give himself a little time away from Nicole. A few days to think about what he was going to do with the rest of his life. Nicole was a crossroads. He needed the dark-haired puritan but he had to decide how badly. Enough to crumple his principles into a ball and throw them over his shoulder? Maybe not, since he was having second thoughts.

At the police checkpoint they played his identity strip and asked him why he was not wearing a receiving bracelet.

"I took off my wristband when I left the City. No use for it out there."

"Please wear it now, sir. You may need it should an emergency occur."

"What sort of disaster?" They were so damned complacent.

"I didn't say 'disaster', sir. I said an emergency."

Smug, self-satisfied and probably right, to a degree.

"Okay." Alex slipped on his wristband and tuned it to soft

music. If an emergency did occur, the police would broadcast on all channels.

Alex wondered if any of the stems ever tried to enter. They had no identity strips, or receiver bracelets either for that matter. All they had were their ragged selves and a faith in a warrior chieftain called Sweyn.

That reminded him. He wanted to visit the House of Poets while he was in the City. He wanted to see Mathew Tse's holovid.

All entrances to London were at Level two and Alex found himself on the smooth aluminium street of the production zone. From building to building the strips sprang out and allowed a person to drive to the office or factory floor without having to leave the vehicle in the street. A girl was running across a third-storey strip, her freckled face frowning old lines into young skin. Alex remembered the youthful dangerous game of "running the strips". An electronic device was used to trigger the electric eye and a hummer strip would zip through the air temporarily joining two buildings at various heights above the ground. The strip could detect the presence of a hummer, but not a person on foot. People did not walk across a metre-wide strip of flexible metal high above the street. If a strip was called forth, and remained unused within thirty seconds, it retracted itself. Zip. In an instant. Thirty seconds was ample time to run across the springy metal path to safety, therefore one had to make the return trip in order to prove that courage was there. *Rückkehr. Revenir. Returns.* They played the game in all the cities. It was probably the reason why his parents had been so anxious to keep him at their side twenty-four hours a day. Indulgent parents were the norm, not the exception. There were not many children around to indulge.

Alex had never been troubled with heights. Even now, as an adult and fully aware of the possible hair-raising consequences of his childish efforts to prove himself, he had only had one or two recollections at which he shivered. He had heard of accidents: one or two of them apparently fatal, but he had never actually witnessed one. The adult world was horrified, of course, at each new (albeit infrequent) accident and attempted to build in childproof safeguards. A futile exercise in a world where children were the electronic innovators of the age, producing new methods of circuitry, new devices, day by day in home and school laboratories. Their minds were sharp with the state of the art. Theirs was an era of the early induction of knowledge. They could beat the adults hands down at retaining the game of touch-death-and-run.

He watched the girl reach safety and shook his head. Didn't they ever tire of it? Surely there was something new by now?

On the fourth level Alex found the House of Poets, a perfect cube of white covering an acre of the City's precious top layer. He parked the vehicle inside the entrance and walked down the main corridor to the Room Index in the centre of the building. Finding the hexagonal index he waited patiently while two people before him in the queue found the references they needed, and then scanned the names of the Holy Poets for that of Mathew Tse. He found the code beside the name and entered the reference into the chart. On the flat screen of the hexagon a route through the maze of subsidiary corridors traced its white-light lines.

Memorizing the paths he had to follow, Alex eventually found the small room dedicated to Mathew Tse. He entered.

At the back of the room stood Mathew Tse, Asian Poet of no fixed religion. His poems ranged from Christ to Buddha to Mithra.

"Come in, friend," he said, "and listen to the pantheistic word of Tse."

There was a stool in the centre of the room and Alex sat on it, giving his attention to the animated holovid image before him.

"There are always two sides to a story," said the artificial phantom, using its hands to express itself.

"How original," commented Alex drily.

The poet frowned.

"If you came here to mock me, you may leave now," it said.

Hell, a free-programmed image, thought Alex. Those who prayed through Mathew Tse, and poets like him, were supposed to immerse themselves in that particular poet's philosophies, his ideas and interpretations of God. That way one did not have to think too hard for oneself. One just adopted the thoughts of one's favourite poet—be he atheist or devout Hindu—and saved oneself the trouble of delving too deeply into heady matters.

"Two sides," continued Mathew Tse. "I look at the reciprocal of the story. You are familiar with my poem 'The Long Drop Upwards', which deals with the fear of falling into the sky?"

"Yes." Tse's image was on safe ground and was well aware of it. Aware? An image? Never mind, just listen.

"In this poem, 'Tree Messiah', I deal with the reciprocal of the crucifixion of Christ. I recite . . ." And the tones were liquid, like the sea murmuring over the warm sands of a beach:

> "When trees can talk
> they will tell how brutal hands
> cut down their tall prophet
> from its sentient slope—
> they will speak of pagan tools
> that scissored away the gold-green arms
> from the holy son of the forest,
> and how the bark-robed trunk was split and crossed—
> they will tell patient judges
> how their lord was dragged
> through jeering crowds, and crucified
> against the body of a man."

Alex stayed for some time listening to the verses, which he liked, but still could not accept as religiously inspiring. In the end, he began an argument with the image which ended, on Alex's side at least, in a slanging match. A priest was secretly summoned to throw him out. Physical ejection was unnecessary. Alex left the building, shamefaced, hurrying in front of the grim-looking official and bearing the disapproving glances of other visitors (*pious* visitors) with embarrassment. So much for Nicole's deity!

He drove back down to the third level and to his flat in the suburbs. Outside his apartment stood a familiar figure. It was obviously not going to be his day.

"Hello, Lila." Resignation.

She smiled and made the sophisticat's gesture for "hi".

Her face was hollow with lack of sleep. The Greek nose

(Greek again? Maybe it was permanent this time?) pinched at the nostrils, which meant she was going to cry as soon as the smile faded. Yes, there were the tears, genuine enough unfortunately. She really *did* miss him when he was away, but, just as unfortunately, she soon tired of him when he was there for any length of time.

He kissed her cheek, tasting the salty wetness, and she followed him through the door into the room.

"Is that all I get?"

He sighed, then kissed her lips, holding her tightly. She moved against him then and he thought what the hell? So long as she was there they might as well. She had broken the three months again. He always did make love to her when she came to claim his husbandry.

Afterwards, lying amongst the pool of clothes on the floor, he said, "This is getting a little monotonous, Lila. Don't you think we could meet without *meeting*, so to speak?"

"Why?" she asked simply, the blue eyes wide and frank.

"Because it's repetitive. Don't you find it boring? You usually do, you know—find the echoes, the harmonics, boring."

"Don't use communications jargon to belittle me. It's not clever. As a matter of fact, making love to you cleanses me—for a while. You're so . . . straight."

"Is that supposed to be *immature* in your world?"

She shook her head.

"No. Not that. Not anything. If one hasn't had straight sex for some time, it almost becomes a perversion to try it again. I always enjoy it with you because I know you're enjoying yourself too. Mostly it's the act with the others. . ."

"Oh God, you're not in *love* with me again?" he groaned.

"Don't be such a bastard. Of course I am. I always am. I just . . . can't stay, that's all. We have a good life. You can have me any time you like, you know, you only have to call. . ."

"Well, what do we do now?" asked Alex. "We can't very well lie around here all day."

"I'll make you something to eat."

She stood up and went into his kitchen closet, presumably to heat something for him.

What the hell am I doing with my life? he thought, as her

lithe, small-breasted figure disappeared into the recesses of the closet. Chasing a woman that has no interest in me—at least not any passionate interest—and offering myself as the willing buffer of a woman who can find no satifaction in ordinary, everyday living?

A few minutes later, Lila's naked form reappeared and she set down a tray between them. There were two dishes on the tray, each filled with a brown jelly.

"Vestil. Everyone's eating it at the moment," she said.

Alex replied, "You don't mean that. You mean one or two of your friends like it."

Lila shrugged. "If you say so. You know what I mean better than I do, I suppose." She was not being sarcastic.

Alex again looked into her large blue eyes. It was her eyes that had once attracted him so strongly. Or was it those slim legs?

"Look, Lila, I'm going back."

She seemed preoccupied and began eating.

"Back? Back where?"

"To the Angles." He knew he did not mean it but he was curious to see what her reaction would be.

She continued to spoon the vestil into her small mouth. Suddenly her voice was low and hard and, still looking down, she said, "Back to *her*. That woman?"

"So your nuisance has already reported? Yes, if you like, back to her."

"Do you love her?"

"What do you care? You have dozens of lovers."

Lila's breath was sweet in his nostrils.

"But you're my anchor," she said, simply and with desperation in her tone. "I need you here."

Suddenly he saw how unhappy his wife was. It was in those eyes, in the curve of the mouth, in the slump of the slim shoulders. Unhappy? Maybe that was the play for today? How could he be sure this was the real Lila? She was so good at playing games. He took a spoonful of the vestil. It was heavily perfumed and, while a week ago he might have enjoyed it, right at this moment it was like tasting sugared mud.

Without saying anything else to her, he dressed himself and walked towards the door.

"Where are you going?" she asked. Her tone was flat.

"I thought I'd take a trip to the library. There's something I want to look up. You're quite welcome to stay as long as you want. I shan't be back for a while."

She made her gesture for goodbye—the kind of indecent finger movement a whore might give a client who had underpaid her.

Alex drove up a spiral to Level Four and into Museum Street, at the end of which was the largest library in the City. Once inside he found the reference section of the memory banks and began searching for data on the history of the Outer Angles. His search led him to an old book within which was a passage on Sweyn of Essex. He read:

"Sweyn (d. *circa* 1086) son of Robert, Standard Bearer to Edward the Confessor, held fifteen lordships in Essex. He served as Sheriff of Essex under both Edward and William the Conqueror. Know as the 'greatest sheepmaster in Essex' his castle in the south-east was at Rayleigh.' (Not Hadley?) "He was succeeded by his son, Robert Fitz Sweyn, but his grandson, Henry de Essex, was accused of cowardice in a battle against the Welsh, fought a trial by single combat and lost, ending his days in penury at Reading Abbey."

There was more but Alex had read enough. It was the "sheepmaster" phrase that obviously attracted the stems to the man, though how that sort of information had passed to people who were as far away from books as the Moon from the Earth he had no idea. What worried him was the fact that they had chosen a warrior, rather than a man of God, or even a poet. Were they planning revolution one day? And if so, for what purpose? They had no need of the city, they were left well alone and went about their business unhindered by any government. True, they didn't *own* the land they farmed but then nobody, as far Alex could see, was considering moving them or removing the right to farm.

A shepherd-knight. A man who owned vast—by stem standards—tracts of land. A man whose roots were in the marshes of the Angles and whose people were country folk. Stems.

The ownership of land was something Alex did not fully understand, so he burrowed through more reference works, some of them subjective and opinionated, after which he began to comprehend that to a farmer land was everything. It was not just a way of life—it was the source of life. Not to own the land one farmed was intolerable. A man needed to feel part of the soil he trod. It had to be his; in him and he in it. The man and the mud, one together. Every bird, every plant, every fox, coming under his ownership. Each leaf of the elder, each berry, each globule of amber sap or white cuckoo spitball, the farmer's own. In *his* fields the hares should box each other before mating, the grass snake feign death and the fang-like toothwort grow in hairy ugliness. Even the sky above the land was part of the land.

Right. Now while he was about it he might as well look up "empathy". He found the psychological definition: "Imaginary projection of one's self into the consciousness of another—the capacity to identify with that person without losing one's own identity."

Alex was *beginning* to understand.

He left the library, deep in thought. It was only when he found himself outside his own doorway that he realized he had headed home. The door slid back to reveal the watery paleness of the professional nuisance. Shocked by the sudden nearness of the face, Alex stepped backwards and lashed out with his fist. The knuckles connected against something hard and pointed, and for a moment a feeling of irrational triumph flooded his body.

A split second later, something hit his chest with tremendous force, smashing him back against the corridor wall. He thought for an instant that he had been struck by a weapon, a hammer, or at least kicked by a heavy boot, but when he could see again through the mist of pain, the nuisance was crouched before him like a cat and he realized it had been the man's fingertips that had delivered the blow.

"Again! He hit *you* first. I'll vouch for you if the police ask questions."

The vengeful, acidic voice, which came from the room, was Lila's. He had not enough time to say her name before a second attack took all the wind from his lungs. It hurt. It hurt like hell and he kicked back in anger, connecting with something soft. Then he stumbled away from the danger zone and began running along the corridor.

There was a screech from Lila and footsteps pounded after him. Alex felt cold fear trickle alongside the agony inside his chest. The nuisance, despite his sickly appearance, was obviously no weakling. In fact the man was trained in some form of martial art and, if he caught Alex, would no doubt practise that art upon Alex's vulnerable body. He glanced quickly behind him and saw that his pursuer was limping slightly. Good and bad. Good, that he had given the man a taste of his own ability to hurt. Bad, that the man would now want revenge for that hurt.

Alex reached the lifts, jumped inside, and watched with relief as the doors closed before his antagonist could reach them. They were on the third storey and Alex alighted on the second, hoping that the nuisance would think he had gone down to street level.

The second lift came down, the doors opened, and the nuisance came out like an eagle from an open cage, his pale skin glistening under the artificial light. There was a determined expression on the hawk-like features which made Alex glad he had put several metres between them.

There followed a seemingly endless chase round and round the corridors of the second floor, with the nuisance gaining all the time. Finally, Alex felt his chest was going to explode. Only the terrible thought of suffering a possible bone breakage kept his feet moving under him. At one point he even felt the situation was farcically funny and turned to laugh, only to see the viciousness in the face of his athletic pursuer undimmed by any humour or possible exhaustion.

Then, suddenly, Alex took the wrong turning and found himself in a hummer chute leading to a strip. The outside doors remained closed at his approach and he realized he was trapped. With unreasonable terror, he clawed at the hairline crack between the doors. Miraculously, they opened, not because of his efforts but because, simultaneously, a hummer was crossing the strip outside and they had slid back to allow it an entry.

Alex flattened himself against the wall to let the hummer pass. He received a curious glance from the driver but he paid no attention; he was busy counting. "Ten, eleven, twelve, thirteen, fourteen. . ."

Alex had reached seventeen when the nuisance appeared at the entrance to the chute, walking slowly because he knew there was no hurry. Alex could not escape.

"Eighteen, nineteen, twenty."

Alex stepped out on to the springy strip, his heart pounding in his breast, and began crossing. Half-way between buildings he look back to see the nuisance hesitating in the gap between the doors.

Too late. Only five seconds left. I've made it, thought Alex excitedly.

Then the nuisance stepped on to the strip and began following him across.

"No!" he shouted. "Go back! Back, you idiot!"

Then he ran himself, reaching the far side, and stepped into the chute. Christ, hadn't that fool ever played the game? Didn't he know how long . . . ? Just as Alex turned to look, the door hissed shut and he knew the strip would have retracted itself in the same instant.

Alex imagined the mangled heap lying in the street below, bones crazed and blood oozing through abrasions. His stomach heaved.

Feeling giddy, he made his way down to the street below and approached a ring of curious people standing around the body. Alex elbowed his way to the front and, to his immense relief, the nuisance was still alive. In fact—incredibly, and quite out of character— he was grinning. Their eyes locked and Alex suddenly realized that it was not a grin, it was a grimace. The man's lips were drawn back over his teeth in agony and Alex could now see that one of his legs zig-zagged from the hip.

He pushed his way back again to the fringe of the crowd and returned to his apartment in a daze. What was he going to do? He had caused a man to break his leg (or perhaps even worse?) by provoking a fight. Or had he? The nuisance had, after all, been in his flat. But, on the invitation of his wife who, it could be argued, had a half-share of the accommodation. Christ, what a mess.

If the nuisance brought charges, it would be a long struggle through the courts. Once the police had a hook in you, they were reluctant to let you go. Would the Ministry support him? He would not want to put it to the test.

The best thing to do was get out of their reach. Go back to the marshes of the stems. Join Nicole at Manston House. Take the damn job, for what it was worth.

The police were less anxious to establish his identity since he was not entering their jurisdiction, but leaving it. Alex drove out into the open spaces of the country, but this time the emptiness was comforting, not frightening as it had been on that night he had driven out with Peter. He felt sorry for Peter now—an enclosed, encapsulated mouse—and pleased with himself. Pleased because he no longer cringed from the sun, or hunched below distant stars as if they weighed heavy on his shoulders.

Following the marker posts, he drove across the fields rather than round them. Folk lore, taught him by Jamie, had made him anxious to witness some natural but unusual animal event —like a weasel dancing on its hind legs before a rabbit in order to hypnotize its victim, or wild stallions battling for supremacy of the mares. His eyes flickered keenly over the unkempt bushes and long grasses.

Once, he stopped the hummer and braved the fresh air in order to whistle. Jamie had told him that on a stretch of flatland a hare will hide in a hollow. A sharp noise will encourage it to stiffen its ears, thus exposing itself and its hideout. Alex was disappointed when the landscape failed to sprout ears. In fact, not a single pair could be seen.

What he did see were the obvious remains of a hedgehog and once again his old fears returned. Only foxes and badgers ate hedgehogs, and of the two the badger left no tell-tale skin. Therefore a fox was in the neighbourhood.

As he stood in thought, a partridge whirred from a bush,

frightening him. The comfortable feeling had gone. He *was* an alien in these surroundings.

Once on his way again, Alex felt more secure. The countryside was all right, it seemed, on the other side of a windscreen. The swishing of the reeds below and alongside the craft had a calming effect on his nerves and he could look at the day's turbulent happenings with a certain amount of detachment.

First of all, he had felt a psychological tugging at his heels on leaving the Angles for the City, quite apart from his feeling of contempt for the police at the entrance. Next there was the argument with the artificial ghost of a long-dead poet—humorous now that it was behind him. Following that incident, the lovemaking, the library finds and the running fight with his wife's hired help. The last experience made him physically shudder. He could not throw away the image of Lila as he had stood behind the nuisance, her angelic features twisted into a knot of hatred. Only an hour or so before she had been telling him how much she loved him. Life had once been like that on a permanent basis, when he had first married her. One day a clawing, spitting cat whom he loathed; the next a soft, gentle kitten. One thing he would say for her, she was never, never boring.

Half an hour later the hummer was flattening the giant hogweed near Polgrove's farm. Tomorrow Alex would go to Manston House. He could contact the Minister later. Jamie came out of the barn with a wrung chicken dangling from his hand. He grinned when he saw Alex's face.

5 The Tests

Strecker had influence: that much was obvious. Not only had he cooled the nuisance incident from a criminal charge to a civil lawsuit, but he had also had Alex's equipment installed in Manston House before the month was out. The case—for which Alex had no doubt that Lila was responsible—would not come up for another seven months at least, and by that time anything might happen. The police had been reluctant to drop their charges but pressure from above was applied to the arteries of the force and the nuisance was left with the choice of sueing or forgetting. Strecker was convinced that because the nuisance had retaliated there would be no case to answer. Alex was not sure, but hoped his new boss was right.

Around the Polgrove farm, November was flexing its icy fingers. Dawn skies had those smeared blood streaks at which farmers nodded sagely and then fussed about their livestock, making sure the fodder store held enough to last the winter.

Even with a hummer Alex maintained a respect for the broomway, especially at high tide. It would not do to get lost or take a dive during the winter months. Exposure would kill him within a few minutes. This morning the tide was out and he made good time, arriving at Manston House at around seven o'clock.

Alex went directly to the blue room where Odell schooled her twins, two boys of Swedish extraction. Nicole had explained that male twins were not expected to perform well in the tests because their *closeness* factor was less than that of females. There was empirical evidence to prove this claim, she said. But then Nicole had girls and Alex had noticed an element of possessive jealousy around the place when it came to the children. Nicole was no more above such feelings than any other foster-mother.

The classroom was empty so he sat on one of the child-sized chairs until Odell entered with the twins. They laughed together at his clowning.

"Morning. Everything all right?" he asked.

She frowned.

"Yes, I suppose so. I don't like these tests."

"Well, that's what it's all about, I suppose."

He liked to hear her talk. The accent was strong but not unpleasant. He studied her face. Her hair was so blonde it was difficult to see where the hair-line began. It gave her a high forehead, an intellectual look which did not disturb the somewhat square-featured handsomeness of the woman.

"Come on, cheer up," he said.

The boys were beginning to look worried now. They were six years old—Peter and Petre—and they had been told there would be some games this morning.

"What's the matter, mummy? Can't we play the games?" asked Peter. (Or was it Petre?)

"Yes, we still play the games, but you must be *good* boys and not ask too many questions."

"You always say we *should* ask questions."

"Not today. Today is serious—a time for serious games, that is. Uncle Alex is going to help us."

"Uncle"? He wasn't sure he liked that.

"Peter will come with me", she said, "into another room while, Petre, you will go with Auntie Susan. What I want you both to do is think very *hard* about your brother while you are away from him. Okay?"

She had squatted down between them, her arms around each of their shoulders and their faces pressed to her cheek.

"Is that the *game*?" said one, pulling away in disappointment.

"Some of it—but it gets much more exciting," replied Alex.

They looked up at him, their angelic expression trustful. He felt a bastard. These two poor youngsters had been conditioned to react to a fairy-tale nightmare—a normal child's black witch on a broomstick—only for them the tale was true, the nightmare real. In the sound-proofed room down in the basement, the holograph projectors would produce a life-size gin for one of these children, and his terror was expected to be felt instantly within the breast of the other twin.

"Okay, boys, see you later," he said.

The twins smiled and left the room with Odell, who couldn't keep her hands off them, touching their hair and cheeks continually. They were sure to sense her nervousness but that wasn't his business.

Alex went to the monitoring room and sat down before his electronic scanners. There were five screens before him, one on top of the other, each ten by ten centimetres. The scanners behind each screen would automatically run through all the frequency ranges within a few minutes. There would be an electronic screening bubble around the house to prevent interference from outside signals. The five separate scanners would begin their cycles at different levels on the frequency ranges: VLF, MF, VHF, SHF and EHF. When they reached their starting point, they would begin again. After the tests were over, Alex would replay the cycles, only at a much slower speed and with the major part of the dry-run scans automatically edited. *Then* they would be able to pinpoint any likely transmission between the twins. If it was a foreign transmitter, such as a grasshopper between the floorboards, he could eliminate it at that stage.

Alex knew there would be interference from rogue signals *within* the house: human voices, bugs, beetles and anything else that vibrated, resonated, emitted, or blew its nose within receiving distance. He would run through the cycles several times before the actual test and separately identify most foreign disturbances.

The red opal glowed.

Alex's thoughts dissipated immediately and he began concentrating on the monitor screens.

For twenty minutes he allowed the rogue signals to collect within the memory banks of the mini-computer, and, when the opal was extinguished, he began replaying them through more slowly. He had asked John Strecker not to interrupt him for a few hours. Those rogue transmissions he had identified before the run he had programmed for dark green. He could have eliminated them but should the transmission from the twin have been on the same frequency as a rogue he would have lost both. This way he identified the locations of the separate sources and programmed bright red for any that appeared on the actual run.

There were several, of course, but he pinpointed their source. None appeared to come from the room in the basement. Several hours later he emerged from the room, dark-eyed and carrying a dull thudding in his head. Strecker was in his office.

"What's the matter?" asked the weary Alex. "Aren't you interested? It was damned hot in there—and hard work."

The other man shook his head as he fiddled with a handkerchief.

"No, sorry. It's not that. It's just that there was no reaction in the second twin. I let you carry on, just in case, but Peter didn't even flinch while his brother was screaming blue murder. Whitman, but that child's face. When we let him out of that sound-proofed room, he frightened me. Didn't you hear him?"

"I received the audio-wave."

"Well, he quietened down when he saw Odell. I think we'll have some trouble tonight. Echh! I hate this . . . Anyway the doctor's with him now. She'll dose him up, probably, but still, not a nice thing. . . "

"So, it's all over then? The tests?"

Strecker looked guilty, his boyish face wrinkling in distaste. "Nope."

"No? Why for God's. . ."

"Because it's important we try them all. Every one of the test pairs has to go through with it. Today it was a couple of boys—they're not as sensitive as the girls."

"What's so *important* about it?"

The dumpy man shrugged his shoulders.

"Well, ah, might as well tell you something. They may be heading for a confrontation on New Carthage. They don't know for sure but they've picked up evidence which points to a big event in the lives of the gin. What it implies, no one is quite sure."

"Bit vague, isn't it?"

"Whitman knows that's true, but that's all they've got at the moment."

Alex pulled in a deep breath and drummed his fingers on the desk.

"Which set next?" he asked very casually.

"What? Oh, the Kittoe twins."

The sigh of relief gave Alex away.

Strecker said, "What was that for?" Then his keen blue eyes studied Alex's face and he nodded thoughtfully. "The Lo twins. You're worried about Nicole? So am I but I've scheduled them according to what I consider to be their potential—which is high. I'm leaving the most likely until last. The Lo twins come just before the Koreans. There's not much to choose between the two sets but that's the way I'm playing it. You don't need to worry for at least a fortnight."

But Alex was worried, especially after passing Odell in the corridor. She did not reply to his greeting. He guessed why. Odell was not the most logical of people and she aligned Alex with the management—possibly because he was a man, like Strecker, while all the others in the establishment were females. Or maybe it was because Alex reported directly to Strecker, was an advisor rather than a line employee like the women? Whatever the reason, he was zero-rated according to Odell's assessment. Nicole might take the same attitude after the Lo twins had been "processed". He shuddered at the thought. Peter could relax now and begin to grow out of his nightmare. On Lo or Ti Lo had her turn to come. *Bright little round faces, screwed into a ball of terror below the black fringe of hair. Shrunken pupils robbing the liquid softness from a pair of dark eyes. Small mouth, round with screams for mother.*

Mother. That was Nicole. She knew of the necessity to find a telemetry system that would beat the distance problem. But would she condone the tests when she saw Peter and the other children going through hell, flopping around on the floor like mindless fish afterwards and waking the house with the noise of cold-sweat dreams? He thought not. In his opinion, Nicole would join the ranks of the unbelievers quicker than fast light.

"How *do* you feel about it?" he asked her that evening. They were walking along the shore of Feerness. Alex had decided to stay at Manston that night. He felt washed out, used.

She turned to look at him and he tried to read those brown eyes in the near darkness.

"I try not to," she replied. "It's best not to think about it."

"That's okay if you can manage it. Whenever I tell myself that, I end up thinking about nothing else. It must be a weighty problem in the beginning to make such a promise to yourself."

"True, but there are circumstances. . ."

"New Carthage. Christ, there must be some other way."

She took hold of his hand and gave it a tug.

"Why do you stick to that outmoded prophet? Better still, why curse at all?"

A quick change of subject? Still, better not press her too hard, he thought.

"I like him. He wasn't outmoded in his time. God, wouldn't *I* like a pair of sandals and a beard—then to follow some poet over hot sands, listening to his stories. . ."

"Jesus wasn't a poet."

"What makes you so sure? Maybe he's just been badly reported?"

She giggled and he realized she was still holding his hand. Progress. With any other woman he would have given up in disgust but with Nicole . . . well, he could afford to be patient. The prize was a big one.

Ht strolled along in the dark, conscious of the contact between them. Marsh samphire formed a spongy carpet beneath their feet. Occasionally the crystal rings of a salt pan gleamed in the starlight. The stems used the samphire and another prolific seashore plant, saltwort, to make washing soda. They harvested them in heaps to burn over large holes into which flowed semi-fluid alkaline. The smells from the weed-covered stones of the shore were strong and a little unpleasant, but bearable.

Everything about this primitive place was becoming easier

to handle, except possibly the people. The stems were a strange people. That youth, the blond boy—they had seen him several times lately, wandering over the marshes or crossing the broomway, and always he wore that mocking smile when he saw Alex. It was infuriating that a country yokel should radiate self-confidence the way that boy did. Alex had always imagined that a lack of sophistication would rob a man of self-assurance, give him ingratiating utterances and servile manners in the presence of a man from the City. Not a bit of it. The stems were the worldly, jaded ones; the people from the City, the frightened children. At least out here, under the stars.

He looked up. They still produced a giddy sensation in his loins when he stared up into their distant tunnels of light.

"Maybe we'll make it to those stars one day, you and I?" Nicole said.

"Together?"

She was silent for a while and he heard the sound of a fish breaking the still surface of the bottle-glass sea.

"If we *are* still together," she finally replied. "You may want to go on your own."

"Never."

Her small pointed breast pressed against his elbow. An accident? Could he feel the warmth through all the layers of their oversuits? Suddenly he pulled her to him and kissed her on the lips. Cold lips, but an outer cold was responsible. Underneath, the feeling was warm and moist.

"I'm sorry," she said. "It's a bit unfair, out here. We can't really do very much. We'd freeze to death."

"Why this sudden change?" he asked, stroking her hair, damp from the November atmosphere, its blackness part of the night.

"It's not really. I just thought . . . well, we don't have very much time, do we? I'll soon be quite old and you're close behind."

"I'm only twenty-seven."

She laughed. "Yes. Oh, I don't know, I've got a doom complex at the moment. I feel the world has taken a wrong turning somewhere. I mean, where *are* we going?"

"We're trundling along the same way we've always done. We just trundle a little faster some times, a little slower others."

"You mean technology."

"And new places, new discoveries."

But she was right. They were like the cold of her lips, those bright baubles of the 22nd Century; they were on the *outside*. What Nicole was concerned with was the inner man and woman. The soul? He didn't like that word. It sounded too biblical, but he hadn't a replacement.

When they returned to the house, he asked her if she would leave her door unlocked that night. She said no, but promised a future time.

"Everything is too close at the moment—with the tests and the twins. Once it moves back a bit, then perhaps. I'm . . . a little afraid, too. I need to be. . ."

He said he understood. It wasn't the right time. *Later*. And then he went to bed, bitterly disappointed. If he could joke about it, he could still be saved. . .

Over the next few days, Strecker carried out further tests on the children. They had one or two glimmers of response from girls. However, when they tested the set of twins before the Lo girls, there was a positive reaction from the receiving twin. She stood up the instant the image appeared before her sister inside the sound-proofed cell, and her face registered such terror the adult with her cried out. Then she screamed high and loud, stopping every heart in the house for an instant in mid-beat.

Alex, who had one piece of equipment tuned to audio frequencies so that his omnidirectional aerial could pick up the pleasantly diverting conversations around the house, was almost deafened.

Strecker was ecstatic, the women much less so. Later Nadine —the foster-mother of the Thai twins who had "produced" for Strecker—Nicole, two more foster-mothers and Alex all crowded into Strecker's tiny office The host himself was busy handing out drinks.

"We did it—we really cracked it. And no transmission, eh,

Alex? Not one wiggly line on any screen. Whitman, I knew we'd do it . . ." Strecker's face beamed below the whispy-haired pate.

"They're still frightened . . . the children," said Nadine.

Strecker became serious. He nodded gravely.

"Yes, that's the unfortunate side of our work—but once we establish the link, we don't need to do any more tests, do we? I mean, if it works, it works. Further tests might even weaken the emotional contact . . . with your particular set, that is."

There was a sigh of relief from Nadine.

Strecker looked down into his glass.

"Well, your two next, Nicole . . . well done, everyone, so far." He took a swallow.

There were white spots on Nicole's cheeks. She fumbled with a handkerchief, wiping her palms.

"Tomorrow?" asked Alex.

Nicole answered, "The sooner the better. Let's get it over with." Her voice was very quiet.

Alex looked at Strecker's face and saw the faintest of shadows pass over it. *Strecker had passed through the crisis more easily than he thought he would.*

"Well, that's settled then," said Strecker. "Let's drink to another success tomorrow." He raised his glass. Alex noticed Nicole hesitate, then take a little sip of her drink. If Strecker let it alone now, it would be all right. Reluctant acceptance was there.

"Wow, it's really getting colder now, isn't it?" said Strecker, moving to the window and staring at a darkening, thunderous-looking sky. The willows were stark, printed upon their marshy background.

Alex's admiration for Strecker's ability to handle people increased. The quick change of subject had taken the foster-mothers unawares and they began to talk to one another about winter in the Angles. The possibility of snow, the certainty of frost. Ice, hanging from the willows. For many of them it was the first time.

The thought of winter outside the City was abhorrent to Alex, yet he felt he had to run the experience. Besides, what choice was there? At least Lila would stay away.

What do foxes do in the winter? he wondered. One of the Lo twins would meet her fox tomorrow, in a locked room. He shivered involuntarily. *If it was me, I would go mad.* Yet he was subscribing to this madness, this manipulation of a child's phobia. Cruel? Primitive? Ugly? Yes, those. But not malicious. For the *good* of those people on New Carthage. For their safety a child had been fashioned to suffer.

On Lo was to be the one to face the gin. Ti would be receiver because sister On had the more extrovert personality. Quiet ones are deeper, noisy ones radiate. If an emotion had to be projected then Nicole felt On was the natural choice. On's presence in a room was always the most influential of the two.

She kissed On's cheek and nudged the little girl into the test room. On looked up at her with dark eyes and then suddenly the child smiled. Instead of reassuring Nicole, it gave her a cold sensation inside. She glanced up quickly towards the malevolent-looking eye of the projector and then down at On again.

"You play with the toys, dear. Mummy will see you soon—when the . . . the game is over."

"Okay. Is Ti playing too?"

"Yes, Ti's playing. You both have to think very hard about each other. Now I'm going to close the door, but I'll be just outside."

"You won't switch the light off?"

Nicole's heart pulled inside her.

"No, I won't switch off the light, darling, but don't worry anyway, because . . . because I won't be far away . . . okay?"

The little mouth was pert, confident.

"Yes."

"Right then, I'll close the door. . ."

She pulled the door shut and, with her heart thumping wildly, she turned the old-fashioned lock. God, why did she have to do that? The child couldn't even reach the handle. She unlocked it again and then stepped back, waiting. She was supposed to wait ten minutes before going in.

Nicole looked around her at the brick walls of the basement. Strecker had made no attempt to decorate this part of the house, or modernize it in any way. The steps were made of some kind of wood and no doubt would fetch a fair price on the black market. Two minutes ago On had insisted on holding Nicole's hand and jumping two-legged down those steps.

Two minutes? It felt like twenty.

Strecker should have had a glass panel put in the door, a little window so that the children could be observed. Perhaps he was afraid that the foster-mothers might try to rescue a child prematurely? Cold. The place felt cold, even with the heater Strecker had installed.

Three minutes.

What was On doing now? God, Mathew Tse, don't think about it! But what was happening?

Nicole listened hard for the screams of Ti Lo but could hear nothing. The sound-proofing was good.

There were some sounds: small scrapings in the brickwork. Insects? Rodents even? (She steered herself carefully clear of the word "rats".)

Three and a half minutes. This was ridiculous. Time was going backwards. They *must* have done it by now. She moved towards the door. Should she? The child might be. . .

Suddenly her body was alive with tingling sensation which increased rapidly in strength for a few moments before dying.

"Uhh!"

She rubbed at her arms furiously. What was happening? Electricity? Static?

Then her body experienced a second heavy wave of needle pricks, stronger than the first. She cried out, frightened of something she couldn't put a name to. *On? What was happening to her child?*

Then a third wave which took the breath out of her body. Not painful, just powerful, and she reeled, clutching at the wall for support.

"Turn it off!" she screamed, without knowing to whom she was talking, or about what. She felt herself being sick but moved towards the door that held the little Chinese girl prisoner. Pulling it open, she saw On, standing quite still before the three-dimensional image of a gin which Nicole had seen during pre-test runs.

"On?" she gasped. Somehow she realized the child was generating the energy and Nicole was reluctant to touch her.

The image faded, and with it the full strength of the power coursing through Nicole's body.

She grabbed at the child and found her absolutely rigid. A plastic doll.

"What have we done?" sobbed Nicole.

Then, slowly, the warmth began to return to the small limbs and a heart beat could be felt against Nicole's breast.

"Hello, mummy," said a voice from below Nicole's chin. "Is the game over now?"

"Yes, it's over, it's over," sobbed Nicole into her hair.

Strecker came running down the steps.

"Did you feel it?" he shouted. "I thought it was something outside but it started the instant I projected the image."

Nicole tried to control her voice. "I felt it. What about Ti? Is she safe?"

"Safe? Yes." Strecker was white-faced, nervous. "She went as stiff as a pole for few seconds. I couldn't get near her—she positively vibrated . . . I could see her. What about On?"

"The same—at least, she was. But I can still feel that . . . what is it? That tingling?"

"I don't know. I just . . . it's something really new, isn't it?"

"You're not doing it again, not to these children," hissed Nicole, clutching On to her chest. The child stared from one adult's face to the other. She seemed perfectly safe. Serene almost.

Alex came next, stumbling down the steps and looking as ashen as Strecker.

"Well?" said Strecker, turning to face him.

"Snow."

"Snow? What the . . . what does *that* mean?"

"The screens. They were fuzzed over with snow—interference. Lots of white dots."

"Did you get a transmission?"

Alex shook his head. "I told you, the damn screens were shot with snow. I couldn't get a reading through that lot, even if there was one."

6 The Winter

Certain people have the facility of seeing others, and themselves, very clearly. Strecker was one of these. He had a penchant for personality analysis, which he carried out in a detached clinical manner. With one exception he cared nothing for type, but accepted people for what they were, no matter what class, creed or culture.

The only type of person he disliked was one who adversely affected his work, whether the interference was accidental or on purpose. Strecker was not just wedded to his work, he was welded to it. The ways and means by which he ensured his work was completed were diverse and infinite. He would use charm, force, tact, rudeness—any method, in fact, which would give speed to the completion of his current task. But he *knew* himself and he *knew* his fellow men. Using his talent for crystallizing human nature, he manipulated weaknesses and employed strengths with the sureness of a skilled puppeteer.

He knew, for instance, that he was a bore; that his thick lips, thin hair and pear shape made him unattractive to most women; and that he frequently failed in showing tenderness and consideration where it was needed.

But he worked diligently and the job was always done well.

This morning he watched Alex Craven and Nicole Toupe as they strolled across the grass below his fern-frosted second-storey window. The man had his arm around the woman and both were exhibiting that stiffness of form which indicates unease. Strecker guessed that Alex was comforting the woman, telling her that her foster-children were not freaks, just unusual. The children themselves were still asleep, or at least in bed for it was not yet eight o'clock, the time that all the children were woken.

The couple walked down by the stream and seemed to be

talking to the water. They were, he knew, talking to each other but they seemed to have difficulty in meeting each other's eyes.

Strecker knew Alex as a man of fairly limited but well-employed intelligence. The young man was, however, very emotional and at times, when his balance was thrown, his usually articulate way of expressing himself became lost in a heavy cloud of emotion.

Nicole, on the other hand approached crises with a calm, almost indolent outward manner. She complained a lot, mostly about small things, but in normal times had an approach similar to Strecker's with regard to work. Her natural bent towards neatness extended beyond her person and she had no time for incompetence. She could be venomous with those she considered in the wrong and was very slow to forgive even a momentary weakness in her contemporaries. She would be listening to Alex's heavy, muddled talk with only half a mind: the other half would be calculating the right move for *her* in such circumstances. It was this cold decision making that concerned Strecker, and not Alex Craven's influence, which in fact amounted to very little.

A rabbit hopped out of the tall grasses and on to the lawn. Its fur glistened with droplets thawed from the seasonal frost and it ran quite near to the couple below, without them noticing. Perhaps they had been so still and quiet at the time that the creature had not noticed them? Were people just large potential predators like foxes, or did the rabbits recognize in men something special, a breed apart from all other creatures on Earth? Animals with souls? What would a rabbit see, for instance, when confronted by the Lo twins?

The test on the twins had created an indefinable field between them which everyone at Manston could *feel* in the atmosphere. Alex Craven had described it as a tangible cloud of charged particles, produced by the energy which was released when the children were empathically connected. Polarized children? thought Strecker. A magnetic field between two humans? He tried to imagine a bar of magnetized iron, the atoms all pointing in the same direction, the lines of the force field curving around from pole to pole. It sounded

78

ridiculous. It *was* ridiculous. Yet something was there. The twins had personified it.

Strecker had had a visitor late the previous evening. Nicole. She had needed to confide in him and had been so anxious to unload her information that she had not been able to wait until the morning.

She said that when she had been putting the twins to bed, she had asked them whether they felt different in any way, now that the tests were over.

Ti had answered, "Of course we do."

"Why?" Nicole had persisted when nothing else was forthcoming.

"Because she's come."

"Who . . . who is 'she', darling? Is it a friend of yours?"

The reply had made Nicole's already disquietened spirit uneasy beyond words. It was, she said, delivered in an "Oh, for goodness sakes" tone of voice.

"Mum*my*, you *know* who she is."

The dark eyes had smiled children's secrets into her adult face and she had finished the tucking-into-bed in hidden confusion and fright.

Earlier the adults had had a meeting and they had all admitted to experiencing the sensation which Nicole had felt during the test. They had also said they *still* felt *something* (though they weren't sure quite what) which lacked the strength of the original experience.

All of them had had the same thought in their minds: *was the last test going to take place?*

Strecker had insisted that it would, and it was for this reason he now watched Alex and Nicole closely, gauging what their reaction would be to his insistence and preparing his own movements to meet them head on.

He guessed that although Nicole would be strongly against the last test, she would hesitate before declaring herself. For one thing, they would not be *her* children this time, and therefore she would feel less obligated to force an issue; for another, she might lose the children she was fostering. Strecker could have her removed from her post. He was the boss.

Alex, too, would be against the test, but for a different

reason. Strecker knew that Alex's scientific curiosity would be aroused by the previous day's events and the monitoring expert would be itching to run tests on the Korean twins. It was doubtful if he would say that to Nicole, however, as they stood by the stream. Very doubtful.

Strecker smiled to himself as he watched them.

The sun came up and warmed Alex's back and gave him an internal buoyancy. He had been told that it was very mild for mid-December, despite the bad start to the previous month. It was a weekend and he was helping the Polgroves around the small farm. The last test had gone badly, from Strecker's point of view: that is, a negative response from the twins. It didn't matter. They had the Thai twins and also Nicole's children. Two sets. Strecker had given his report to the Minister, but it would be some time before the outcome would be known. Alex felt that the project was viewed very much tongue-in-cheek by the officials and he wondered whether in fact the Lo twins would ever be split and one sent to New Carthage. He had told Nicole that it was doubtful.

Staying with the Polgroves was not financially inhibiting. The only use they had for money was sending a stem courier to the edge of the City for chute-order goods. These were specialist items: shells for the shotguns, harness pieces for the horses, and certain kitchen utensils for Mrs Polgrove. The items were expensive, due either to their antiquity or their oddity, but you could get most things in the City, provided you had the money.

Alex had been right about the land. It was all Government owned, and the resentment was deeply embedded in those who worked the fields. It explained the *ferment* amongst the more militant of the stems. But building a castle in the 22nd Century would not sufficiently influence or disturb any City into releasing land. The seeds of unrest had blossomed into what might have been a tourist attraction, had it been well enough advertised. Alex felt sorry for them. The Governments of the Cities were not interested in the feelings of a group of primitive farmers. There was one way he might be able to help.

In the last decade, there had been a revival of interest in

wood. Alex had observed the enthusiasm of young scientists who were studying tropical cane growth with an eye to accelerating forest growth in temperate zones. He concluded that the Angles might be an ideal area to turn to trees. It would give the farming community a sense of purpose—Alex assumed that nobody from the City would wish to act as a forest worker—and, being near the City, transportation would not be a problem. He resolved to mention it to someone.

Alex looked up at the sky as he clipped together what would eventually be a chicken coop. The sun seemed to have found itself a hole in the clouds. Over the rest of the countryside, to the north and west, the cumulus hung black and low. As he was resting, Polgrove and Jamie came out of the farmhouse. They were each carrying something in the crook of their right arms. Long black tubes. Shotguns.

Jamie had been cutting hair that morning. Some young local boys had been brought by thickset mothers to have their locks cropped by the old man. It was not that Jamie was a skilled barber—indeed, some of the hair-styles were more sightly before his inartistic hands had begun their mutilating process—but he alone in the neighbourhood owned a pair of hand clippers. Watching him, one did not doubt that a great deal of expertise was involved. One only doubted afterwards, as the victim was being led away in tears.

"Nearly finished," Alex said as they approached.

Polgrove nodded. "Not a bad job."

Alex pointed with the pliers.

"Going out shooting? What's there to kill at this time of year? Rabbits?"

Jamie said sharply, "Fox. I seen that bugger two morning's runnin' now. Out near the old rail track. We can nail him today."

Alex's heart gave a jump. "I see."

"You want to come along? Have to stay behind the guns but you're welcome to watch."

Polgrove was giving him a treat—in Polgrove's eyes. They both knew of his fear of foxes. Maybe these stems were using a bit of practical rustic psychology and thought this was the way to cure a city illness. Alex cleared his throat before the lie left it.

"I should like that very much. I'll just put on some warmer clothes—the wind may be colder out there on the flats."

Jamie looked around the edge of the sky.

"Ah, could be. But this weather belongs more to May than December."

Nevertheless, Alex went inside the house and put on his oversuit. He noticed that his hands were trembling.

"Idiot," he said to himself. Anyway, it was doubtful they would even see the fox. The habits of wild animals were not as predictable as Jamie would have him believe.

Outside again, he fell in beside the two stems and they started off across the fields towards a small pond some two kilometres away. They passed around the marsh areas, using the edge of cultivated fields as their path. It was difficult walking over the clods of earth and neither of his companions was of a talkative nature, so they clumped along in silence, Alex's weak ankles giving him trouble occasionally.

The unnaturally high December temperatures had thrown the plants and bushes into confusion. Having just dropped their leaves the hedges had now received the signal that spring was close by. One or two still clung to the remains of their summer foliage. It was as if they were reluctant to surrender to the proper season in case something was coming to divert it. There was a vibrant feeling in the air when there should have been a leaden one. The skies immediately overhead were blue and cloud-feathered, not the usual grey wash stirred with a dirty stick. Along the ditches, life was lifting the dry grasses from beneath and there were fresh holes appearing in the banks. A light covering of coleoptile fuzz had been breathed on to the normally barren fields.

The two men walking slightly ahead of Alex had, if not a bounce, then the equivalent of such in heavy-footed farmers. Plastic boots thudded ageless rhythms into the drum of the world and Jamie's grizzled face tilted itself occasionally upward, as if his large nose were a necessary filter for the pleasant country odours carried on the breeze. It was at once an inquisitive and an appreciative gesture.

Polgrove's red neck glowed well-being through its network of fine white creases.

All's right with the world?

Alex knew it wasn't, although the unseasonal weather could hardly be called a problem. Anything that held the winter at bay was bound to be good, especially out in the Angles.

"Polgrove, why have you just *now* decided to kill the fox? Surely it's been around—well, I thought it had—for some time? Since before I came to stay?"

"True. But the winter's coming on. Cold winds and an empty belly make a fox des'prate. He'll get to the chickens no matter what we do to keep him out. Kill 'im is the only answer."

Alex thought about that.

"Aren't there other animals—wild beasts—that will rob a chicken coop?"

Jamie replied, "Oh, there's plenty there if you want 'em." He cleared his nose of surplus fluid and decorated a fence post with the yield. Alex felt himself wincing.

"Then what? What animals?"

"Like a stoat what changes mysterious, into *ermine*." He pronounced it with a long vowel. "Dark coat to snow, just like that."

Alex's eyes widened as he thought he sensed witchcraft.

"Really? What are these ... ermine?" Then he saw Jamie's shoulders quiver slightly and he knew he was being laughed at. He felt both stupid and angry. These stems, these yokels, never ceased to make fun of him.

As they neared the place where Jamie had seen the fox, they motioned to Alex to stay back. The shotguns, covered in ornate centripetal engraving along the double-barrels, glinted a dull blue in the sunlight. They were middle 21st-Century sporting guns with an over-and-under barrel arrangement and real wood stocks and butts made of redwood, highly polished with use. Alex knew they were prized possessions. He himself found them strangely beautiful instruments. Was it that the guns themselves were attractive, or was it what they did? He was inclined to believe it was their awesome destructive power that held his own interest. Certainly the terrible noise they made when fired *demanded* respect and appreciation.

He crouched down in a ditch, to leeward, allowing the farmers to move ahead. They didn't *stalk* their prey exactly, but walked purposefully forward, eyes keen, hands firm, knowing they could hit a fox on the run if he broke cover. Alex waited for some time without hearing a shot; and then finally the men returned, moving silhouettes against the eastern sky, guns like manipulating strips projecting from their waists.

"Not there," said Jamie. "We'll try up by the sea wall."

They searched the earthen bank without success, and then several other likely spots, before deciding to return home. Polgrove killed a fat rabbit on the way back but neither man wanted to waste expensive cartridges, so no further shooting took place. In any case, they were men past the age of finding pleasure in taking pot-shots at targets.

Alex was pleased it was over. His ears still rang with the sound of the single shot and his body ached with fatigue.

As they neared the farm, Alex fell back, his tired legs giving him trouble over the rough ground. Jamie was busy pointing out several types of bird that should have migrated by now and generally discoursing on the vagaries of nature, his free arm waving at the horizon. Polgrove, as usual, listened—or did not listen—to his uncle; Alex was never quite sure which, since the farmer's expression gave no indication of what was happening beneath.

Suddenly Alex stumbled on a clod of hard earth and pitched forward into a depression filled with coarse grasses. Simultaneously Polgrove gave a shout. Something began zig-zagging about twenty metres away and a shotgun blast hollowed out a cavern of sound in the morning air. The animal that had been running jack-knifed and somersaulted loosely against the blue backdrop. Alex was sure it was the fox and his heart began racing wildly. He opened his mouth to call, when something stirred in the grass not far from his face. He turned to stare into a pair of bestial eyes.

Instantly the muscles on his cheeks contracted with fear, causing him considerable physical pain. *Not a metre from him was the face of a living fox.*

The eyes held him. He could read fear in those eyes too. Fox and man searched one another for a sign, each an instant away from bolting, reactions tight springs on their triggers.

Not a movement came from either creature and gradually the fear in Alex began to dissipate. It was as if he could look down through the beast's eyes into its mind, could see the fox-thoughts judging him as a known enemy. Thoughts honed to a double-edged decision: whether to run or to play log. *Had the human foe really seen what was fact, or had it just thought it had seen a fox and was not sure?*

Still, absolutely still. Running is the secondary protection. First comes camouflage: melting into the earth, to appear part of the rocks and soil. When that fails, then run. But when is the instant of positive recognition? That is the prey's constant dilemma. So the fox waited for the sign.

There was a link established between them then. They knew each other's secret, and Alex felt a flood of sentiment wash through his body. He had a companion in terror. A cross-section, a transreceiver, of the same emotion. Hunter and prey, fused into one. The cycle complete. Soft hearts pulsed against the turf. Sinews flexed, muscles stayed primed. The mousetrap minds ready for snap decisions. Eyes remained locked.

It was at that moment that Alex realized that his own experience could be equated to the creation of the trinity. It had not been the *fear* itself which had strengthened the closeness factor between the twins, thus creating the field, but a strong visual image merely *enhanced* by the fear. *The emotional trigger was in the vision centre of the brain.* A physical path between the children had been established by the sudden appearance of a key image which had opened a reservoir of empathy and allowed it to flow.

"I see 'im!" came a shout from the direction of the other two men. The shock of the voice made Alex jerk his head upwards. Jamie began running towards him, yelling, "Out of the way! Out of the way!" Alex stood up but remained in the firing line.

And the fox had had the sign and was now a live smudge of red-brown racing against the dark hedgerow. Jamie raised his gun and then must have realized how hopeless his shot would be. He bobbed a couple of times, then flung his arms down.

"Sweyn's eyes," he cursed, "I could've had 'im." He turned on Alex. "Why'dn't get out of the way? You blocked my aim."

"I'm sorry," Alex mumbled under Jamie's glare. "I guess I'm just not quick enough—my reactions. Not for this sort of thing."

"You almost stood there deliberate," accused Jamie.

"Leave it, Jamie," interrupted Polgrove. "He was just froze. There weren't nothing deliberate about it. The man's afraid of foxes an' that's that. Can't change a man's fears in five minutes."

Jamie grumbled something inaudible, then moved away towards the carcass of the dead fox. Alex felt helpless. He wasn't even sure himself that his interference had been accidental. The intention had been to move but just the same his body had stayed where it was. And he was *glad* the fox had escaped. At least, that particular fox. He thought he knew how it felt, even though he was scared of the animal.

He walked over to where the other two men were standing. They were inspecting their kill. Polgrove turned the body over with a casual flick of his foot.

The carcass was almost in two pieces, the heavy gauge shotgun having ripped open the underside and broken the spine as well, a few centimetres from the tail. Suddenly, to Alex's revulsion, Polgrove bent down and thrust his fingers into the gaping wound, then retrieved them covered in gore.

"See that?" he said to Jamie. Both men then nodded. Alex could see they were puzzled.

"What's the matter?" he asked.

"Vixen," replied Jamie curtly. "In cub. Must have been the dog that got away."

It meant nothing to Alex but Polgrove added, "Well out of season. Something's going on—mild weather, birds and bushes acting funny, and now a fox in cub during early December ... ?" He let his words tail off.

"Is that very rare?"

"Well, let's say it an't usual. It happens but it's not *just* that. It's other things too."

A thought struck Alex and he said suddenly, "I wonder ...

maybe that field the twins created has got something ... no, that's stupid, it was—sorry, *is*—only local."

"Field?" Polgrove screwed up his eyes.

"Yes." He looked at the faces of the two men and then read the incomprehension. "Oh, not a field like this." He kicked the earth with his foot. "A magnetic field—a ..." He searched his mind for a comparison the farmers could understand. "Well, like the sun's radiation. You can't exactly *see* it but you know it's there. You can feel it. And of course it can be measured by electronic devices."

They still looked a little lost, so he said, "Forget it. I'm probably wrong anyway. It was just a sudden thought."

Jamie did not let things go that easily.

"Twins, you say? Up at the school?"

Alex twisted uneasily.

"Yes."

"An' they got this radiating thing which is changing the weather?"

"No. That is, not really. It's nothing to do with radiation. I just put that up as an example. It's merely a sort of *feeling* that passes between them. They're very close, you see." He had to steer well clear of radiation. There were unpleasant connotations attached to that word.

"An' what's a *feeling* got to do with a fox in cub?"

"Nothing," mumbled Alex. "Now let's forget it. I'm bored with the subject. I'm sorry I got in your way. Now let's go home and ... and just forget it."

But it was not easy to forget something that filled their lives in the subsequent weeks. It became very obvious to all in that area of the Angles that they were a special group. The sun shone most days with liquid softness and almost every night a light rain fell to water the winter crops. Those summer birds that had not already left remained in the area to take part in the unnatural springtime. Bushes that had corked off their tips began sprouting green fingers again and the light green of the early crops covered the fields like the fuzz on a stripling stem's chin.

The area became alive with wild life.

There were two reasons for this: firstly, those animals that hibernated, or slept throughout the winter, began waking and nosing around for food; the second reason was that there appeared to be an enormous influx of creatures that normally lived outside the sunlit territory. This was natural, since farther afield it was cold and wet and most of them were starving. In the Outer Angles there was plenty of game for the carnivores and the promise of cereal, fruit and berries for the herbivores.

For humans, who indulged in both meat and vegetables, it was a weird but pleasant sensation. Some of the more industrious—those who believed the mild weather would last out the winter—began to comb their fields with ploughs. Others watched sceptically from porches blooming with convolvulous flowers, and flicked away wasps and flies with a disbelieving wave of their hands.

The children were disappointed at first. They had been looking forward to ice and snow as promised winter toys. But the young soon fell into step with the new situation and fishing poles were extracted from hiding places, nesting began in earnest and others looked forward with apple eyes to the obvious coming of a second scrumping season.

At Manston House, the change was viewed with great concern. If it remained warm, the country's attention would soon focus on the Outer Angles and solutions to the puzzle would be sought. There would be parties of eager students and lone professors wandering over the mainland. Possibly they might even venture out to the island and Strecker was anxious that their presence at Feerness should not be discovered by the media, which would very soon find a reason for them being there. Whether that reason was a true one or not mattered little. Questions would be asked and the Ministry would be embarrassed. It would mean the end of the project. Strecker made urgent trips to the City in order to speed up the decision on when to set up the human telemetry system between New Carthage and Earth.

7 Revolt

On Lo sat complacently astride the animal, full of unfounded trust in Alex, who was nominally in charge of the beast. They made their way from clump to clump of rich grass not far from Manston House, talking in quiet tones.

"I can feel it . . . her, you know," said Alex to the child.

Holding the rein and looking up into the girl's nutmeg face, he was experiencing a gentle vibration running through his body. It did seem sometimes as though he could see a movement in the air around her, the blur of something oscillating at high speeds, like humming-birds' wings. He could not be sure that this was not simply an illusion produced by the sensation, which was at all times present, but stronger when one was close to either one of the Chinese children.

"Yes," replied On to his remark.

"Then why can't my pony feel her?"

This was an insult to all true ponies—the horse was at least seventeen hands—but Alex always used what he thought of as "childwords" for animals and objects when speaking to the young.

"Because . . ." The eyes narrowed with concentration. "Probably because it's not a person. Yes, that's it."

"What, her? Or the pony?"

"The pony. It's not a person, is it?"

What was it that separated beasts from men? Intelligence? A soul? An awareness of death? Or perhaps something completely outside *human* consideration.

"Do you know why she's come? How did she get there, do you know?" Alex asked for the sixth time.

"No, no," said On Lo, smiling. He had asked two questions and she had answered both of them, as she always did, separately. And the answers were always in monosyllables, never an explanation. She was, as Nicole pointed out, only a child, a very small child.

"Why does she make all this nice weather?"

"She doesn't say. She can't *speak*, you know, uncle. She's just *there*."

"Why do you call her 'she'?" he questioned shrewdly. "Is she a lady?"

"She *feels* like one. She feels like my mummy. Can I ride some more? It's just eating."

Nicole? Or On Lo's real mother? There was no *real* mother. Just a donor, unknown and lost in a crowd of a hundred million Chinese.

"Gee-up, gee-up," chanted the child.

"Come on, you old nag," he grumbled, jerking the mare's head. "Once more round the garden."

The mare reluctantly left the grass but managed a last wrench which filled her mouth and gave her green whiskers. Alex pulled the clumping animal along as On Lo shouted to her sister, who had appeared at the main doors of the house with Nicole, "Look at me, look at me, I'm a lady!" She affected an exaggerated upright pose. Nicole smiled indulgently. There was something about that smile that triggered a warning signal in Alex but he dismissed it. There were problems enough without inventing more.

"Has Strecker arrived back yet?" he called.

Nicole shook her head.

"Okay. Does Ti want a ride?"

Even as he said it, he saw the distant speck of what would be Strecker's hummer crossing the water.

"He's coming," he said, lifting On from the horse and experiencing that strong charge as he did so. The child ran to join her sister.

Nicole was wearing her black hair in a tight bun, away from her face. The eyebrows curved slightly upwards at their points and the hair-style made her complexion seem smoother and clearer than ever. She was immaculately groomed, as usual, her lipstick gleaming in the sunlight. It gave her a well-defined, classical look. There was resolution in that expression. She was wearing her yellow summer suit, as befitted the weather. It was the one the twins liked.

"How are you feeling this morning?" Alex asked. He had released the horse, allowing it to graze at will.

"Fine."

"You look fine."

"Yes." She had not taken her eyes from the approaching vehicle. Alex felt nervous for some reason.

"You look as fine as porcelain. You look as though your cheeks would ring if I flicked them with my fingernail."

She smiled then.

"The intrepid horseman."

"Yep. I came galloping across the broomway full speed to see my porcelain princess. Have you eaten?"

"I don't feel like anything at the moment. It's too early. How did you sneak On out without me seeing you?"

"She was already up and playing with her toys. Ti was still asleep so I crept out with her. It was all right, wasn't it?"

Nicole gave him a sidelong glance.

"Well, I was a little alarmed when I found her bed empty. She does wander out into the garden sometimes. You should have told me."

"I thought you were asleep too. I'm sorry. Next time . . ."

Strecker's hummer had stopped and he was climbing from it. The veins in Nicole's neck were as taut as wires. Strecker was smiling.

"No," said Nicole, softly.

"What? What was that?" asked Alex.

Strecker bounded up, and then stopped short.

"Well?" asked Nicole sharply.

Strecker looked at her and smiled.

"Everything's okay. It's all systems go."

"They've agreed to it?" said Alex incredulously. "They're setting up the system?"

"Right. Ha!" Strecker slapped him on the arm in boyish delight. "We did it."

Nicole's face was white. Christ, thought Alex, until now she didn't believe it would happen. She believed the twins would stay together, under her care.

"You can't," she said. "I won't let you."

The venom in her tone drained Strecker's face.

"You have no say," he replied.

"I do. I must do. I'm their mother. Their foster-mother," she amended weakly.

The twins were clutching at her trousers, their faces registering concern.

"You're both frightening the children," said Alex quietly. "Let's go and talk this over in your study, John."

He became the autocrat.

"There's nothing to talk over. They're going to perform the function for which they were . . ."

"Designed? Manufactured?" Nicole's voice was still full of acid.

"I was going to say 'born'."

"I'll bet you were. What the hell do you know about birth?" she said.

"Or you?" he replied coolly. "You're merely their nurse, Nicole. Already you're on the way to becoming a narrow-minded old spinster."

"How dare you say that to me," she choked. Her eyes brimmed with tears and Alex longed to put his arm around her.

"Mummy," said Ti Lo in a little voice. Nicole hugged the girls to her.

"You see?" she said in a small but triumphant voice.

"That wasn't fair, John," Alex intervened. "I think you ought to apologize." He curled the fingers of his hands, not quite sure what he should do if Strecker refused.

To his relief Strecker said, "Sorry," curtly, and brushed past Nicole on his way up the steps. Nicole hung her head.

Alex waited for her to say something. Eventually she looked up, a resigned expression now.

"Well, that's that then."

Alex nodded.

" 'Fraid so. You know, it's funny. When I first came here you convinced me the project was worthwhile—something we ought to do. But now you've done an about-face."

"It's different now. *They* are different." She spoke to the twins. "Go in now, to breakfast. I'll be in, in a few minutes. All right?"

They nodded and dutifully trotted into the house.

She turned back to Alex.

"They're not the same children. They're special. You know that. Have you seen the way the other children treat them? They hold them in *awe*, Alex, and no one has said anything, or done anything to make them think that way. They just *know*."

He knew what she was talking about but it worried him to dwell on it.

"What do you mean, *know*? Know what?"

Nicole became exasperated.

"Don't play games with me, Alex. This weather. This farmer's dream. Whatever that thing is between the children —and I'm not the only one to . . . well, there are some who are prepared to believe in divinity."

"Who?" The word came out like a short, sharp cough. He didn't like the way the conversation was going but felt powerless to stop it.

"The stems. That's who. They incline their heads when the twins pass—when *I* pass. They *worship* them, Alex."

"*Holy Mary, Mother of Christ,*" he said. He hadn't meant it to sound so bitingly sarcastic but it had. Why was he always so defensive, so caustic concerning things he didn't understand? It was as if incomprehensible events clustered round him like phantoms and he had to ignore them, or fight them off with cynicism. If he was nasty enough to Nicole, perhaps he could change things, nullify those unwelcome ghosts.

She was not angry, which made it worse. She affected a sort of holy-sufferance attitude.

"No," she said, "nothing like that at all. I don't believe this is a deity. I think it's some physical manifestation, but one we have not, as a race, come into contact with before. Whatever it is, it seems to have the power—either consciously or unconsciously, I mean it may not even *know* what it's doing—it seems to have the gift of giving us what we most want."

She looked him directly in the eyes and he turned away.

"So I should wish for a pot of gold, and I'll get it? Right?"

"Wrong. You won't get anything but what *everyone* wants, and not everyone wants to be rich."

"Then they're idiots," he laughed. But the phantoms refused to be joked away too.

"Don't you see?" she continued. "It's the undercurrent feeling of the community this—I can't call it 'she' like the twins because I don't think it has intelligence—this entity, then, is diagnosing. Or do I mean *prognosis*? I'm never sure. It's the concentrator for this community desire, a wish . . ."

"The collective desire—hope—or something like that?" Was that Jung? Or was he bending the facts to fit the theory?

Her eyes lit up. "Yes, yes. I knew you would have a way of putting it better than I can." Which was intended to grab him by the ego, and did, of course.

She added, "The stems. This is a farming community and the one hope is that the weather will be conducive to ideal growing conditions. It's happened. The Outer Angles is having a second summer."

"I'm not so sure that's a good thing," Alex replied dubiously.

She shook her head in impatience.

"I didn't *say* it was a good thing—or a bad thing. I don't believe it's concerned with good or evil, right versus wrong. It merely interprets the collective desire and transforms it into reality."

"What if everyone wants civil war? I get the idea that some of these people would like to see the fall of at least one City Government."

She shrugged. "Okay. So it'll happen. But it won't, because people are not *sure* of that particular desire. It's probably got to be deeper than that. Overwhelming. Rooted in many generations—like farming."

"Or peace and prosperity? For all men?"

She nodded vigorously. "And women."

"I was speaking figuratively. People then. But you're forgetting one thing. The effect is only local."

"I know. That worries me, I must admit. But if we were to split the twins then we should put them on opposite sides of the Earth, not send them into space. That way the field they produce may encompass the whole world and we can all benefit."

"What if it all turns sour?"

"Then peace and prosperity—whatever form they take—will no longer be the racial wish. Something else will be. Don't you see, it's foolproof—*it has to be something we all want*. Not just a few. And the politicians can rave all they wish, telling us what is good for us—communism, democracy, Hpasism. We will have the key in our collective conscious, and no one can change that."

"People all want different things."

"Individuals, yes. Groups, no."

Alex looked away from her face. She appeared very militant in her tight yellow suit and with her hair drawn back tightly from her face. Severe. It was almost as if her appearance was deliberate, in order to provoke comment.

"Alex," she said, "please do what you can to make John change his mind."

He sighed. He had had the idea that she intended to solicit his aid. She knew he was unable to resist her when she pleaded that way. She did not do it often, which made it all the more sincere.

"I'll do what I can."

She kissed his cheek.

"Thanks, Alex. In the meantime, I'll take the twins for a walk. They could do with some fresh air."

She left him on the steps and he stared moodily over the grounds to where the waves broke in irregular patterns on the shore. The problem was he was not convinced she was right. But then eight weeks ago, he would have wholeheartedly endorsed her proposals. Oh well, he thought, nothing is ever constant. He had better go inside and tackle Strecker.

Nicole went directly to her room and packed a small bag with some light overwear. Then, making sure the corridor was clear, she went to the dormitories and gathered together some items of children's clothing.

The children were in the dining-hall and Nicole decided to place the bag inside the hummer first, then collect the twins.

Her heart was jumping wildly and she hoped she would not meet Alex or Strecker on the way because she felt sure her face would give her away.

The bag stowed, she proceeded to put Alex's hummer out of commission by removing a piece of the motor. Then she went to collect the twins.

They went without protest, having finished their breakfast. Vibrations coursed through Nicole's body but the feeling excited rather than disturbed her.

Outside the building she made her way towards the hummer. Her legs were shaking a little, but not from fright.

"Where are we going?" asked Ti Lo.

"For a ride, darling. Over the water. Don't you want to come on a ride with mummy?"

On Lo nodded her head gravely and Ti Lo smiled.

"We think so, yes," Ti said.

They scrambled into the hummer, On sitting on Ti's lap in the single passenger seat. In her haste to get away before the men discovered her defection, Nicole almost ran into the horse. It was a stupid action; now that she was mobile, she reminded herself, the men could not follow. She had sabotaged the only other vehicle.

The horse? No, that scraggy animal couldn't manage a decent trot, let alone a gallop. She was safe, except for some reason she did not want to *see* either of the men. She might falter in her resolve or do something silly. She realized she was embarrassed at having to resort to subterfuge.

The tide was in so there was no real necessity to cross by the broomway. Nicole made straight for the beach nearest the house and sped on to the dark sea. It was a little choppy which made their ride bumpier than usual but the twins did not seem to be worried. They stared through the transparent bubble-front down on to the rolling surface of the water, their faces solemn. They were, compared to other infants, composed and submissive. Their IQ's, though a little above average, were not exceptional. They had, to Nicole's knowledge, no special musical talents; they were not brilliant artists nor did they show any signs of being so; and they had no supernatural powers, no second sight or extra-sensory perception. Nothing,

96

Nicole thought, above the very ordinary. Yet, they *were* special. They appeared to be the unwitting hosts for some strange creation or visitation which radiated well-being over the immediate countryside. She had to protect them from Strecker, who was, it was obvious, interested only in his stupid alarm system for New Carthage.

The hummer suddenly hit smoothness and Nicole came out of her reverie to find herself racing the vehicle along tidal creeks covered in saltwort. She slowed down, then drove towards the Polgrove farmhouse, using the broomway gap to cut through the sea wall. On the other side she almost collided with another vehicle, a hummer from the City.

Her first thought was that Strecker had contacted the police: there was a circuit for official calls between the house and the Ministry which he could use. Then she realized she was being foolish. The police could not have driven to the Angles so quickly. As the other hummer drew up alongside, she looked at the occupants. One was a man; the eyes were weak, the hair lank, the face drawn and the colour of subterranean limestone. Nicole recalled Alex's description. The nuisance. His bones must have knitted enough to allow him to venture out—at least in a vehicle.

Sitting beside the nuisance was a slim woman with short dark hair tight against her head. She looked, to Nicole's eyes, sophisticated, vivacious and smart.

"Lila Craven," muttered Nicole to herself, although she had never met the woman before.

The woman climbed out of her hummer and stumbled over the uneven ground towards Nicole. She would, of course, know about Nicole. The nuisance would have told her. Nicole felt some trepidation. She said, "Yes?" through the air vent as the woman leaned forward.

"I wonder if you can help us? Is this the way to a house called Manston?"

The mouth was small, confident; the manner, pert. She did not know Nicole after all. The nuisance had said nothing. Why? Why withhold information from his employer? Or was he tired of being bullied? That was the most likely reason. He was just being contrary. Lila Craven probably gave him a terrible time.

"Manston? Oh yes. Across the water. It's on an island called Feerness."

Lila Craven frowned.

"He was right. I thought he was mad when he said we'd have to cross water."

"Who?"

"My ... companion. I thought he must have it wrong. It looks very dangerous out there. And ... weird. So open." She hugged herself and shivered.

"Don't worry," said Nicole kindly. "The twins and I have just crossed and it's perfectly safe. Just a little choppy this morning."

The frown deepened.

"Crossed? You're from this Feerness place? You don't look like a stem." She studied the Chinese identicals with obvious fascination.

In another moment she would have guessed. Nicole pulled away sharply, just before the nuisance climbed from the other hummer. There was a look on his face which said *"Wait a minute. I know you."*

It was not that he had recognized her and was keeping it to himself. He had not, until that moment, realized who she was.

Poor Alex, thought Nicole. It was not his day, that was for sure. She tried to visualize his face when he saw the other hummer approaching and, expecting a returning penitent Nicole, he was confronted instead with a gloating wife.

Nicole drove towards the Polgrove farm and on reaching it left the twins sitting in the hummer and went looking for Polgrove rather than knock on the farmhouse door. She had no wish to speak to Mrs Polgrove and the farmer would not be indoors at that time of day.

He did not appear to be working around the farmhouse. Nicole took the hummer out into the countryside. She found him after half an hour of searching. He was standing on the outskirts of a field of bright green shoots with a dreamy expression on his face. Every now and then he seemed to sniff the air appreciatively.

Not wanting to harm the crops, Nicole stopped at the edge of the field and let the twins run loose. It was cramped in the small hummer and they had begun fidgeting. Polgrove ambled towards her, a benign giant with a giant's heavy tread.

He nodded towards the two youngsters as they gambolled in the dry ditch.

"Are they the ones?" he asked. There was a note of veneration in his voice.

"Yes, they are," she replied. There was no need for any qualification, and her heart felt lighter than it had done for many weeks. She smiled at him.

"How did you know? Was it Alex who told you?"

"He said something but we had to guess some. It weren't hard. Where are you taking 'em? To the City?"

"No, I'm running away," she replied frankly. "I came looking for help—your help. Anyone's. They want to send one of the twins to a distant planet. They want to split them. I think that would be wrong, don't you?"

"Would it make any difference to this?" He waved a hand over his greening furrows.

"I think so. If the twins were parted, it might destroy their closeness factor. The magic would be gone."

She had chosen the word "magic" deliberately, since she knew the stems were a superstitious people, but his reply surprised her.

"Not magic so much as the hand of God."

"Do you think so? They seem normal enough children. Look at them."

The twins were rolling down a grassy bank, laughing in delight and, on standing up, pretending to be dizzier than they really were.

Polgrove regarded them for a time then said, "I would expect them to be happy. I don't suppose Jesus walked around with a long face all day, or kept himself prettyboy—clean as a young 'un. No doubt he played along with the rest of his pals, just as these two."

"If you say so," Nicole said, smiling.

The farmer became business-like.

"What we'll do now is take you to young Pagey. He'll look

after you. You can stay there the night then go on to the castle in the morning. Sweyn's castle. We'll hide you there till they stop looking."

"That's the blond youth? The one that saved Alex from drowning?"

A muscle was palpitating in her forehead, just above the left eye, and she wondered whether it was visible to Polgrove. He looked at her hard. Then he said, "I know what you're thinking and you can rest your pretty little mind. He would no more touch you than he would defile Sweyn's statue."

"Did it show that easily?" She gave a little laugh. "I'm very silly."

"No. I can understand your worry, but it isn't needed. He knows what'd happen to him—and anyway, the boy is one of your followers. To him you are the mother of the holy twins. Were he to even *think* of touching your person, he'd cut off his own head to stop the thought flowing. Be sure of that."

"Thank you," she said quietly.

"No need. That's the way it is."

The smell of fresh earth was in her nostrils and the sound of childish laughter in her ears. A stream trickled somewhere nearby and off in the middle distance was a group of white seagulls. They were clustered in a loose circle in the centre of a field, most of them with their heads turned towards the ocean. She felt strangely peaceful. Alex had called her Mary. He had meant it to be sarcastic, but to these people it was a serious consideration.

"Can I touch them?" asked Polgrove.

She looked round. He was standing near the twins, looking down on their small, dark heads.

"Of course."

Gently he placed a hand on each head, and such a look of ecstasy came over his face it made tears spring to Nicole's eyes. The twins rolled their own eyes upwards, towards the farmer, and they giggled in unison. He laughed. His big-boned, cartographic face fractured with creases of laughter. Nicole began laughing too. The fine, warm air carried their happiness over the green furze and hid it in the blanket of the whin.

8 Sweyn's People

Pagey was a good host. He was considerate and able to predict needs, especially those of the children, which was unusual for a young, unmarried man. A hot drink was available half an hour before bedtime and a night-light was provided.

"They might get frightened in a strange house," he explained to Nicole.

The "house" was little more than a two-roomed hovel, built of stone and with a thatched roof. It was strong, though, and kept the winter firmly on the outside—when there was a winter to be excluded. The furniture was sparse.

Despite Polgrove's continued reassurances on their journey to the small dwelling, Nicole still felt apprehensive about spending a night in a strange place with a young, primitive youth. She watched him continuously once the children were asleep, until he looked up from beneath the shaggy, blond hair and said, "I'm not likely to do anything. I know my place."

"Sorry," she replied, blushing. "I can't help it. It's no good me saying I'll relax because I won't. It's just the way I am, with anyone. Even Alex."

"He's a fool, that one."

She flared. "Don't talk like that. You don't know him. Just because his ways aren't yours."

The youth looked taken aback. So much so, she was instantly sorry for having attacked him.

"Is he special? To you, I mean?" he asked. He fumbled with something—a fishing line—as he talked, the artificial light printing silhouettes of struggling monsters on the wall behind him.

"A little. He's a very good friend of mine and I won't hear of him being maligned, especially in his absence."

Pagey looked up and said frankly, "I don't know what that means. What's it mean?"

"Don't talk badly of anyone. It isn't nice."

Staring into his face, she saw that his eyes were slightly crossed; the left one was weak, which only served to make him appear more sinister than ever. Her words had been delivered in a forceful tone but towards the end of the sentence she had faltered. The youth before her was tall and heavily set, like a shire horse. He could break her in two if he wished. It was best not to provoke him, no matter what he professed his intentions to be.

"What's the matter?" he asked.

"Nothing. No, nothing. I'm sorry, I can't help staring. You're new to me, altogether. Tell me," she said in an effort to change the subject, "what's this Sweyn business? Why do you look up to him? He was only a man, and not a very extraordinary one at that."

"There's men and men."

Good, homespun philosophies. Oh, God.

"But what was special about this one? I mean, I use a man through whom I direct my prayer, but I *know* what was special about him. He was a man with extraordinary foresight and insight into future generations' environmental problems."

Pagey furrowed his brow and twisted his mouth. Thought processes given shape and texture.

"He were a man that lived strong and feared no government."

She smiled. "When Sweyn was around, he *was* the government. Only one other person was more powerful and that was the king."

"But he were a shepherd. It says so in some old books."

"A very broad description. It means he owned sheep but you can be sure he didn't look after them himself. He had people like you to do that."

Once the words were out she regretted them. She knew he identified with Sweyn himself and not with his serfs. It was silly to shatter harmless illusions. The boy looked puzzled, though, and she realized she had not reached him. She could still repair any damage.

"You see," she continued, "he owned so *many* sheep he couldn't possibly look after all of them by himself."

A satisfied expression replaced the bewildered look.

"That's true. I heard that said. He were a warrior too, and a good 'un. Good with the sword. I'll show you my sword tomorrow. Fine steel. I can cut a pig's head through with one chop. I'll show you," he offered obligingly.

"That's all right," she said too quickly. "I don't want you to go to any trouble for me. I can *see* you're very strong."

"It an't strength, it's the way you do it."

"Technique? Skill?"

He nodded, the mouth pursed. He really did wear his feelings on his face. It was then she realized she was perfectly safe. This was one youth who could never lie and get away with it. She smiled at him again.

"Where am I to sleep tonight?" she asked.

"You can go in there with the holy twins. I'll stay here. Don't sleep much anyhow—only when I been drinkin'."

He grinned at her boyishly and she laughed. Then she stood up and stretched.

"Well, I think I'd like to turn in. You don't mind?"

"No, of course not." But he did; she could see he was disappointed that the conversation was at an end.

"We can talk more later," she said. "We'll have plenty of time. At the castle, and on the way."

"Yes. Okay. I'll put out the light."

He did so. They both stood in the dark for a few moments, unmoving, then Nicole felt her way to her bed and lay on it fully clothed, allowing sleep to overtake her.

The following morning she allowed him to show her the sword, and he demonstrated his skill in wielding the blade, cutting down imaginary foes and roaring like a bull as he did so. The twins were fascinated and clapped every time he completed a series of strokes, slicing the morning shafts of sunlight with the stamps, yells and grunts of a man releasing pent-up energy. He finished, smiling and perspiring, the blade flashing fire as he threw it up to complete a final weaponry somersault. It landed point first, buried itself in the earth between his feet and swayed like a metronome, backwards and forwards. Nicole was very impressed.

"Where did you learn to do that? Who taught you?"

He looked shy.

"Nobody *taught* me, though some of them strokes were showed me by a friend of mine. He's dead now."

"Oh, I'm sorry."

"No need for that. He died of old age an' happy too."

She nodded, not wishing to probe any further. They ate some breakfast and then set out for the castle on foot, Pagey leading a horse laden with their clothes. The hummer was left behind, hidden in some bushes. On the way he told her details of the change to countryside and of the many animals and birds that now inhabited the area.

He told her that it was not *all* good, for the pests and vermin had increased along with the game, but added that he would rather have too much than too little life in the region.

"I seen some terrible fights too," he said, as they strolled along in the early morning, over grassland paths. "You see, each animal has its own piece of land, like a farmer ..."

"Its territory."

"That's right. You got it. An' if another animal of the same kind starts hunting on the same piece of ... territory, then they fight. 'Course, all this weather's brought in beasts from all over."

"But, accepting that, each animal's territory will shrink in these conditions, won't it? I mean, a fox will patrol as much land as it takes to feed him and his vixen. If more game is available within that area then he doesn't need as much ..."

Pagey nodded his tousled head.

"That's right, I suppose. Seems to make sense ... but you should see some of the fights."

She asked, "Do these combats ever end in death?"

He shook his head this time.

"Never seen that. One of 'em usually ends up on its back, laying bare its belly and throat, see. *I surrender*, it's saying. *You can rip me from neck to knackers* ... but they never do. They let 'em go, off somewhere else, to find a weaker animal."

He chatted on about life in the marshes and she listened with interest.

They had to stop quite often for the twins to rest but the going was not arduous. Occasionally Pagey carried one twin, or both, but he could not keep it up for very long. It was not that he was not strong enough. He had the strength. It was the direct contact with the energy from the triad that forced him to place the children on the ground after a few hundred metres. He confessed to Nicole that they left him physically weak after each carrying session. Nevertheless, by noon they had reached the castle and were admitted immediately. Nicole was embarrassed by the treatment they received: the bowing, the humble gestures of welcome, the whispered "Thankyous". The twins themselves were a little afraid of the size of the reception committee: it seemed that every stem in the Outer Angles had arrived that morning to pay homage to them. Clearly they considered the twins in the light of a theophany.

Now that they had the twins, the stems did not seem to know what to do with them. They gave the three newcomers a deferential tour of the castle and then showed them to a room in one of the towers. They had even thought to provide toys for the children, which the twins fell upon eagerly.

The room had been furnished quite lavishly by stem standards and Nicole felt guilty for imposing upon these generous people. She felt she was being treated kindly under false pretences. Still, there was nothing she could do about it. She needed them—and they *seemed* to need her. Or at least, the twins.

Left alone, she considered their position. What, then, she thought, while staring through one of the arrow loops at the blue sky, if she was right? What if that "goodness" or whatever one liked to call it (perhaps it was just a *reflection* of a racial longing, the field being the mirror for that which was termed "good" in the minds of the people) was loose energy of a sort that was spread thinly throughout the universe? And then, occasionally, someone came along who attracted this energy and acted as a concentrator for the "goodness" of the universe? Did it collect around a place, thing or person to form an essence of holiness?

Consider history's holy prophets, such as Christ and Mohammed. Consider the holy places such as Lourdes. Consider holy objects like the Black Stone of Mecca or the Shroud of Turin. Perhaps these people, these places, these things had the facility of absorbing holiness and re-broadcasting that concentration of energy in the way the sun radiates heat? Perhaps it was an optimum assemblage of atoms which created this attraction? An accident in chemistry?

She wondered if her theory of divine energy was new. She decided it couldn't be—it was too simple to be original.

It would explain, though, the difference between faith healers and the men with true divinity. Two ends of a vast scale: at one end, those with weak magnetic properties and, at the other end, the strong men like Christ Jesus radiating "goodness". A man who attracted holy energy in vast quantities and allowed it to pour forth upon his people. Surely that was it? The twins were a split whole. Perhaps their chemistry was such it needed the turn of a psychological key to link them into the most powerful projector of divine energy the world had ever known? Science and divinity, interwoven. Even Einstein had called in God to substantiate his theories on the nature of the universe.

Mathew Tse had written "Tree Messiah" with the thought that "goodness", being in all things, could be concentrated in a single object, be it a tree or a man. The leaves soak up the sunshine, the roots take in their water by osmosis—*the Christ-tree's soul draws its holy energy from the now of space and time.*

When night fell, the castle became a Christmas tree, with torches lighting the hallways and candles festooning the walls of the rooms. Nicole put the twins to bed after a light supper of oatcakes and lemonade. Then she began to wander over the great stone giant by herself.

Wherever she went, down corridors where flame-lit walls jumped and leaped in primitive dances or into halls strewn with straw, the stems nodded and smiled, their warmth reaching out to her. She was not altogether convinced by their apparent friendliness. She knew, from experience, they could be a cold, forbidding group of people and it was only because she was the foster-mother of their Messiahs that they opened the summer of their nature to her. On the island they had passed her with stony faces and the merest hint of a nod to acknowledge her greetings. She did not trust them completely. Not yet. Perhaps when she had been in their company for a while she might.

They were certainly a busy crowd, always bent over some task or other. In the evening—or at least, this evening—most of the women appeared to be sewing. Nicole had never held a needle in her life. Clothes were sealed, not sewn, in the City.

"Hello . . . ma'am."

The last word was delivered awkwardly, as if the user was unsure whether it was correct form of address. She turned to see Pagey sitting quite near, a litre pot in his fist. He smiled shyly, looking a little uncomfortable between two of his contemporaries. One of them, a dark-eyed youth with an eager expression, jumped to his feet and offered her his seat. She took it gracefully.

"How are you, Pagey?" she asked, pleased to be near someone she knew, if only for a short while.

"I'm fine, thank you. This here's Brendon." He indicated the youth on his feet. "And this is Jan. They're friends of mine."

"Pleased to meet you both. I'm . . ."

"Yes, we know. You're the mother of the twins," said Jan. He was freckled and sandy-haired. One side of his nose seemed to have collapsed in on itself, closing the nostril. It gave his features a dented appearance.

"How did you get that squashed nose?" she asked. "Fighting?"

He smiled. "Naw. I were born like that. Mam had a quick fright while I were still coming out."

The boys all laughed, though they must have heard the same witticism a hundred times before.

Looking round, she noticed that people were preparing for bed. One or two had already laid their heads on bunches of straw and appeared to be asleep. A pair of lovers were curled in each other's arms, like kittens. She envied them the security they gave each other. It was while she was considering this lack of shared support in her life that she noticed the fat man standing in the archway. He returned her stare and then suddenly turned up the corners of his thin-lipped mouth, as if in pain. It was a few seconds before she realized he was smiling at her. She smiled back, weakly.

"Pagey. *Pagey*!" she said, interrupting the youth's flow of conversation.

"What?"

"Who ... who's that, there? Over there, in the doorway. The fat man."

"What? Him? You don't want to have no dealings with him. That there's Necka, the witch."

"*Witch*? I thought witches were female? He ... Necka looks like a *man*."

Pagey laughed. "Well, you could say that. Then again, you could say he don't look anything like a man. He looks more like a pig ..."

"Hush! He might hear you."

Necka still wore the smile she had obviously provoked, like a red crescent slashed in his face.

"So what," said Jan loudly. "Give him a thick head, if he comes over here."

The witch nodded and awaited a response from her. He was dressed similarly to most of the other stems in the long tabard worn by both men and women, tied around the waist with a cord. There were boots on his feet and, over the tabard, a sleeveless jacket. Suddenly he crossed the room to where Nicole was sitting and she felt herself trembling involuntarily.

"Have you need of my services?" he asked her.

One of the young men looked up.

"She don't need you. This lady is the mother to the god twins."

Nicole was horrified.

"Don't say that. That's not true. They're just ordinary children ..." But that wasn't true either, and they all knew it.

Necka ignored the youths. Around his neck he wore an amulet of coloured stones that shone in the candle-light. He touched it with a chubby finger when he saw her staring at it.

"For protection," he said. "Do you want one?"

Pagey sneered. "If I wanted to lift that head away from that fat body, no bunch of stones would stop my blade."

Necka still paid no attention to the youths. That is, he continued to look at Nicole. Then he said, "They're just boys. Impolite and arrogant, like most young men. I could make them whimper and sweat in their beds tonight, but I won't because there's no help for them. Tomorrow they will have forgotten and would be insulting me once again. They forget so easily, and the night is another world away." He smiled.

"I don't suppose they mean it anyway," said Nicole. "What can a witch do?"

When he had first crossed the floor, she had been afraid that Necka was going to make trouble. What was witchcraft after all, but a religion? The arrival of the twins might have caused local devotees of witchcraft to change their allegiance, although that didn't seem to be the case. At least, if it was it didn't worry this particular witch.

"You are wondering about the effect of your children on Wicca," he said quietly. "That is a problem, but only temporary as far as I can see."

Nicole felt hot under his candid gaze.

"What do you mean?"

"I mean this is not going to last. I see a change coming soon—the power of the twins evaporating . . ."

Pagey jumped to his feet and Necka backed away slightly with his palms up.

"Leave him alone, Pagey!" cried Nicole.

Necka said, "I'm only giving you the benefit of my ability to foretell events. I don't have any influence over them. They'll happen whether you cut off my head or not. Do you believe me?" Necka looked directly into Nicole's eyes and for a moment she felt a little dizzy.

"Do you believe me?" The voice seemed very far away. The other side of a void.

"No," she replied flatly.

The smile came into focus again.

"You will. Tonight you will."

"What's all this? Is someone disturbing our guest?"

The speaker had come up behind Necka, and Nicole had seen that the witch had been startled by the voice. Apparently his fortune-telling was not easily manipulated.

Necka had noticed the triumph in her eyes but he merely said, "You will believe me," and turned on his heel to trot away.

"Has he bothered you? Pagey, I thought you were to see to the lady. What's all the commotion?"

The latecomer was a grizzled elderly man, but big and strong-looking. In his prime he might have been a wrestler or a blacksmith, something of that nature.

"I'm the Keeper here. Anything goes on in the castle—that's my responsibility. Please let me know if you're not well treated . . ."

She recognized him then as one of those people who had swept her along like a wave when she had first arrived.

"It's all right. The discussion got out of hand, that's all," said Nicole. "I don't think anyone meant any harm."

"Don't be too sure of *that*," replied the Keeper, his blue eyes fixed on the three youths. "Those three can be troublesome when they've had a bit to drink. And the witch—well, he's troublesome in other ways. He worries people."

"I'm sure I'll be all right."

The man nodded, gave the youths a final look full of warning and then strode away.

Nicole quickly wearied of her own company and since most of the castle's occupants seemed to be settling down for the night, she decided to do the same. She stood up, murmured a "Good night" to the youths and crossed the floor to one of the passages without waiting for an answer.

The torches in the passageway created a heavy atmosphere, a mixture of smoke and stale air. The light they gave out was poor and Nicole found herself stumbling once or twice as she tried to find her way back to the room in the tower. At the meeting of two passageways she was undecided. The smoke was burning her eyes and throat and a feeling of exhaustion began to overcome her. She finally took the left-hand corridor, which terminated in a locked door some metres further on.

She retraced her steps to the intersection—and found herself confronted by a choice of *three* exits.

She took the middle one, hoping to find her way back to the large hall, where she could ask for a guide. Some way down the passage the light seemed to dim and suddenly she could smell a peculiar freshness in the air. What was it? Salt air? Ozone? There must be a window somewhere near, facing the coast. Yes, there was a breeze on her cheek! She felt along the walls but found no arrow loop, no opening of any kind. The light was almost non-existent now.

No window then. *But she could hear the wind.* Surely not? The walls were at least a metre thick. How could she hear anything through solid stone?

She stumbled forward as the floor heaved beneath her feet. Heaved? Yes, yes, it was *moving*, rolling from one side to the other. *She wanted to scream but was afraid the stems would laugh at her silliness.* Surely she was just over-tired, giddy with the heavy atmosphere.

But it wasn't heavy. It was clean and fresh. It howled above her and blew cold on her face. It blew with many notes, in several keys.

The floor lurched again, and she could hear the sound of waves now, beating against the side of the ship. The vessel rolled from side to side in the storm, and pitched as waves broke over bows.

Ship? She was in a castle. A solid, stone-built castle perched upon a mound of clay.

She screamed then, and the ship threw her to the deck as she tried to keep upright in the violently shifting craft. Falling to the floor she slithered across the lower deck toward the starboard bulkhead. The body of the sea smashed its shoulder against the side of the craft, and broke into tall white arms above her head. She tried clinging to the bulkhead but her fingers slipped and slithered across its surface.

Suddenly there was a strong hand on her shoulder and a deep, concerned voice asked her if she was all right.

The ship stopped rolling. The sea grew calm.

She was back in the castle once again and looking up into the eyes of the Keeper.

"Are you all right?" he repeated.

"Yes, yes. But I thought . . ."

"Please, you'll be better when you get to bed."

Soaked in sweat and still feeling unsteady, she allowed herself to be helped to her feet.

"Something . . ."

"I know," said the Keeper. "Don't worry, we'll punish him." She was faintly surprised.

"Who? Punish who?"

"Why, the witch of course. Hypnotized you, that's obvious. I'll break his back in two when I find him."

"Please. Please don't do anything like that. I'm sure he meant no harm."

"Of course he did, and he'll be brought to account. Come, I'll take you to your room."

The Keeper took Nicole's arm and gently guided her to her quarters.

9 Helmets

The world changes its aspect, viewed from beneath the peak
of a combat helmet.

Adam Rice was eighteen, and that said almost everything
about him—except, perhaps, that he was a policeman, but even
that did not feel right on him yet. He was all too new. He was
well aware of his deficiencies as a person of experience. He
was eighteen. Sometimes he felt that he was the only eighteen-
year-old policeman on the whole police force.

His hand was hot and damp from gripping the stun-rod too
tightly.

This morning he was supposed to be off duty, but the dawn
had seen him and about three hundred other dewts standing
shoulder-to-shoulder before a ... *castle*? And he for one was
churning inside. Not because he hadn't eaten, but because
around the battlements of the fortification were wild-looking
stems waving steel weapons and shotguns.

There was that feeling, too. In the air? Almost like a constant gentle electric shock. He wondered if the others felt it.
Maybe he was sickening for something?

He had thought it would be an exercise. He had also expected it to be cold. It was *hot*, for Reikersakes! The sun
burned the back of his neck like a fired iron. If he wasn't
careful he might keel over.

Rice went up on to the balls of his feet; he had heard that
helped when you feared you might swoon. No, "drop"—that
was the word. A man dropped. A lady swooned. A whore
passed out. He must be careful not to fall on his stun-rod if
he did go. Otherwise he wouldn't see the rest of the weekend,
and afterwards his head would be full of noise and pain.

If they got this thing over with tonight, he would hit the

mooby bars with Jacobs. Obtain some experience in that field too.

But by tonight he might be dead. And he didn't want to die a virgin. He should have gone with Jacobs last night, then he could have stood toe-to-toe with a stem and said, "I'm a man, probably better than you."

"What was that, Rice?" asked Jacobs, who was standing next to him.

"Nothin'," he mumbled, and went up on to the balls of his feet again.

The Chief of Police removed his gloves. He was perspiring. He knew now that he should have ordered shirt-sleeve dress, but Craven ... well, no one had told him about the weather. Still, too late for remonstrances. He had a situation to deal with. He raised his megaphone to his mouth.

"Stand to," he said to the sergeants in the front ranks.

"Men," he said, "we have a kidnap situation here, coupled with some kind of, let's say, *resistance* against the forces of law and order. There are some misguided people who believe that by living outside the boundary of our City they live outside the reach of the law. A lesson must be taught. Is that understood?"

There was no reply. None was needed.

Someone was at his elbow. Craven, and another civilian.

"My name is John Strecker. I've just arrived. I'm responsible for those children up there in the castle. May I ask what you are planning to do?"

The man was seedy-looking but radiated self-confidence.

"How do you do, Mr Strecker? As you can see, we don't have a lot of choice. We can wait, but that may take a long time. I understand the stems have water and provisions enough to last several months. On the other hand, I can hardly order a few hundred lightly armed policemen to scale those walls. I've sent for a squadron of riot drones. Unfortunately, the troops that will be dropped behind the walls of that fortification will not be as gentle with the inhabitants as my own people ..."

Craven said, "Can I use your megaphone?"

The Chief hesitated.

"What do you plan to do?"

"Try to persuade them to open the gates."

The Chief released his hold on the instrument. After all, Craven had been living like a stem himself for some months. Maybe he could get the stems to listen to sense?

"Nicole!" Craven blared. "Come out. Bring the children. Someone's going to get hurt—a *lot* of people will be hurt. Maybe you, Polgrove, the twins. *Please*."

No answer apart from one or two catcalls from the battlements. Certainly not a woman's voice.

"Are you sure she's there?" the Chief asked.

"Most definitely," replied Strecker.

The megaphone bellowed again.

"You're a selfish bitch, Nicole. Think of the twins. They're dropping in gongheads to sort the stems out."

While the Chief approved of direct speech, he bridled at the use of the popular civilian nickname for riot troops. While these were not his own men that Craven was talking about, they did wear uniforms, and he felt that any smear on a uniformed man besmirched him also.

"Please do not use the word 'gongheads', Mr Craven. My men don't like it," he said, keeping his words precise and evenly spaced.

"I have to use words they'll understand in there. Let's not mince terms. I want to scare the hell out of them."

"Right, Mr Craven," he said. "But what next? If I'm not mistaken, I can hear the sound of the drones. They'll be landing soon and I'll have to hand over command to their leader. He'll probably be young, eager and bloody-minded. When they select gonghead officers they don't look for compassion."

A flicker of a smile passed over Craven's face and the Chief added, "I can say it. You can't."

At that moment, six huge wingless insects came whining around the western towers of the castle and dropped to the turf, one by one, with almost perfectly even time spacing. After a few moments, the motors died and a small black parasite emerged from the leading craft. It strutted towards the group of men.

Lila Craven pulled her husband aside and the Chief heard her say, "If it were me you called a bitch, I'd drag you into bed laughing—but *her*. She'll never forgive you."

"Colonel?" said the Chief, by way of a greeting. The black insect was now a fully grown officer in combat gear who answered the Chief with a grunt. A broad-faced, handsome man in his late thirties, the commander of the riot troops appeared to be in no mood for talking.

"When do we go in?" he asked in a clipped accent.

"When I hand over command to you," replied the Chief, "which I shall do once we have attempted all else."

"Have you," he began in an imperious tone, "have you any idea what it costs to send out six drones packed with highly trained men?"

"No," replied the Chief calmly. "I've no idea and I'm not interested."

The Colonel's mouth twitched.

"I see," he said, and then fell silent.

"If you do go in," said the Chief, "please leave me something to arrest at the end of the day."

"I'll do my best."

"I'm sure you will."

At that point the Chief noticed that Craven had shrugged off the clinging Lila and was bellowing at the figures on top of the walls again.

For a few minutes after he had finished, nothing happened. The policemen, unused to standing still for long periods, shuffled their feet and inspected the grass. Most of them were reluctant to look up at the sky. It gave them unpleasant feelings.

Lila Craven's nuisance blew his nose.

The world ticked around on its axis like the globular wheel of a clock.

A large bird wheeled overhead and landed on the highly polished surface of one of the drones.

A policeman fainted, falling on his stun-rod, thus ensuring twenty-four hours of unconsciousness.

The vibrations the Chief had been experiencing in his bones since arriving in the area were beginning to worry him. In his opinion, there was a huge power leakage somewhere and he was concerned about radiation effects.

"We're going in," said the Colonel suddenly.

The Chief put out a restraining arm.

"Wait a minute. Someone's coming. Look, from behind that tower."

The sun was behind the small figures but they were recognizable by at least two of the group. Strecker called out and Craven began running in their direction. Reaching them, Craven led the children back to the Chief.

"The twins," said Craven. It was a superfluous statement.

Shouts came from the walls of the castle, followed by a scream. A woman's scream. Craven looked alarmed.

"Not Nicole," said Strecker, glancing up. "Some hag with grey hair."

"So these are the twins," said the Chief. Two small round faces beamed up at him. They didn't look so special. Children's faces. Children's eyes. What was so unusual? The Minister had merely said, "They are important."

Strecker interrupted his thoughts.

"I'll get the children away now."

The Chief nodded and patted the nearest on the head, receiving the strangest sensation when he did so. A stronger version of that power leakage. Was it coming from these two infants? He withdrew his hand slowly. Strecker nodded.

"Yes, it's the children, but don't ask me what it is. None of us know."

"Unusual," said the Chief cautiously. "Yes, better get them away. Take them home—wherever home is."

"What about mummy?" asked one of the children, hanging back.

"She'll be coming soon. I'm going to fetch her," said Craven.

The little girl nodded gravely and followed her sister to Strecker's hummer.

"Are we going in?" asked the forgotten Colonel petulantly.

"I don't think it's necessary now," replied the Chief, knowing full well the stems could not be left without punishment. "We can deal with the situation."

"How do you propose to do that? Blow the castle down?"

Craven interrupted.

"That's not necessary either. They're opening the gates. See, the doors are swinging back."

Alex watched the approaching stems with some trepidation. He wondered what had been happening behind the high walls while he and the police had laid siege to the castle. Certainly he could expect a rough reception from Polgrove. The farmer might even consider his action in calling the police one of betrayal. And how had the twins become detached from Nicole? They surely could not have wandered off by themselves and just happened to find their way out of the castle by a back door? Someone had let them out. Lowered them from a window perhaps? Or used a secret passage which had its exit in the outer brickwork or adjoining fields?

The stems were dressed in various pieces of armour and some carried swords. They looked angry. Then he saw Nicole, being helped along by Pagey. A flash of jealousy went through Alex.

"Nicole! Nicole! Over here!"

She saw him. Her face looked worn and tired. How long had it been? Three days? Lila had given him the direction of her flight, but that had been *away* from the castle. They had searched farms in the area of the Blackwater at first. Then Alex had noticed the lack of young men around the farms. His guesswork had led him eventually to the castle.

"Hello, Alex. Where are the twins?"

"Strecker's got them. They're okay. He's taken them to Manston. Are you all right?"

Pagey glared at him.

"Of course she's all right. You think she'd come to harm with me?" He wore a horned metal helmet and the cloak Alex had seen him in the day he had saved his life on the broomway. A pantomime character. They all were.

Alex shook his head.

"No."

Alex saw Lila staring at Nicole from a few metres away. Lila smiled. Alex recognized it as her nervous smile—the one which came to her face involuntarily, when she was unsure of herself. He noticed that Nicole was looking at her too. Suddenly Nicole did something quite out of character. She hugged Alex to her, pulling his face next to hers.

"Take me away from here," she whispered.

He was puzzled and a little embarrassed.

"What?"

"Take me away from these people. I'll go mad if I stay here much longer."

The tone was fierce. She was pleading with him, almost in tears. A totally unpredictable situation. What was he to do? He had officials to talk to. He couldn't leave the stems to the mercy of the police, no matter how understanding their Chief might seem. And then there were the riot troops. Yet she seemed desperate, almost on the edge of hysteria. If he failed her now she might never see him again. He presumed by "these people" she meant the stems. They had obviously upset her, if not actually harmed her.

He made a quick decision.

"Lila!"

His wife came across to him and he felt Nicole stiffen in his arms. Possibly he was making a mistake but he had no choice. Besides, he was gambling on the soft side of Lila's nature coming to the fore. Whatever kind of wife she made, she was not an unfeeling woman.

"What is it, Alex?"

"Can you look after Nicole for me? Take her back to the house—Manston House. I'll follow you later."

Lila was slow to answer. Had he misjudged her?

"She's not well, Lila. She's obviously had a bad time one way or another."

Lila shrugged. "Okay," she said, in a resigned voice. "Okay."

"I'll be all right on my own," said Nicole in a tight little voice.

"Sure you will, but we'll be company for each other," said Lila. "I've had my bellyful of this lot. I need a drink and a rest. What the Reikering hell I left the City for, I'll never know."

"You don't have to use a policeman's curse to jolly me along," said Nicole, but she allowed her hand to be taken and the two women made their way towards one of the several hummers parked at the foot of the slopes.

Suddenly there was a loud yell from nearby. Alex realized it was Pagey. The young man was pointing at another stem who was standing some distance apart from his comrades. A short, fat man wearing a robe and beads.

Nicole stopped in her tracks.

"No, Pagey!" she cried.

The young man paid her no heed. His hand went to the sheathed weapon on his back and it sang out of the scabbard, into the sunlight. The fat man cowered.

"His head!" screeched Pagey and began running, the sword scything the air like the blade of a rotary engine. Alex ran after him, a sick feeling in his stomach anticipating the youth's intended action. *A beheading was unthinkable in such a day and age.* Some of the police had begun moving too, but they seemed slow, ungainly creatures. Everything appeared to be happening at quarter the normal speed.

"Pagey, don't," called Alex.

The fat man's face was a white mask of fear. He knew he was about to die, and fell to his knees, either from the pure funk or from blind acceptance of his fate.

Pagey planted his feet firmly in front of the kneeling man and brought the sword, double-handed, round in an arc from behind his own shoulders. Alex threw himself forward. He hit Pagey in the area of the kidneys and heard a scream of pain. For a moment he was winded, unsure of who was crying out. Then he picked himself up. A policeman leaped on to Pagey.

The youth was pinned to the ground but still struggled violently. Finally his captor stepped back and touched him with a stun-rod. Pagey jerked once, and then lay still.

It was the fat man who was wailing. He was holding the side of his head, blood dribbling through his fingers. In his other hand he held something circular and equally as bloody.

It was a second before Alex realized the object was the man's ear. He felt ill.

"This man needs attention," he said, to no one in particular, and then felt he had done his duty. After all, if it had not been for him the wounded stem would be headless. Alex walked over to Nicole and Lila.

"Who is he? Do you know him?" he asked Nicole.

"The witch, Necka. He's been giving me some trouble over the past few days. For no reason really."

"Jealous of the twins?" suggested Alex, jumping to the obvious conclusion.

"He said not. I challenged him with the same accusation."

Lila interrupted, "But surely, they weren't going to decapitate him just for annoying you. What did he do? Try to bang you? Against your will?"

"Certainly not," said Nicole, haughtily.

Lila shrugged.

"Stop that, Lila," warned Alex. "What was it, Nicole?"

The three of them looked across to where the witch was sitting. He was receiving medical attention. The ear could probably be replaced later. The nuisance was hovering over the injured stem as the latter received treatment; possibly there was an affinity of recently injured souls blossoming.

"They think he led the twins out of the castle by a rear exit. I left the children in the room allocated to us while I tried to find the Keeper—he's the man in charge of the castle. When I returned, they were gone. It doesn't really matter now." There was a weary tone to her voice. Alex could smell the sweetness of blood in the air and he felt he had had enough too.

"Okay. I'll see the pair of you later. I've got to talk to the Chief."

He spent the next hour with the Chief of Police, trying to persuade him to prosecute only the ringleaders. The Chief was reluctant to return to the City with just two or three prisoners but eventually agreed that if they began rounding up stems, the job would never be finished. The chosen three were Polgrove, the Keeper and Pagey, of course. Alex felt like a traitor as they took Polgrove towards a police vehicle. Nothing was mentioned about prosecuting Nicole, the real abductor, which said a lot for the sort of justice meted out to stems.

"I'll do my best for you," he murmured to his former landlord.

Polgrove nodded, eyes downcast. Jamie was nowhere to be seen, thank God. He would not have been so reticent, and—on Polgrove's behalf—would probably have talked himself into a cell too.

The storm troopers, or whatever they were, prepared to leave. Their Colonel looked angry. But then he had looked much the same on arrival, before being thwarted. The morning's sport was now out of his reach. He looked the sort of man that cracked his knuckles while people fell on all sides.

"Can I come with you?" he asked the Chief.

"Certainly. You can ride in my vehicle if you wish. Isn't this weather glorious? I've been cooped up in the City for so long, I'd forgotten what the countryside could be like."

"I don't think it's going to last," said Alex. "Somehow I sense a change in the air."

10 Starbound

Miami airport lounge was close to the transparent, tinted ceiling of its encapsulating hemisphere.

There was a small, twinkling light overhead. Not a star, though, as Alex well knew, but he allowed himself to indulge in a little fantasy for the sake of the children. He recited for them the age-old nursery rhyme, which has never failed to lose its impact upon five-year-olds. It was one way in which he could communicate to the infants his own excitement concerning the coming voyage. The "star" was in fact the celestial platform from which the photon ship would be launched.

After medical preparations, the four of them had already made a conventional journey, albeit only an hour long, from London to Miami. The shuttle to the space platform would leave the Cape in three days. Until that time he had to amuse On, and Lucy, one of the Thai twins. The human telemetry system would soon be in operation between New Carthage and Earth. Also with them was Nadine, the Thais' foster-mother. Nicole had stayed with the other two children. It had hurt Alex that she had not wanted to go with him. She had made all sorts of excuses, and had promised to join him at a later date, but there had been no conviction in her voice.

"I must see that Ti is well cared for, before I follow you. If both of us go, she'll have no one she trusts."

"There're the other mothers—Odell. What about her?"

"No, Alex, please. I wish you would understand. She's friendly with Odell, but she doesn't regard her as *family*. You and I are different. We're their parents—oh, you can wince, but we *are*."

He had given in, of course, but he doubted Nicole's resolve to follow him to New Carthage. Leave Earth for a strange planet? She would need him here to add the motive force, he was sure of that. Perhaps once On Lo was settled he could return for Nicole? He comforted himself with that thought. At least he was escaping from Lila and her nuisance. The civil lawsuit had been withdrawn. Life was not so bad, taking into account all that had happened.

The four of them had supper in the lounge and then retired to bed at the airport hotel. The following morning they were taken by the joining vehicle to Cape Kennedy. The officials who escorted them were friendly enough but Alex was attacked by an overwhelming bout of homesickness. On seemed all right, as did Nadine and Lucy. He was obviously one of life's unfortunates.

His thoughts centred on the Outer Angles and its inhabitants, and he wondered if he would ever see any of them again. They were not a bad people, despite their attitude towards the Government that controlled the lands they worked. Alex had fought hard to keep the Government from pulling down the castle. Finally a decision had been made to remove the huge gates and leave it at that. The stems had been forbidden to replace them.

Polgrove and the Keeper had been put under close arrest for two years. They were not permitted to leave the City and were forced to live in a charity-backed hostel: punishment enough for two bewildered rustics. Pagey had been sentenced to three years in a Youth Retraining Centre. However, the boy *was* tough and Alex rested his hopes on that doubtful advantage over the other trainees. Certainly, Alex could not worry about it for the whole of his time on New Carthage.

He looked at On sitting placidly beside him. The poor child. She was still going to be placed in a goldfish bowl, despite the fact that Strecker and his team had kept the secret of the twins' apparent gift from the authorities. Alex wondered what the journey to New Carthage would do to the field between the twins. It might stretch it until it was too weak to be detectable, or it might leave the force lines as they were and encompass a whole eight light-years of space. The vibrations were still with them now and the twins were several thousand kilometres apart.

This was the first time Alex had ridden on an airwheeler

and he noticed how much quieter and smoother it was than a hummer. The airwheeler was developed on New Carthage—Stingray Raft was one big airwheeler—and the principle was now being used in vehicles on Earth. Without being aware of the technical details, he knew that the craft was carried along on artificially created "rollers" of hot air. He was not sure whether the air needed to be hot to add to the buoyancy, or whether it was that temperature because the motors that produced the rollers incidently transferred their heat by convection.

They were passing the Okeechobee now, having made a detour for the sake of the two children. However, the girls themselves were almost asleep. Lucy was curled up on the seat with her head in Nadine's lap, although her eyes were still open. She was sucking her thumb. On, eyes half-closed, was leaning against Alex.

Nadine said, "Beautiful, isn't it?"

Crystal tree-forms had been planted around the lake shores to produce a magical forest of colour. The sun rays angled through and off these natural-shaped sculptures. It was a brittle, geometric piece of artistry created during a time when city states had not become the main way of life. The machines that produced the crystals still continued to operate, and the tree-forms flourished, snapping off when they grew too tall, to form banks of *lapis lazuli* and beryl debris at their roots.

"Very nice," said Alex, using the traditional English understatement.

"Not many people see *that*," one of the escorts remarked.

"True. I suppose it's because you have such a tight security net around Florida?" said Nadine.

"Not at all. It's because no one *cares* any more. They're all too concerned with being comfortable, see. The City is part of their person—their exoskeleton, if you need a picture for it. That's my idea. Turtles, all of them. Scared to leave their shells, let alone the water."

"You mustn't blame them for that." said Alex, wondering why the man had suddenly opened up into conversation. Maybe the Okeechobee had a special significance for him?

The escort shut himself up into his own shell. Alex was impressed though. The man had something. Maybe the whole human race was retreating further and further into itself. Houses were shells, so was Stingray Raft and its cabins and working cells. Even now they were in a shell and although it was necessary for purposes of speed, a time-saving device, one could find justifications for every movable or stationary carapace.

Suddenly he saw some people moving around the far end of the lake, black dots against the glittering jewellery.

"I thought you disallowed entry to this area?" he said.

"What?"

"There're some people out there. By the water."

Alex pointed and both escorts stared.

Nadine said, "Yes, I see them."

An escort said, "Ghosties. They shouldn't be there."

"What's that?" asked Nadine.

"People who live outside the Cities. Sometimes they slip through our cordon. The water draws them."

Alex stared at the American equivalent of the stems as they drew near to them. The ghosties were dressed in singlets and shorts, and they looked more sinister than their European counterparts. Alex thought for a moment that the vehicle was going to be stopped and a confrontation take place. He was relieved as they went on past the group. The ghosties stared, hard-faced and unafraid, at the airwheeler. One or two of them were carrying what looked like home-made firearms.

"Nice."

"Yeah, very nice."

There the conversation ended. Alex was relieved to see the Cape buildings come into view. He was half expecting the rocks to turn into ghosties at every corner. He could easily imagine the origin of their nickname.

The shuttle craft was due to take off at noon so they had a few drinks in the bar. Then the escorts left and Alex, Nadine and the two children went through so many medical and security checks they began to feel like criminals.

The time came to board the craft and they were herded out behind their limited luggage, along with ten other passengers. Not many people wanted to go to New Carthage, it seemed.

Either that, or most of them were already on board. The shuttle craft was cramped inside but they knew the trip would be comparatively short.

The take-off was like a thump in the spine with a cloth-bound sledgehammer. During the actual flight there was nothing to see except the back of the next passenger's head, and all Alex had to worry about was whether the field created by the Lo twins would interfere with the shuttle's flight-deck instruments or its communications. His own instruments at Manston had been affected a great deal during the test between the twins. After the test was over there had been only a very small degree of interference. He hoped the sensitivity of the shuttle's systems was not such that they would be thrown into confusion by the trinity. Or that the distance between the twins weakened the field. There were no indications of any flight-deck problems, however.

They docked in the space platform some hours later and after disembarking were taken, strapped in tube cars, through corridors of weightlessness to the starship. Once there, the gyros gave them back their co-ordination and several kilo-grammes of personal flesh and bone.

The photon ship was plush indeed. The reception area, beyond the elevators, was not unlike the foyer of a very luxurious hotel on Earth. Thick-pile carpets, potted plants and soft furniture added to the impression. What surprised both Alex and Nadine most was the amount of spaciousness within the ship.

"Well, I suppose when you consider it logically," said Alex, "there's no need for restrictions. Why not build a huge luxury liner? Then if you do have to transport troops, you can rip out the furniture and cram marines in every area of the ship." He was thinking of the event of an emergency situation on New Carthage.

"True," replied Nadine. "And I know for certain that some people pay a fortune just to make the trip. Often, they don't even set foot on the new world. They just use the *Dido III* as a retreat—an away-from-it-all."

They were shown to their cabins by a lean-faced steward. The children were taken to the nursery where they would be cared for by round-the-clock nursing staff, although Alex and Nadine could visit them whenever they wished.

The cabins were less plush than the reception area but were nevertheless more comfortable than either of them expected. Nadine appeared at Alex's door a few moments after he had unpacked his bags.

"The artificial gravity is making me feel a little queasy," she said.

Alex looked up at her from his sitting position on his bunk.

"The spinning? Yes, it can affect some people, though I'm told it's psychological to a degree . . ."

"Tell that to my stomach."

She was small and neat—almost flat-chested, but not quite. Her breasts were small sharp points beneath her tight under-suit. Why was she looking at him like that? *Why was he evaluating her barely-existent breasts?*

"Would you get me some ice-water, please?"

She sat down on the end of his bunk.

"I could call the steward."

"No, it's not that bad. Just a flutter. Don't you feel any-thing?"

"We're not even moving through space yet," he said, wryly.

"Ho, ho. Not much. We're zooming around Earth at I don't know what sort of speed."

He moved up on his bed, away from her, and put his feet in her lap. It was a comradely gesture.

"We're geostationary. We're not zooming anywhere."

"Well, it feels like it."

She began playing her fingers across his ankles, which was not what he wanted at all. At least, he didn't *mind* so long as it stayed on a friendly basis.

"There aren't many women on New Carthage," he said.

"What about my ice-water?"

"Oh yes." Alex jumped up, nearly kicking her under the chin as he did so. As casually as he could, he closed the cabin door. Nadine was less casual in turning the lock. The ice-water was forgotten.

Afterwards Nadine said, "I may as well move in here."

"The bunk's not big enough."

"I don't take up much room." She snuggled her nakedness into the cavity of his stomach as if to prove the point.

Alex swallowed.

"I could never love you, Nadine. Like you a lot, yes. But never ..."

She dug him in the ribs with her elbow.

"Who asked you to? Anyway, don't never say never—you might wake up one morning and find me gone. *Then* you might change your mind. We won't be allowed to bunk together on New Carthage, you know. Captain Alexander's a bit of a puritan. These colonial types often are."

Some hours later, at a time appointed by the tides of space, or whatever governed the launching of starships, Alex was informed that the photon craft was leaving the platform. She would head for the Launching Station where she would enter the light core directed at Wolf 359, accelerated by the Hartpole Units into a fast light stream. Alex had a vague picture in his mind of light waves that were projected by the Hartpole guns around the ship. The whole integument of the ship would undergo a change of state and become a ball of white brilliance. The light-enclosed *Dido III* would then be carried towards its destination inside the fast light stream. Light, faster than light, within light. In four calendar months, real time, the ship would, barring accidents, reach its journey's end.

Time aboard the photon ship was measured in hours and the passengers and crew kept an artificial day for the sake of regularity. At least, *most* of the passengers followed the ship's routine. Certain elements—the joy-riders—kept their own hours, which would have been no different had they still been on Earth.

There were a great many distractions and pastimes on board: games, gambling, holovid shows. Alex found Nadine satisfied with his company, although he had half expected to lose her to one of the jaded starship crew, who appeared to have little to do but move jauntily around their playground in sharp-looking uniforms.

Alex had hoped to be able to watch the stars from an observation point within the ship, but he was informed (complete with a smirk) that all one could see was a white blur. It was possible that the projection platforms for the Hartpole guns would be visible from the control room—if the ship had any portholes (another smirk) which it did not.

So, for four months, Alex's universe was to be a large in-limbo hotel. Glad that the Government was paying for his ticket, he wondered what the stems would have made of all the luxury around him.

One thing was bothersome: the floor was concave beneath his feet and he could visualize the spinning sphere which was his new world. He wondered about the stability of the systems but his enquiry was met with a claim that the artificial gravity was finely tuned to produce a constant effect. While it was below G, it was not supposed to vary to any perceptible degree. It was the use of the word "perceptible" which concerned Alex. A man of his sensitivity might perceive that which others did not. So, on some days he bounded confidently down the gangways, and on others he clung to the inside of his bunk convinced that if he let go he would smash heavily against the ceiling. At certain times, the insecurity he sensed with the low gravity was exacerbated by a feeling of paranoia. On those occasions, Nadine was banished from his cabin, and stewards who arrived to try to persuade him to leave his bunk were aware of deep undercurrents of suspicion and were subjected to overtones of abuse.

The truth was, he was homesick for Earth.

Two months out, Alex was resting in one of the three lounges, the one that allowed the presence of children. On was asleep, her head over his knees, when suddenly she jerked fitfully, and Alex was aware of a sensation like the snapping of a taut cord across his legs. The child woke, cried tearlessly for a few moments, and then fell into an exhausted sleep again.

Alex knew, instinctively, that the field had gone. The magic between the twins had ceased to be. He could no longer feel the vibrations from the child's body and he wondered what was happening to the other terminal—Ti. Was she with Nicole and was the foster-mother grieving at the loss?

He stared down at the little bundle in his lap and stroked her hair. Poor On. Not once had she asked for her mother or sister. Lucy had cried herself to sleep when first parted from *her* twin, but On seemed unconcerned at Nicole's and Ti's absence. Maybe it was because she had been with them— spiritually—while the field existed. Now that the trinity had been broken, she might miss them terribly.

When the child woke, she confirmed Alex's fears.

"Where's Ti?" she asked, looking round the starship lounge.

The remnants of a cocktail party that had turned into a twenty-hour bender regarded the little Chinese child with obvious amusement.

"Sweet thing," said a slender girl in an evening gown, smiling, before her facial muscles returned to their slack positions.

PART TWO
People of the Dawn Country

God is an expressive person;
has dimensions, gestures:
when an eagle
vaults the sky
or intricate Man
spears deep Space
at superhuman speed
or a seed
bursts like a bomb
and expands
God is talking
with his hands.

From "A Photograph of God" by Mathew Tse
    (Born: 2013 Died: 2060)

11 Stingray Raft

The only city on New Carthage was a floating raft and it had no mayor. Instead, it had a captain by the name of Alexander; the same captain who had commanded the first starship to the several planets of Wolf 359; the same man who had discovered the thinly oxygenated atmosphere of New Carthage. Alexander was now sixty-seven Earth years of age.

With the oxygen, and an ozone layer, the similarity with Earth ended. New Carthage was somewhat smaller than the Captain's birthplace. The inhabitants had an atmosphere close in quality to that breathed by the Indians of the Andes mountains. The *siroche* was not an uncommon complaint amongst those who ventured outside the raft without backpacking their own supply of oxygen. New Carthage had a 254-Earth-year day, which was in its favour since the hemisphere that faced the sun reached temperatures well over 100 degrees centigrade, too hot for normal habitation. Even the natives had not evolved in order to be able to withstand that degree of direct sunlight. Instead, they lived a nomadic existence within the dawn strip, cultivating their crops of fungi, bushes and roots, and moving slowly in the opposite direction to the planet's rotation.

Surprisingly, the mass of New Carthage was greater than that of Earth, and the human colonists found their bulks were heavier to handle on the new world. They trod with the grace of elephants that have undergone the same contraction as a collapsed star.

The planet was mountainous in places, especially on and around the poles: a geological thorn in the side of Captain Alexander, who had to plan well ahead to avoid these natural obstructions. Stingray Raft, named for its resemblance to the fish, kept pace with the dawn on airwheels, or rollers. Its long whip stretched behind it and out into the sunlight where solar cells at its tip gathered energy for the raft's needs. Once in a while the Captain enjoyed travelling to some high distant place in order to view his raft in all its shining splendour. A gigantic silver manta ray sliding imperceptibly over the sea-like plains of New Carthage.

This morning (the habits of several million years are hard to throw: Stingray acknowledged an artificial twenty-four-hour clock) Captain Alexander sat in his cockpit on the flat, forward-sloping head of the raft, and surveyed the plains. His reflection stared back at him from the instrument panel. There were no secrets hidden by his appearance—he looked what he was: an engineer elevated to a command. His sleeves were rolled to reveal thick, hairy forearms and the rest of his body fell into the same line: the legs trunk-like, the waist heavy, the chest a drum. His bald head was decorated with a laurel-leaf crown of grizzled, closely-cropped hair. As a plumber, his overall appearance would have filled one with confidence. Here was a man who could use his strong hands to bend the kinks out of dented pipes. Although he had never actually used a spanner in the course of work, he was fond of this image of himself as a nuts-and-bolts man. As an engineer he had been a designer, but he now referred to the early part of his career as his "nail-bending" days. He was an affectionate man, he knew, and, with no single female in his life, any fatherly excess of this kind was directed towards favourite junior officers, males and females.

Captain Alexander sometimes wondered whether there was anything sexual in his fondness for his crew. It was not an aspect of character on which he cared to dwell at length be-cause he felt that to *think* about sex too much, while one seldom *practised*, might lead to an unhealthy state of mind. Instead, he channelled all his energies into his work and tried to leave these small indulgences for the early hours of the middle watch, when almost everyone but the duty crew was asleep.

Although he knew he could not stop copulation altogether, he carefully fostered the rumour that he was a puritan which resulted in any sexual encounters between unmarried couples being kept carefully under wraps. While he understood the desires of hot-blooded young men and women, he did not want

Stingray Raft to appear in history books as another Gomorrah, and himself as a debauched satrap allowing unlimited sexual licence.

There was a light tap on the cockpit door.

"Yes?"

"Williams, sir. Would you like a drink? We're just going off middles, well, fifteen minutes. The morning watch will be taking over soon."

Captain Alexander automatically glanced at the chronometer on the panel—0730 hours. The new shift was due on at 0800 but regulations argued a fifteen-minute hand-over period. Not that it was always strictly adhered to. Mostly there was nothing to hand over and the old watch went directly to bed.

"Okay, thanks. I'll take it in here."

"Right, sir. Black coffee, two sugars?"

"Williams, you check every single time. Do you think I'd change a lifetime habit just to annoy you?"

There was humour in his voice and Williams smiled.

"You never know, sir. One day you might ask for a drop of something in it."

"And *you* know I forbid the drinking of alcohol on watch."

Williams was never beaten.

"You're not on watch, sir. I am." The young man shut the door.

The dawn country stretched out in a grey-gold crescent either side of the raft. Captain Alexander could see the many gin working at their fungi crops. The aliens had no mouths; they inhaled their food as powder through their huge nostrils or siphoned liquids through spikes on their forelimb joints, their elbows. The Captain was very tolerant of the natives, although they were difficult to communicate with, an aspect of their nature which gave cause for mild alarm. Furthermore, there were very few deaths amongst them. A dead gin had never been examined, since the natives, like Earth men, revered their deceased relatives and would not allow the bodies to be defiled. The deaths amongst them seemed to be caused entirely by accidents. Old age was not apparent; they appeared not to age at all, physically.

Were they immortal?

He knew they could not be, though it was a beautiful and romantic idea. Perhaps they had the secret of longevity? Certainly that would be consistent with the slow breeding cycle. The frequency was unknown to Stingray but very few gin young had appeared since the first landing. It was to everyone's bitter disappointment, both on Earth and New Carthage, that the gin had proved to be of low intellect. Captain Alexander, probably more than most, had hoped for a race close to the human level of technology. It had almost ruined the expedition to find a ground-grubbing near-animal instead of an advanced race on the planet. Only Captain Alexander's personality and powerful friends on Earth had ensured the founding of a small colony.

Behind the raft was the knife-edge of the day—a sickle blade of bright sunlight honed to an intense white edge. There were bush fires along this strip. The idea was to remain ahead of the day and never allow it to overtake. To do so the raft had only to maintain a speed of seven metres per hour; not a difficult task, even allowing for breakdowns. However, the raft carried many spares and maintenance was *the* priority employment. If the inhabitants of the raft ever lost their transport, they would be in trouble. There were children among the occupants; to have had to live like gin while the shuttle ferried a few at a time to the starships (which had a capacity for 2,000 passengers each at the most, in any case) might cause a few problems. There were emergency life-rafts, of course, but not enough to cater for a complete failure and the loss of Stingray.

Ahead of the raft was the night hemisphere, where the gin went to rest and planted their fungi crops. Out of the night came the strong headwinds with which everyone and everything on the planet had to contend. On one hand the raft benefited from these because the power of the rushing air was used to a certain extent in keeping the raft up on its airwheels. On the other, the headwinds created the need for more solar power to drive the rear jet-streams and move the raft forward. The wind was something they cursed but accepted—an alien-world devil about which they could do little. New Carthage was the only planet in the dozens explored around Wolf 359 and other stars—from Proxima out to Epsilon Eridani—which housed alien life, albeit of a low-level intellect. A little wind was not going to keep scientists away from that kind of uniqueness.

The winds were warm on dawnside. On eveningside they were a great deal hotter. Somewhere near the middle line of the night hemisphere the surface gases peeled away to the west and east to form the two separate tidal waves. There was heavy turbulence around this atmospheric watershed, and also out in the day hemisphere where the two winds met head on. The Captain could never really picture meteorology except when looking at the charts produced by his experts—maps covered in curving lines, symbols and figures which he was shown every evening and which varied only in composition, never in content. He left them to it and accepted their forecasts with faith, if not with understanding.

At least the raft did not have to contend with a great deal of surface water along the equatorial belt. Vast underground seas kept the gin supplied with liquid which they obtained mostly via insect-like creatures the size of a man's foot.

To the north and south of the equator, water bubbled out on to the surface to form wide shallow lakes, around which grew shrubs and succulent plants. The dawn nurtured these areas of life during its relatively brief hold on them. Once they moved out into the day, the water evaporated and was blown back into the night as cloud. The bushes and other plant forms shrivelled and died under a merciless sun. Life cycles were finely tuned and seeds formed and dropped before the bush-fires took their toll. Somewhere in the night it was raining.

The raft could manufacture an emergency supply of water out of oxygen and hydrogen but mostly it drilled its own wells which the gin had recently begun using for themselves. Captain Alexander encouraged this alien use of his facilities. He felt it fostered good relations between the raft people and the natives. Others on board, he knew, disagreed with him. They maintained that the gin had a completely selfish attitude towards the pumps and that gratitude was not part of their nature.

There were some anthropologists and zoologists who lived amongst the gin from time to time. A few of these agreed with the popular image of the "indifferent" gin. Others reserved judgement. No one had yet cracked the language completely, so communication was very limited, but there were men and women who could "get by" to a degree with certain colloquialisms. The golden rule was *non-interference*. This was a wise policy from a long-term point of view but it meant that the gin remained an enigma. The largest life form on the planet (skeletons of other largish creatures had been found but now appeared to be extinct), the gin were truly uninterested in the visitors from Earth and would not allow themselves to be inspected or used in any way. Not one had been inside a human's vehicle or habitation of any kind. They barely tolerated close human society. Contact with the visitors was obviously distasteful to them. Consequently, their history was unknown.

Other life forms had been "tapped" by computer for historical data—at least back to conception. Everything on Earth, even plants, had a memory which could be transferred to the storage banks of a computer and studied. So it was with New Carthage. It was unfortunate for the visitors that the dog-like skeletons they occasionally found, whose cranium cavities suggested a large brain, were no longer around in the flesh to be questioned.

Lord, send us a highly intelligent alien, the Captain prayed silently. And if you can, make it a *social* beast. Human society was stale, sterile. It needed a stimulus to begin living again.

There was a buzz from the door which interrupted the Captain's thoughts.

"Come in," he called.

The man who entered the cockpit was of average height with thick, black, untidy hair. He was lean and lissom, using a springing step, despite the gravity, to bring himself to the centre of the room. The eyes, set in a dark-skinned face, had a sullen look.

The Captain sighed. "Dresnig."

"You didn't call me here to tell me my name. I already know that."

"Don't be insolent," snapped Alexander. "You know damned well why you're here. This is a small ship . . ."

"Raft," came the interruption, softly.

"As you say, *raft*, and as such we have to all be considerate of each other."

Captain Alexander looked away from the man, picked up a sheaf of papers and let them drop again on his desk.

He said, "Your guitar playing is annoying the other occupants again."

"All of them?" Incredulity in the tone.

"One or two. That's enough. I've decided to sound-proof your cabin—it's the only way to protect innocent ears. Where you learned such filthy songs . . ."

"I made 'em up."

"Yes? Well, that doesn't surprise me. You're in 1374, aren't you? Who's in with you?"

"What?"

"Who bunks with you?"

"No one. I'm on my own. The last guy moved out after three weeks. Peterson. We didn't get on."

Captain Alexander grunted. "I've yet to meet someone with whom you are compatible. Well, space *is* at a premium. You can't be allowed to occupy a double bunk alone for long, and you don't yet qualify for a single."

"Pity."

Once more the Captain tried to reason. The last time, a week ago, he had failed miserably.

"Dresnig, you're a civilian and I can't order you to behave, as I would one of my own men, but I can report you to Earth."

"You already have."

"No—I told you I would, but I didn't do it. Your pictures —your work as an artist is a needed source of income to the colony. We have to be able to support ourselves. I appreciate that help and I know you—no, dammit, you *don't* appreciate us. You're an ungrateful bastard and, what's worse, you don't seem to care that you're here because of my goodwill. You've been given the chance of a lifetime; other artists would grovel at my feet to be given an opportunity to reside at Stingray, to paint an alien scene, an alien people."

"Okay, I'm grateful," said Dresnig, not looking as if he had an atom of gratitude in his body. "I'm grateful that you let me sweat my guts out producing masterpieces which sell on Earth for thousands—*of which you get half*. I'm very, very grateful, see? The fact that I'm *better* than anyone else you can name is beside the point. Hell, man, you're lucky I'm *me*! I know half-assed painters who drain a bottle a day and grow higher than pines on topsy . . ."

The Captain was getting out his depth for about the seventh time since Dresnig had arrived as many months ago.

"I know you're a very clean-living person . . ."

"Straight as a goddamn light wave."

Captain Alexander sighed.

"I wish that were true—I've yet to meet a reasonable artist. You're all type-cast, and you do it to yourselves. Those of you who aren't born eccentric copy those of you who are, either because it looks fun or so that you can wear a uniform . . ."

"Audacity is the mother of a good painting."

"I bet you were a nice boy to your mother, Harry. I bet you wore clean socks and combed your hair. When did you look at yourself in the mirror and say, 'My God, I'm an artist. I'd better start practising to become a mean, unpredictable son-of-a-bitch or I'll never make the grade'? When, Harry?"

"Harry?" Raised eyebrows. "What happened to *Dresnig*?"

It was becoming a farcical interview. He had wanted to reprimand the artist quietly, and he was getting nowhere. Worse, he was back-pedalling.

"Harry," he persisted, "you know the way things are run on New Carthage. It's a bit like the old old days when generals used to pay for their own armies, captains for their own ships. Finances have tightened up again, and while the Armed Forces are prepared to put a certain amount of money into this project, it's a fixed amount. It's not enough, Harry. It was sufficient to pay for the raft and the two ships but not for the running of them. The ships run themselves—Mississippi riverboats . . ."

"Say again?"

"Gambling joints— they pay for their own running expenses out of the joy-riders' pockets. And here, on the raft, we have a number of enterprises, of which you are one . . ."

"I pay your wages?"

Alexander shook his head.

"You'd like to think so, wouldn't you? Truth is, I come free of charge. So do my men. It's the anthropologists, zoologists, archaeologists—in fact, all the '-gists' we've got. Sometimes a society or two throws in a few coins but it never covers for its member. I believe in this project, Harry. I'm not a scientist, I'm a common navy man with a desire to further the knowledge of mankind . . . "

The Captain could see the edges of an impatient yawn being stifled behind his listener's hand and he felt more than a trace of irritation at the young artist's poorly concealed contempt for his—yes, he had to admit it, even to himself—his *pompous* reprimanding.

"Okay, Harry. Just remember, don't . . ." There was an embarrassing pause. "Why did I call you in here?"

"My guitar."

"Yes. Keep the noise—the playing—down. That's all, Dresnig." To finish on a formal note was good. It re-established the Captain's authority.

"I can go now?" asked Dresnig.

"Please do."

"Thanks a bunch." Dresnig went out flicking a mock salute and once more Alexander had to grit his teeth. Wisely, he remained silent. A reopening of the discussion would have added nothing to the morning's work.

Captain Alexander was tired. A starship was due to go into orbit in a few days' time and he wanted to be fresh and ready for his visitors—a man, a woman and two children. These were part of the human alarm system he had been promised. He had reservations as to its effectiveness, of course, but what choice was there? Mankind had outreached its own technology once again, and had to look within itself for an answer. He stretched, and decided to rest on the cockpit couch rather than go to his bed. His officers would not hesitate to wake him if they needed advice. If he was in his cabin they would be reluctant to disturb him. A doze was as good as a sleep in any case. The couch was quite relaxing. There was just one job he should do before lying down, though. The ship's log was not quite up to date . . .

Ooma lifted the limbs to allow winds to blow pleasure

through the underarm holes in the skinflap. Pleasure was felt at the discovery of a new nest of drinkbulbs in the adventitious oneroot. Drinking would take place and there would be a linking between the *vilpa*. Drinkbulbs were becoming scarce. Soon would come the *manaha* which would make a better life. A less crowded life.

In the dim light of the dawn, the fingers used a scraper to bare a piece of the tubular oneroot which covered the sub-surface of Ooma's planet. An incision was made into the one-root and a hole cut for the hand to search inside. Oneroot was present everywhere just below the ground, and its hollow centre was the home for many varieties of creatures, mostly multi-legged and hairless. Long, serpentine animals also oc-cupied the endless tunnels within the oneroot, which had its millions of root hairs and caps dangling in the great under-ground oceans of the world. Ooma's *vilpa* obtained liquid food from the abdomens of certain paw-sized creatures, piercing that part of the body with their drinking spikes and draining the bulbs of their contents. Ooma jabbed a bulb now, drank, and then allowed the creature to crawl back into the root. It would replenish the liquid content of the bulb in time. The fluid was sickly and sweet, as it should be.

The wind was a twisting creature at this time, creating eddies in the blue-grey dust. It was strong, but not too strong. At certain times it was difficult to move against the wind, which was a frightening thing. The day yawned with a white, burning mouth—waiting to swallow the *vilpa* whole, if they ever let it.

On occasion, Ooma's people had been taken by accident into the day and one or two had survived the experience, only to return half mad. It was possible to stay alive by digging deep into the soil and curling beneath raw oneroot. Provided that part of the root was frequented by a colony of drinkbulbs, a food and liquid supply was to hand. It could be done, but seldom without the loss of one's mind. If you were not able to dig, however, the heat would hammer you into the ground with its paw and the drinkbulbs would end up eating *you*.

There were some dark foothills coming from the distance and Ooma tried for a recognition. Had they been seen before?

The *vilpa* had such poor memories, which was not surprising for the surface of the planet had little vegetation, its geography was unstartling and there was no day or night by which to mark the passing of time. Everything had a "sameness" about it which dulled the memory into a useless tool; there were no triggers to serve as useful aids to its mechanism. Only the memory stones provided a record of progress.

Most vegetation was fungoid in nature and sprang up in the night region. In places along the dawn strip the oneroot would sprout a small brittle foliage but as these entered dayside they caught fire and burnt themselves back down to the surface level again.

Only incidents remained in memory-print and these were not fixed by time scales. They jostled each other for space in the mind and often changed places by accident. It was not unusual for Ooma's people to return to the wrong mate and be confronted by a second partner. Not that this really mattered, since they were hermaphrodites and three could mate as easily as two—it was the triadic relationship they could not cope with.

A second, not of Ooma's *vilpa*, joined Ooma at the root. This young one delved into the hole made by Ooma's instrument and extracted a drinkbulb. The bulb was pierced before Ooma's double-lidded eyes and golden fur bristled as the other drank heavily. It was a wrong action but nothing could be done. They stared at each other, both sniffing heavily, the juice drying to crusty flakes around their spikes.

Ooma lifted the armflaps and buzzed annoyance through the nostrils. A question was nasalized.

"Have you anything for me? Some food-dust perhaps?"

Something should be given as compensation for sharing the bulbs. Dried fungus was inhaled as powder by the *vilpa*, yet the thief offered none. Instead there was an answering buzz which was plainly insulting. A derogatory remark was not what one expected in exchange for hospitality, however reluctantly given.

They stared at each other again, two golden beasts fashioned for speed and agility, each knowing that there would be no fight. Recriminations perhaps, but no violence.

Frustrated, Ooma did a full stretch, thin arms reaching for the sand-coloured sky. The wind screamed annoyance through the orifices in the five or six centimetres of skinflap beneath the armpits. Large eyes narrowed to deep slits and nostrils flared red in the opponent's face. An alarming note issued from within the olfactory organ.

The other merely buzzed hard at this show of passion and, after a few contemptuous passes of the sign hand, ambled away.

Ooma was left to wail at the loss of the drinkbulb. Although there were many more in the hole, passing by the spot all the time, Ooma could not help but feel anger at the other's lack of manners and breeding.

A little while later, another shape loomed over Ooma's smaller frame. It was one of the visitors. The visitor pointed to the hole in the oneroot and opened the horizontal slit in its face to reveal white. Ooma knew this to be a sign of pleasure and stretched forth a furry hand to be touched. The visitors liked to hand-touch on meeting and parting, but they would not allow exploration of other parts of their body. One of them had once screeched in Ooma's large ears when the hand had found a sensitive part below the abdomen. There were two types of visitor but they were difficult to tell apart. There were odd bits about their bodies which gave clues, but Ooma had long ceased to be interested in which was which. It did not seem to mean very much in any case. Both kinds of visitor seemed to have authority to do as they wished, to go where they pleased. It did not matter to the *vilpa*. The visitors used to collect drinkbulbs and other creatures when they were plentiful, but recently had ceased to hunt them. This was fortunate from the point of view of the *vilpa*.

The visitor sat down to watch Ooma in the act of eating. There were containers on the visitor's back from which a long black tube issued and the end of this tube was occasionally inserted in the visitor's face-slit. A food of some kind? Ooma would like to try it sometime. Ooma reached out for the tube but the visitor drew back shaking the head. Possibly a food which was in short supply?

Another thing about the visitors. They wore those peculiar

146

loose skins. It was almost as if they were in the act of shedding the outer layer and forming a new one—but they never did; at least, not in the presence of the *vilpa*. No one Ooma knew had seen anything like this happen. It was just that they were *almost* skinless. Most ugly.

Another white look from the visitor. What did it want? To speak? Ooma buzzed a question.

"Have you come for food or talk?"

The visitor became agitated at this and made the hand-sign for a repeat of the question. Ooma decided to concentrate on the main sounds.

"*Food* or *talk*?"

The visitor mimicked the buzz through its face-slit using that strange vibrating flap of skin that filled its redness. A fair attempt at *talk* but the sound would have been unrecognizable if Ooma had not been expecting it. The visitor gave Ooma a look of excited enquiry.

"*Talk*," buzzed Ooma, clearly. "Talk, talk, talk, talk talk . . ." The sound became a tune and the companion was forgotten for a while as Ooma buzzed softly to the wind.

Below the two creatures, just beginning the upward slope, was the home of the visitors—huge, flat, silver container full of many caves. From its back rose tall fins that reached up into the light, glistening and sparkling like stars. And from its rear ran the long copy of the oneroot, only it was segmented instead of having a continuous single casing. The tail went out into the hot day. What use it was or what it did there the *vilpa* had no idea. Nor did they care very much. Anything that went out into the day was a lost, forgotten object unless it was well hidden from direct heat—like Ooma's *nirna*, which was hanging safely in a cavern. When the time came the cavern would be found, but at the moment Ooma could not place its whereabouts in the mind.

The visitor pointed to the container.

"*Home*," buzzed Ooma, losing interest.

The visitor copied the buzz and Ooma left it, sitting by the hole in the oneroot, and went to fetch the *vilpa*. The visitor would not move since Ooma had made the "waiting" sign. It was to be hoped that if the intruder from the other *vilpa* returned, then the approach might be slow and hesitant if a visitor was seen to be guarding Ooma's claim. Probably it was a vain hope, but then there was no real choice.

Ooma ran, down beside the floating home of the visitors with its wind-makers blowing up the dust beneath its form, strong as the turnings of dancing single-winds. Ooma's people lived in shallow depressions in the ground. They had no need for solid structures. A nest was scraped out just before one needed to mate, or rest, as the case might be. Otherwise one spent one's time searching for food.

Ooma had the wind behind the body and the long string-muscled limbs reached a high speed naturally and smoothly. A long neck stretched forward as if the small round head was straining to reach the destination well ahead of the torso. Arms and legs moved rhythmically and strongly, gracefully pushing the sleek, wind-toned body across the dawn strip. Long, wide ears rolled into thin, pointed tubes which flattened against the neck. Twin-layer eyelids, one transparent, one coarse and opaque, worked independently from the bottom and top of the eye in order to maximize protection against dust particles in the atmosphere.

The wind and Ooma were not one, but two complementary parts of a moving scene. On Ooma's planet movement was life —everything obeyed that law. To remain still for longer than necessary was to court death. No wonder that movement was joy. A fast run was sensual, sexual. Ooma knew that a mate would have to be found before returning to the oneroot.

12 Arrival

The starship was a gem imbedded in the blackness behind
them as they sped towards the surface of New Carthage. Alex
could see lights dancing along the wings of the shuttle like the
silent static-electric footsteps of some fantastical creature from
another reality. This was another world and all things here
were, or seemed, different; even imported commonplace objects and actions. Everything was impregnated with a newness
that deserved imbibing. Excitement surged through his breast
in waves, threatening to drown him in successive draughts of
intoxicating emotion. The senses battled against exotic tides
which flooded his normally level-headed and cautious approach to fresh ventures. If someone had asked him, "How do
you feel about going to New Carthage?" he would have stut-
tered that it was the most wonderful thing that had ever
happened to him.

He gripped On Lo's hand on one side and Nadine's on the
other. The little one was grave, the woman as feverish as he
was himself. Clearly it was a time for adults to indulge in half-
beliefs. The children were submissive and uninquisitive: insecurity born of strange surroundings.

The pilot executed a vertical landing not far from a huge,
steel monster that hovered above the half-lit hill.

A vehicle was sent to collect them, its windows blanked to
prevent the children from seeing at close quarters any gin that
might be passed on the return journey. Alex and Nadine were
soon standing before Captain Alexander in his cabin. Alex
introduced them.

"This is Nadine Seerman. My name is Alexander Craven."

"Captain Alexander. We appear to have something in
common, Mr Craven."

"The name, yes. It's not a coincidence. I was named after

you. My mother gave birth to me at the same time as you discovered New Carthage."

"Still something of a coincidence that we should meet."

"Again, I don't think so. It was a popular thing to do at the time—name children after you. You're a famous man."

Captain Alexander appeared to enjoy this remark. Why not? It was true.

"And these are the children? Couple of sweet-looking cherubs."

"They're girls, Captain," said Nadine.

He looked confused. "I know—the closeness factor."

"Cherubs are male," she explained.

"Ah. I see. Well, just a figure of speech. Perhaps you could enlighten me on one or two other points. I've read all the reports, of course, concerning the children's tests, but what happens in the event of a false alarm? I mean, how ... I'm not sure I know what I mean, but how do you prevent nightmares? Perhaps I shouldn't be talking about this in front of them?"

"That's all right," replied Nadine. "I'm sure they don't understand anyway. No, there shouldn't be a false alarm. The children's brainwave patterns have been remotely monitored and logged in a computer since birth. Those patterns that came out of the tests are very different from those taken during bad dreams—even though they may be dreaming about the gin. The peaks of terror are far higher and sharper during a real confrontation with their phobia. Besides, their Earthside counterparts will *know* what is causing the fear."

"I see. Presumably the Earthside twins are being monitored at this moment ..."

"Continuously," replied Nadine.

"Okay, at least I have it straight now. Well, the children look as though they're getting restless."

The two girls were hanging on to Nadine's slacks and were looking fatigued. On Lo was singing softly to herself, a folk song Nicole had taught her.

"I'll bed them down. Will I have some assistance with them? They should be watched night and day ... I mean ..."

"That's okay. We have a night and day here. It just never changes colour, that's all." Captain Alexander smiled at her.

"Grey all the time. It's day now ..." He glanced at the digital clock on his wall which depicted the calendar date and the time, GMT. It was 1400 hours.

The Captain continued, "You'll have two nurses to assist you. I've put you in charge, so how you work your rota is up to you. I suggest a three-day watch—that'll entail each one of you working shifts over two days, with the third day free. I'll explain it to you later if you wish."

"I do wish. Thanks."

"That's fine then. I'll call someone to show you to your quarters. You'll soon get to know your way around. And you and Mr Craven will be allowed to visit the surface, but, of course, not the children. They will see the gin from the cabin portholes but the living accommodation is on top of the raft, too high for them to recognize details. The natives will just be distant figures to them."

Alex interrupted. "We understand. Um, is there any chance I might be near them—Nadine and the children? I have to help with their schooling and care   ." he coughed. "Father, so to speak."

Captain Alexander looked at him coldly.

"I understand your duties, Mr Craven. Unfortunately the single quarters for males and females are at opposite ends of the raft ..."

"Ah!"

"... and therefore, you see, it's not possible to put you together. As I've already explained, nowhere is very far, and you'll need all the exercise you can get. Incidentally, we have a very good—small, perhaps, but well-equipped—gymnasium, in which case one can work off any excesses. Do I make myself clear?"

"Perfectly."

"Good."

The Captain pressed something on his desk.

"Now, Miss Seerman, I'll get someone to show you the way."

"Thank you, Captain. You're most thoughtful." She glanced out of the corners of her eyes at Alex while she spoke. He thought he noticed a smug look in that significant passing expression but he couldn't be sure. The protected virgin? Bit late for that.

Nadine was duly collected and a short time later a young black officer came for Alex. In a way he was glad to get out of the Captain's presence. There was something oppressively old-fashioned in the man's manners, yet he gave the impression of being extremely efficient. He had been very smartly dressed in a grey shirt and slacks and his hands had been manicured to perfection—yet there had been nothing effeminate in the man. From his build he had looked as if he could punch holes in aluminium panels. Not a man to tackle physically if one could avoid it. It often helps a man in authority—especially in the military or navy—if his subordinates respect him for his physical strength as well as his power to command. Discipline, that was the outdated word for which he had been searching. The Captain looked like a well-disciplined man, which was something that annoyed Alex because he himself was a spontaneous person.

Alex asked his escort, "Do we have to wear receiving bracelets here? So that the Captain can contact us?"

The officer shook his head. "If you go outside for any distance, you're expected to carry a transceiver, but here in the raft we have a tannoy system."

Alex nodded.

The main alley-way seemed endless, but eventually they branched off and the young officer reached a cabin door marked 1374.

"This is your bunk. I'll leave you to introduce yourself to your cabin mate. His name's Dresnig. Harry Dresnig. Please excuse me, but I've got to get back on watch." There was an expression on the officer's face which Alex could not recognize but hc said, "Yes, okay. Thanks."

"You're welcome."

Alex stared at the officer's back as he walked away and, just before the man turned the corner, he looked back at Alex with that same in-between expression. What was it? Like a cross between sympathy and the anticipation of a brawl. The sort of look the Romans gave the underdog before a gladiatorial confrontation?

Alex shrugged and pressed the door-release button. The door slid back and he stepped inside. The cabin was very small. There was a flap-down table, two folding chairs and two over-and-under bunk beds, the top one of which contained a dark-skinned, completely naked man who was openly appraising Alex.

Alex put down his bag and stretched out a hand to be shaken.

"Alex. Alex Craven. I've been assigned to this bunk."

"Assigned?" The hand was left untouched.

Now why the hell did he go and use that word? It was military jargon.

"Allocated." The hand returned to Alex's side.

Alex was not used to naked men and he looked away, embarrassed yet mentally kicking himself for being so.

"I'm a junkhead," continued the man.

"What?" Alex had heard, but it was one of those sentences one needs to have repeated.

"Yeah. And I'm glad they sent me someone at last. I need to share my experiences with another person, you know what I mean? Most of the men here are straight—straight as goddamned light waves . . ."

Alex swallowed hard. This was what the young officer had been waiting for—he had known what was coming.

"I don't have the habit," he managed to say at last.

The other's eyes grew hard as flints.

"Listen, I hope you have nothing against us. I mean, I don't like prejudice . . ."

"Certainly not. Each to his own, but . . ."

There was an interruption from the visiphone on the cabin wall.

"Okay, that'll do, Dresnig. I thought you'd pull something. It's all right, Mr Craven."

The man Dresnig punched angrily at the buttons on the visiphone.

"There's no privacy around here!" he shouted when the picture failed to fade.

The Captain's image said, "You know I can override the main system from my cockpit control panel. Now listen, Harry, you are going to have to share your cabin, whether you like it or not, so get used to the idea. You can have a single in several months . . ."

"They're too small."

"Then you have to learn to share."

The image faded and Harry Dresnig was left glowering at the blank screen.

"Mother . . ." he began, but then glanced at Alex and, with a heavy scowl distorting his handsome features, turned his face to the bulkhead and lay down, presumably to sulk.

Alex timidly began to unpack the small amount of personal effects he had been allowed to bring with him. Homesick, and feeling insecure now that the excitement was starting to wear off, he reflected miserably upon his situation. There was no going back for a while. He was stuck on a raft full of strangers in a cabin with an occupant who clearly resented his presence. Since there were no other available cabins, and no one in a single bunk was going to be fool enough to change places with him—(they presumably all knew this man Dresnig)—he was going to have to make the best of it.

"How did you know I *wasn't* taking drugs?" he said to Dresnig.

There was silence then a muffled reply.

"Pardon?" asked Alex.

"I read your file," said the other, loudly.

Alex coloured and felt the anger rising in him.

"Who allowed you to do that? Aren't they supposed to be for the Captain's eyes only?"

"I screwed his secretary."

"Oh." There did not seem to be much more to say after that. He could report the incident but it didn't appear to matter very much.

He flopped on to the bunk, which was surprisingly comfortable, and fell asleep.

Sometime later, Alex woke and glanced at the clock. 1807 hours. Cautiously he stuck his head out and looked upwards. The top bunk appeared to be empty. Relieved, he got up and rinsed his face in the small metal basin attached to the bulkhead. He thought about calling Nadine on the visiphone but decided against it. He could not remember her room number and was too shy to call someone and ask them for it. Besides, what did he have to say except "I hate this place"?

He had just finished arranging his worldly possessions in the small cabinet provided when there was a buzz at the door.

"Yes? Come in."

He was disappointed to be faced by the black officer who had shown him his cabin. He had hoped it would be Nadine.

"Hello."

"Lieutenant Peter Jameson, remember? I've come to take you to the mess-hall. Called earlier, but you were asleep, so I left you to it."

"That's okay, thanks. Yes, I could do with a bite."

"Okay, let's go. It's off the middle of the Burma Road."

Alex said, "What?"

"Oh yeah, you probably don't know. This centre alley-way that runs the length of the raft, it's nicknamed the Burma Road—long and straight, see? We have to walk. There's no room for vehicles on the raft but nowhere is more than one kay."

Alex nodded.

"The rest of the alley-ways fork backwards off the Burma Road, like the backbone of a fish. You'll soon get to know."

"I'm sure I will."

They began walking and Jameson said, "I'm from Morristown, New Jersey. Used to be a town once but it's a city state now. You're from London, England, right?"

"Used to be, when there was an England."

They both smiled at this.

"Listen, what's the matter with this man Dresnig?" asked Alex. "He seems to hate my guts already and we've only just met."

Jameson waved a hand.

"Don't sweat over that creep. He's an artist the old man had shipped in. Paints the gin and local scenery. Nobody will scream if you smack him one in the mouth. He doesn't hate you any more than he hates me, or anyone else."

"Then why ... ?"

Jameson interrupted, grinning, "Trouble is, he does hate me and everyone else. Here's the mess-hall."

They branched off and entered a long narrow room with fold-down tables and attached bench seats. The first thing Alex saw was Dresnig talking earnestly to Nadine. It was so obviously a set-up. They were positioned right in his line of sight as he entered and he noticed that Nadine looked away from him quickly as he stared at them. Dresnig was trying to rattle him.

"Over here," said Jameson, steering him towards the serving hatches.

"Just a minute," murmured Alex.

He walked deliberately up to Nadine and said, "What's this man been telling you?"

"Nothing," said Nadine, with a little toss of her head. "Well, nothing *bad*, that is. It's all quite exciting." Her hands fluttered.

Alex bunched his fists.

"The Captain doesn't allow fighting on the raft," said Jameson, but there was an intimation that this rule could be bypassed somehow. The rest of the mess-hall had gone quiet. All chatter had ceased.

"Be my guest," said Dresnig, smiling.

The words were spoken in undertones but there was such malice in the voice that Alex felt his face drain of blood, and he blinked rapidly.

"Just be careful," he managed to get out. Then he stumbled away from them, Jameson on his heels.

"You don't want to worry about him," said Jameson. "He's not as tough as he makes out. Guys like him make a lot of noise and then flop around like fish after the first blow lands."

"I've got to sleep in the same cabin as that nut," Alex said, the strain evident in his tone.

"Which is, of course, exactly what he *doesn't* want to happen," replied Jameson. "He knows he can't get away with anything. Someone's bound to report this *non-incident* to the Captain. He wants *you* put somewhere else so that he can have the whole cabin to himself, so he'll do anything to further that course, even make up to your girl . . ."

156

"She's not my girl."

"Well, your travelling companion then. Trouble is . . ."

"What?"

"Well, the Captain seems to *like* him. I mean, anyone else would have been shipped home long ago, but though they square up to each other and verbally hammer one another into the ground, the Captain and Dresnig seem to have this thing going . . ."

"Great. Great. That's all I need. The Captain conspiring to aid and abet my murder."

Alex grabbed his meal and sat down at the nearest table, shovelling the white substance down his throat without even tasting it. He tried to take his mind off his troubles by asking Jameson questions. He asked about religion. Who was the favourite poet of the New Carthaginians? Did they believe in Mathew Tse?

"That's hard to answer. Each one has his own private thoughts, but here . . . ? I don't think there's much of a revival going on at all. Guess we're happy to see each new hour, without concerning ourselves overmuch with eternal problems. We have a service every now and again. It's supposed to be ADAC—all denominations and creeds—but you don't find many of the orientals attending. They like to meditate, or whatever, alone. Like I said, it's something you hold to yourself here. There's not much else you can keep private. By the way, the Captain's a puritan—I don't mean for real, I mean in outlook. Don't blaspheme in front of him—*anybody's* God— and don't let him catch you with a woman . . ."

"But Dresnig . . ."

"I said, don't let him *catch* you. Dresnig's careful about that. Why the hell do you think he wants the bunk to himself?"

"Ah! Okay."

"You'll have gathered by now the Captain's all-powerful. Omnipotent and omniscient. Perhaps that's why we don't really need a God up here. We've already got one. This is a sailing ship—and he's John Paul Jones."

"Horatio Nelson."

"Have it your own way," said Jameson.

157

"Let's talk about the raft. I understand the power is solar-generated."

"Yeah. Comes from the tail which stretches back into the day."

"What about those thin metal sheets I saw on top of the raft then?"

Jameson took a sip of his drink before replying.

"Photon sails providing ancilliary power. Water heaters, etcetera."

At that moment, Nadine and Dresnig stood up and prepared to leave. Nadine gave Alex a half-hearted wave when she saw him staring. Then they went through the doorway together.

Alex gripped his drink container.

"Your knuckles are turning white," remarked Jameson.

"I'll give them five minutes, then I'm going to break in on them."

"Surprise, surprise."

"Yes, well it's my cabin too. I'm not going to let that freak get away with murder—or anything else."

"Good luck, pal. I'll look in on you later. Maybe I should bring some plastic bags." Jameson was wearing his lopsided grin.

"For him or me?"

"I'm betting on you, buddy. I like the way your jaw sticks out. Shows determination."

"Okay. See you later."

Alex left the hall and retraced his steps to the Burma Road. Eventually he reached his cabin and paused outside the door. Having come this far he knew he would have to go through with his plans but his courage was beginning to ebb. Dresnig was thin and brittle-looking, but he had a vicious streak and that was worth a barrelful of muscles. Still, Alex had bested the physically superior nuisance on Earth. He could do the same with this artist.

Without any further hesitation, he pressed the button and entered.

The cabin was empty.

Deflation followed rapidly, and then frustration. They were

probably in Nadine's cabin. Alex could hardly go breaking in *there*. He was still staring angrily at the empty top bunk when a hand descended heavily on his shoulder. Fright made him skip sideways quickly.

"Hello, room-mate," said his assailant. It was Dresnig and the man was actually smiling.

"You want the top pit? I'll sell it to you, for a block of topsy."

"I told you, I don't take drugs," answered Alex, unsure of his ground once more.

"You don't have to—I'll do that."

"Well, I don't have any."

"Pity." Dresnig swung himself easily up on to the bunk in question.

Alex was left standing, stupidly, near the door.

"How long have you been here, Dresnig?"

"Harry. Harry's the name. Father French, mother German. Born and raised in Cairo. Touch of the black in me somewhere—from my father's side, probably. Surprised you want to share a cabin with me . . ."

"Why, because of that? Most people are mixtures these days. My fiancée's originally from Panama." Nicole would object to being called his fiancée, but one could afford to be reckless, light-years from Earth.

"And you?"

"I expect I've got several nationalities under my skin. You won't get rid of me that way."

"How long have I been here? Forever, man, that's how long a minute is in this place. If you took all the hours I've been here and shuffled them, then spread 'em out on the table like playing cards, you would still have a pack that's in order—because they're all the same. Each hour is as full or blank as the next one, and they slot in anywhere. A deck of blank playing cards, that's what we've been given here."

That was all Alex could get out of Harry Dresnig for the time. He was already beginning to feel that drag on his tail which Dresnig prophesied. For the rest of the evening he moped around, exploring the raft in a desultory fashion. There were shops on board and one or two small entertainment centres but mostly the mess-halls and common-rooms were the communal meeting places. Late in the evening, Alex went to the nearest common-room bar and bought himself a drink. He looked around the half-filled room for Nadine or Jameson, but could not see either of them. So he sat and mooned over the drink thinking that if this was all life had to offer them, he would return to Earth on the next starship.

There was a sinking sensation in Alex's stomach. Then a sudden lurch moved his drink a few centimetres across the table. The speaker above the clock murmured softly, "Duty crew, duty crew. Cable break." A man and two women rose and left the common-room immediately. The rest of the patrons resumed their interrupted activities and, even when the gentle bump occurred some few seconds later, they appeared to be completely at ease. To Alex it was obvious that something serious had happened and that the raft had settled on solid ground. It was not until the constant gentle hum died that Alex actually noticed it had been there at all.

He leaned out and spoke to the couple in the next booth, a young man around twenty and a woman some few years older. The woman was a high-ranking officer.

"Can you tell me what's happened? I mean I realize the raft has stopped—I only arrived this morning."

The man smiled in a superior fashion.

"Sprog, huh?"

"What?"

"Sprog—spring frog. New man."

The woman seemed irritated by the young man's attitude. She gave him a look of annoyance. Then she turned to Alex.

"We've had a cable break," she explained. "It's not serious but if the raft continues to move forward, we get further away from the segments on the other side of the break. So we stop until it's repaired."

"Does that mean we've lost all our power?" he asked her.

"No, just the source. There are storage batteries. And we have the photon sails."

"Thanks," Alex smiled. "Sorry to butt in."

The man shrugged. Alex returned his head to his own booth and contemplated the young man's attitude. It seemed Alex was going to have a lot of trouble making friends in this place. Everyone appeared to be so aggressive. No, that wasn't true—Jameson was all right.

Just then the woman from the next booth came and sat on the opposite seat.

"Hi. My name's Maya. Maya Kleppel. Silly name, isn't it?"

Alex studied her face, trying not to be obvious, as he acknowledged the greeting and gave her his own name. She had heavy-boned features, and an untidy head of woody-blonde hair. She was, he guessed, about thirty years of age.

"I'm thirty-three," she said.

"You a mind reader?"

"No. You're obvious."

"I'm sorry. Anyway, what about your friend? Won't he mind you leaving him?"

She tossed her head in an expression of contempt.

"No, I don't think so. Anyway, he's gone to look at the break. Nothing much exciting happens around here, so when it does, it becomes a sideshow. Not that a cable break *is* anything. It happens fairly often—about once in every three months."

"I don't think Maya is a silly name."

"No, but Kleppel is. Do you want to go outside? I'll take you to see the break if you like."

"Why not? Now?"

"I'll just get some tanks. You won't like the thin oxygen. Then we'll hitch a lift on one of the airwheelers going out there. Okay?"

"Okay."

Their greyness turned gradually to brilliance as they sped along towards the dayside. Apparently the break was inside the day but the vehicles had air-conditioning. Also the windows were photosensitive. There would be no need for the oxygen tanks. No one could leave the airwheeler.

On the way Alex studied the natives. They mustered on the slopes like herds of antelope. No, not antelope, that was only suggestive of their numbers—more like leopards or cheetahs. Since the landscape was almost barren, Alex wondered how they existed in such large groups. He mentioned it to Maya.

"Well, I've been here seven years and in that time alone

they've increased their young but none of them seem to die of old age. The old man is getting worried about it."

"I suppose that's why I'm here," said Alex. "I've brought a little girl—On Lo—with me. She's a twin . . ."

"I know. The telemetry system."

"Yes."

They travelled parallel to the thin segmented cable, with its flattened underside which was normally supported by its own miniature airwheeler system. All around it dust storms raged, but they were erratic and clouded the vision only intermittently.

"Doesn't seem thick enough to provide all the power the raft needs," said Alex.

"The cable contains thousands of fibre optic circuits," Maya patiently explained. "The energy is transmitted in the form of light until the raft converts it into thermal power and electricity."

They reached the break but there was little to see. The duty repair craft had split like a pea pod and folded itself around the two separated pieces of cable. Inside the craft, repairs were being carried out in refrigerated comfort. Alex was disappointed. He had half expected to see men and women in huge cumbersome suits clumping around the frayed ends of the broken line.

There were no gin out here where the sun breathed on the surface like a dragon with incendiary lungs. Even from within the craft the outside atmosphere and screaming airborne grit seemed charged with heat. They made their way back to the raft. By the time they arrived the raft was afloat again.

Alex said goodnight to Maya and then visited On Lo. She was still awake, chattering happily to a nurse.

"Are you all right, sweetheart?" he asked the child.

"Yes, uncle. The lady has given me lots of toys. Look!" She showed him. "Ohhhh! Stupid Tinta," she remonstrated with her doll, for reasons known only to her.

He nodded, patting her head. Then he said to the nurse, "Don't let her stay up too late. She's had a long day."

Back in his own cabin, there was a surprise waiting for him. His heart stopped at the sight of a fully grown carnivore sitting on his bunk, bright-eyed and bushy tailed, in the dimmed light of the cabin. Harry Dresnig was lying on his own bunk, looking at him expectantly. Then Alex noticed the lasers.

"Piss off, Harry," he said wearily.

"Vulpephobia. It's on your file," replied his room-mate gleefully.

"I've been cured. Now grow up, sonny."

Dresnig switched off the hologram of the fox and turned to face the bulkhead. His sulking position.

The funny thing was, thought Alex before dropping off to sleep, the fox had not scared him. Surprise and alarm at the unexpected, yes, but not that mind-stabbing fear he was used to experiencing. Familarity breeds contempt. An old but still serviceable truth.

13 The Sun Rock

On Earth, each new dawn had been characterized by some subtle change in the atmosphere: a ruby-inspired streak running obliquely to the sea; a foaming buoyancy on the horizon. Here on New Carthage, there was no newness. There was just the dawn: grey, unchanging, interminable. High cloud banks sped across the sky giving the impression of a fast-spinning world. The inhabitants followed doggedly behind.

In such situations men and women function inside a dreary vacuum with the feeling that they are experiencing an unwanted immortality. Life slows almost to a stop. The minutes from waking to sleeping are stretched into unrecognizable time spans that separate a mortal from sanity. In this kind of situation, people tend to withdraw into themselves rather than seek entertainment amongst others. They shun society and begin taking lonely walks where they can philosophize without interruption. They begin to pick away at their souls, search for poetry and original thought. It becomes enjoyable to sit and watch the distant gin labouring at a food problem. (It was policy not to interfere with the natural order of the planet; the gin did not receive provisions from the visitors and their efforts to survive provided a kind of uneasy entertainment. Captain Alexander had told Alex, rather enigmatically, that he did not want another John Frum Cargo Cult on his hands. On investigation, Alex had discovered that during World War Two an American quartermaster had supplied Pacific Island natives with rations from military aircraft. After the war the rations obviously ceased to arrive but the natives continued to attempt to seduce overflying aircraft with graven images: crudely made replicas of DC3s.)

Alex wondered if the gin really did have a long life cycle or whether the grey, apathetic life they led had made them remiss. Perhaps they had just forgotten that some of them were supposed to die sometimes?

As he stared through one of the portholes at the open plain they were crossing, Alex reflected upon how little he knew of the "outside". Not just on New Carthage, but anywhere. Those few months in the Angles, including his initial unpleasant re-actions to the countryside, had merely whetted the edge of his keenness to experience more of the vastness of the outside. The confinement of the raft would not have bothered him a year ago. Now it was like wearing a tight suit of armour. He took every opportunity to shed it.

Most mornings he helped with the schooling of the six children on board, an occupation that was pleasant at first but which rapidly palled. The afternoons he spent in his own company, when possible, and only in the evenings did he seek society. He disliked room parties but often accompanied Maya when she wished to attend one. Mostly he joined his male friends in one of the bars or common-rooms.

After four months of his company, Harry Dresnig had finally abandoned his attempts to winkle Alex from the cabin. They had even come to like each other in a strange off-hand fashion. There was no admittance of friendship—merely a silent acceptance of each other.

Now Harry had promised to take Alex outside with him. Alex had been out before, of course, but Harry had something special to show him. The artist was excited about his dis-covery, and living with an excited Harry was like setting up home in a fairground.

"I think I've found something that could be really im-portant," he had said, arms ferris-wheeling, eyes like sideshow firebrands.

Alex had asked, innocently, "Have you told the Captain?"

"What? Are you crazy? This is *my* discovery. As soon as I tell that prig, it'll be *his* find."

"Okay," said Alex, dubiously, "but we may have to tell him sooner or later. I mean, if it's that important."

"Yeah? Well, I'll see about that later. In the meantime, keep it to yourself. Don't go blabbing about it all over the raft."

"I don't even know what it is yet."

"Good, good. That's the way I like it."

So today they were going outside. Alex wished that, instead of the dull half-lit plain, outside consisted of snow-covered forested slopes, or burning deserts; neither of which he had experienced and which he could only imagine.

"Where are we going?" he asked Harry, as they walked the length of the Burma Road.

"Outside," said Harry, in his usual irritating manner of disclosing as little as possible until absolutely necessary.

"Who are we meeting?" Alex joked, hoping for a slip, a name, but Harry did not like to brag about conquests and Alex did not really want to be reminded about what he was missing. Nadine was long gone, to young officers and uninterested in him any longer. Nicole was on Earth. He had formed a relationship—of a kind—with Maya, but she had turned out to be no less than Captain Alexander's Second-in-Command, which was inhibiting. At least, it was to Alex. Presumably Maya would take over in the event of Alexander's departure or demise, and the thought of sharing a bed with the Captain designate was not appealing. It created a feeling of impotency even before the event. She was wholesome but no beauty.

They collected their tanks, then passed through the airlock and into the thin oxygen on the outside. Harry Dresnig leaped to the ground with a loud exuberant "Whoopee!" and began to dance.

"Wait a minute, Harry. Shouldn't we register with Admin Control so they'll know where we're going?" Alex quickly became breathless and took a delightful whiff of his back-packed oxygen.

Alex knew that Harry had a heart murmur and it worried him to see the artist doing violent exercise. He was afraid Harry would keel over, clutching his chest, while there was only him around.

Harry stopped his dance and pulled on the oxygen.

"We're gonna see some *art*, mister. That's where we're going. To those rocks in the distance."

Alex nodded, wondering if he should go back and tell Admin Control. Like mountaineers or pilots they were supposed to register any outside movement and give an estimated time of return. He shrugged his shoulders. There were two of them, after all. They would hardly both meet with an accident at the same time. He followed Harry, who was now walking ahead.

"Where did you learn the dance, Harry?" he asked, catching up with the artist.

"I didn't. It's natural. In my bones."

"Balls, Harry. That was a traditional dance, with set steps. Besides, you haven't got any Red Indian blood in you."

"Why not? I got most other kinds."

Harry Dresnig claimed he possessed all sorts of natural talents. Like his wild, abandoned guitar playing—which was good, Alex admitted. Harry had said that he picked up a guitar at the age of six and just extracted a tune from the strings. Alex suspected the "six" was borrowed from the stories of Mozart's early genius for composing. Harry would consider that little familiar details like that gave his stories authenticity.

They passed several gin crowded around a oneroot hole. There seemed to be some sort of argument going on amongst the natives as there was a lot of arm-high wind-holing going on. It was best to ignore such a fracas.

Alex enjoyed the sound of the gin arguing. There was something both sad and comic in the sounds they made. They haunted the plain with their ghost-like hooting and wailing.

"Come on," Harry called. "It's about them—where I'm taking you."

The wind cut around them and Alex complained loudly at its attempts to erode his body. Sand blew into his mouth and nostrils, and he ground his teeth on its grittiness.

"Why didn't we bring a vehicle?" he asked. "Or suits?"

"I've told you. We're taking to the high ground. Vehicles can't get up there and suits are cumbersome. Now stop staring at those cicadas and let's get moving."

Cicadas. Harry's personal nickname for the gin. He always had to be different. He named them for their whirring noses.

To Alex, Harry was full of light—a Turner painting. He was an irregular whorl of white, snow-like brightness that obscured his definite self in its attempts to portray his soul. Like a Turner, Harry was a vague, hazy outline that only suggested what it was supposed to represent—the rest, the precise shape of his character, was hidden beneath that swirling dust, snow, steam and fire which even obscured others when they came too close to Harry. It was Harry's soul: too large for its mortal housing, its influence spread beyond his body. Like the heat from white-hot metal, or a magnetic force field.

Alex recalled a typical story Harry had told him the previous evening while they rested on their respective bunks. It concerned, Harry had said, Omogan, the great African dictator who had ruled absolutely the middle decades of the 21st Century. A whole continent had fallen under his powerful black hand at a time when Africa was leading the world in ideas. Like most tyrants he had begun his reign with good intentions, which had proved impossible to fulfil, and had, finally, fallen into despotic ways.

There had been many assassination attempts but Omogan survived them all—save one. No conspiracy had brought his downfall. The plot had been hatched and implemented by a single person: Lavinia of Lagos.

Omogan had demanded of all in his presence that they should be naked and weaponless. He had cleared his palace of any ornaments and furniture which could conceivably be used as missiles or clubs. Fingernails had been inspected for poison by the outer guards. Omogan's programme had been changed frequently, and an audience with him might take weeks of waiting to mature—or merely minutes. His behaviour had been unpredictable.

He had been a classic megalomaniac.

Like many absolute rulers, he had enjoyed as many women as he could manage. Lavinia of Lagos was one of his general's daughters—an only child. She was seventeen with a skin like black silk. Her breasts were high and taut. They curved upwards towards the nipples like twin rhinosaurus horns. Omogan had had the father executed to get to the daughter, and surprisingly she had come to him willingly. Omogan had been suspicious but his security was impenetrable.

Like all others she had entered his room completely un-clothed. Her nails had been inspected at the palace gate. Omogan's fifty-year-old loins had ached for her and his arms had folded around her warm, smooth body as she came to him.

Minutes later he was writhing on the mosaic fishes of his palatial floor in the throes of death.

The goodbye kiss had come from the fanged mouth of a bootlace snake.

Lavinia had drugged the snake and inserted its head in the nasal passage at the back of her throat, in order that it could breathe and remain alive. The rest of the tiny body she had curled under her tongue. Once in Omogan's arms she had deftly tongued the head of the bootlace to the front of her mouth. By this time the effects of the drug had almost worn off but in her mouth the snake had had no room to rear and strike. As Omogan had bent to kiss her, Lavinia allowed the snake to serpentine through her closed lips. Then it had struck at the descending face. The instant the death blow had been delivered Lavinia bit down hard, severing the snake's head from its body, thus preventing a strike at her own face.

As the story had ended, the light had faded from Harry's expression. Alex had tried to read the other man's face but it had been impossible to discern whether this had been another of Harry's inventions or a true historical account. If it was the latter, Alex's education was incomplete. Officially Omogan had died of a heart attack while in the company of a courtesan.

They reached the outcrop of rocks which was their destination. They had moved out of the dawn and into the edge of the night, but the stars offered enough light to see by. The boulders were, like much of the planet's rock, obsidian in nature. The starlight picked out silver webs on their surfaces. These were formed of needle-long crystals lying upon the rocks in the disarray of jack-straws loosed by a careless hand.

"Is this it?" asked Alex. Harry was excited now and the generation of his feverishness was beginning to affect Alex.

"Over this side. Look!"

The south face of the rock was smooth, as if the whole block had been split to give one side a gloss surface. Alex trained a flashlight on the spot indicated by Harry. The light picked out hundreds of white-lined fractures on the glinting face.

"What is it? Some kind of art form?" he questioned.

"More than that. It is—but look deeper. Look for a meaning."

Alex was confused by the vast array of powdery indentations. It was as if someone—or something—had struck the surface time after time with a heavy object. A spike of some sort, or a pointed stone. Harry was watching his face intently and Alex knew he would have to make a guess. The artist would soon give way to his impatience and become annoyed with Alex's stupidity.

'Stars," he said at last, hoping for a miracle. He *almost* made it.

"Yes, yes. But what star? What?" shouted Harry, and then had to take a whiff of oxygen.

"I don't know. You tell me."

"The sun!" said Harry, eyes afire in the light shining from Alex's fist. "A sunburst."

Alex was incredulous. "Our sun? Earth's sun?" What was Harry saying? That the gin had been to Earth?

"No. God, no. The sun over that shagging horizon, you great . . ." There was a wild waving of arms towards the dayside.

"Calm down, Harry. You *tell* me. Why should this be our sun? Our star?"

"You're the first one I've told about this, Alex."

"I'm not going to run to the old man—tell me."

Harry said, "They are suns, carefully produced by an artist's hand. Look at the similarity between the images. The point is —how does a gin know what the sun looks like? They've never been out there, under that thing. How do they *know*?"

"The stars," said Alex, but Harry was already shaking his head.

"Not the stars. Look. The stars have no points of light here. They're just dots. Besides, look at the *whiteness* of the nuclei. That's heat, Alex. White heat. Suns."

"Okay, so what?"

"So, I have a theory. What're you doing?"

Alex was nodding his head at the images. He stopped.

"I'm counting them."

"What for?"

"I don't know. Just practical, I guess. You're the artist. You see it from your angle. I look at it more from an engineer's point of view."

"Do you want to hear my theory or not?"

"Go ahead," said Alex, with an apologetic note to his voice.

"Good. Well, I believe that once upon a time this whole planet was habitable. That's why the gin are crowding each other at the moment. They're not used to living on such a narrow strip of land. They've been forced into a corner. Probably it happened a long time ago and they have some natural mechanism to deal with it now ..."

"Like what?"

"Use your imagination! Like racial suicide. Like ingestion of the reproductive organs. War. Plague. I don't know *exactly* what. But something to cut down their numbers. A culling factor."

Alex nodded. Harry had obviously thought this all through, if not very carefully. It was certain he had not found the rock art yesterday.

"Harry, have you seen other examples of this?" He pointed to the sun rock.

The artist nodded. "I've taken some pictures. I'll show you later. The important thing is, I think I know what's happened. How they managed to see the sun—way back in their dim and distant past. I believe, listen, I believe that Wolf 359 went nova ... is still doing so."

"Yes?"

"Well, don't you see, man? Only those on nightside survived and this group eventually formed the clans that live in the dawn country. Before that they roamed the whole world— *and were able to see the sun.*"

"A less bright sun."

"Right." Harry slapped his left palm.

"Wrong. Harry, a nova doesn't last that long. It's usually a very brief flare. It wouldn't still be in nova condition now."

It was the kind of major mistake Harry would make as he sniffed around the edges of an idea. He was a bloodhound, not the master of the pack.

"What do you know about it? You got a better theory? There must be slow novas."

"Nov*ae*—and I don't think so. Jesus, I don't know. Maybe, but I've never heard of one. Have you?"

Harry looked crestfallen. "I don't know anything about novas *or* novae. What do you know?"

"Next to nothing."

"So I could be right?"

Alex tried to be gentle. "I don't think so, but, okay, *perhaps.* What about a decreasing ellipse? Possibly they've moved nearer the sun?"

"That sounds even wilder. I think I'll stick to my nova for a while. Anyway, the main thing is, the culling factor. If it's a war between the clans, it could mean we would be dragged into the fight. I wanted to show you this," he said, indicating the rock, "before going to the old man."

"I think you're right. He should be told—but how much credence he'll give to your theory ... Well, just expect to be disappointed, that's all, Harry. Don't expect him to leap up and down and call you a brilliant detective."

Harry scowled.

"I'm not looking for kudos," he said, but Alex knew he was lying this time. They made their way back to the raft in silence.

The trouble with Harry was he wanted the old man's respect, not for being an artist—his painting came relatively easy to him because of his extraordinary talent—but for being *like* the Captain. He knew this but he didn't know *why* he wanted the old man to think of him as an equal, and it made him very angry. Mostly he was angry with himself but it did not stop him from taking it out on people like Alex Craven. This morning, however, a day after showing Alex the sun rock, he was savaging his latest "painting" instead—spraying sand over the moulded collage of the New Carthage landscape with ferocious abandon. "Texture," he snarled to himself, "the whole thing needs plenty of depth and texture." He reached into his multi-pocketed apron and produced a glob of red mud which he smeared lightly along the horizon.

How many variations of a sky can one do? he thought. The

stupid light varied only slightly from day to day, depending upon the raft's position. He needed new subjects, new life. Then he remembered the sun rock. Should he paint the new one? He had already turned out several angles of the one he had discovered some six and a half months ago. Then a thought struck him.

Harry left the landscape painting and began sorting through some completed works that he had stacked against his studio panel. Eventually, he withdrew two paintings of a tall rabbit's-ear rock. He began to count the markings on the face of the rock. Halfway through the count, he realized his efforts were futile and let the paintings fall to the floor. For one thing, the original holographic images would be clearer and for another —well, he never painted a truly accurate picture of anything. It had to have some of Harry in it and Harry was not a precise, exact person. He was an artist, not a photographer. Therefore, it was entirely possible that he had not painted every single sun on the rock face.

He extracted his hologram plates from a cupboard and, despite his poor filing system, managed to find a good reproduction of the first sun rock. With the image finally in the equipment he counted the suns, three times to make absolutely sure.

There were 499.

The figure disturbed him for some reason and he counted them once more.

Four nine nine. No mistake.

What was the significance of that? Nothing, except that it was a peculiar number Why 499? Why not 6 or 600?

Alex was using the cabin today. He had wanted a long talk with Maya, he had said. Harry thought about interrupting them, certain that *talk* was an accurate description of their activity. He decided to wait, though. Alex would become suspicious if Harry called him, especially since he had expressly asked not to be disturbed. Alex was good at latching on to insignificant queries and considering them important.

Then Harry had another idea. A brilliant one, that outshone Wolf 359. He calmed himself before calling the duty watch.

There were thousands of photographs in the archives, all microfilmed for space-saving purposes. These were the products of several official photographers who had snapped away at anything and everything since humans had arrived on New Carthage. Harry ran them through the viewer, reel after reel, and found he was not the only one to have discovered the sun rocks. After a long, gruelling search he found several photographs of similar rocks to his own finds—most of them labelled "Native Artwork", then a category number (55/3/1/440).

Harry took hard copies of the photographs back to his studio, ostensibly for art-research reasons, and began sorting them into date order. Then, with the aid of a magnifier, he counted the suns.

Damn Alex! He had to hit the thing square in the centre. Accidentally, of course, Harry was sure. He put the photographs in one of his small cupboards and carefully locked the door on them. There was still an hour to go before he could speak to Alex. Besides, the collage needed finishing.

He relaxed and considered his calling. He knew he was lucky to be able to paint well. Not that it was not hard work! It was, and he strove for perfection—painting for others came easy, but painting to his own satisfaction was a nightmare of frustration, sweat and tears.

Only occasionally did he reach one of his goals and, having reached it, set the next target even higher. The man that satisfied himself with every piece of work was a fool without personal ambition. Harry was not a fool. He always wanted to reach, even though the agony of that stretch would never be recognized outside of himself. He felt sorry for others, though, like Alex, who were touched by the fringe of art but could never wallow in its beauty. There were people, like Maya and the old man, who would not know a sculpture from a block of virgin marble, and these people were outside pity. They were the blind-from-birth incurables in Harry's book.

Harry had seen the "Venus" of Laussel—a limestone relief of a fertility goddess from the Aurignacian Culture. He had touched the smooth lines of the marble Cycladic Head of Man from Amorgos in the Aegean. He had *held* in his hands the Bird-snakes from Ch'ang Sha, China. Those who did not seek out such beauty, and steep themselves in the liquidity of its mysterious past, were souls without the hope of afterlife. How could one appreciate the beauty of Heaven, having remained unaffected by that of Earth?

The day ended, but no night fell. Through the studio porthole (enlarged, courtesy of Captain Alexander who was aware of light and panoramic scenes, though not through an artist's eyes) Harry could see a silver lake emerging from nightside in the far distance. Though he could not discern its movement, it was the first time he had noticed it. Well, at least that was something different to paint. He unfolded an easel. There would be bushes around the banks of the lake, though at that distance they would appear as a blanket of gorse upon a hill: formless and without detail. Now there were tufts of water, lifted by the strong winds, which feathered as they grew taller. Harry could not see the far side of the lake which dipped down below the horizon.

He began painting.

Shortly afterwards the door slid open. Harry knew it was Alex without even turning to look. He could smell Maya's perfume.

"What are you doing, Harry? It's almost 2400 hours. Aren't you going to sleep?"

"Nope. I'm going to paint. I got the fever on. Can't control it—comes and goes as it pleases."

"Okay. Well, I'm going to sink into my pit."

Harry grinned and, without turning around, he said, "Had a hard day?"

"Not the way *you* mean. Well, see you."

Harry nodded, then said casually, "Oh, by the way. How many suns did you count on the rock?"

"The rock? Yesterday?"

"Yeah." He paused in mid-stroke.

" 'Bout five hundred. Yes, five hundred. Why?"

"No reason. I just wondered. It just seemed like a lot of work and got me thinking. Five hundred, eh? That's a lot of suns."

"It is indeed. Goodnight, Harry."

"Good-whatever it is to you too, pal."

14   A Letter

The mail-room was open and Alex called in as he passed. There was a straight lettergram from Nicole. It was like her to send lettergrams unaccompanied by a sound-track. She was becoming too inhibited to record a personal message for him, even though it was usually only business letters that omitted the sound-track. That's what separation did for people.

He took the letter with him and went to On Lo's cabin. The little girl was busy doing nothing—watching a visi-program. He gave her a hug and then sat on her bed, showing her the stud.

"Letter from mother, want to see? I'll read it to you."

"Yes please, uncle."

Switching the visiphone to "local", he fitted the stud into the empty socket and switched on. Nicole's words flowed across the screen. He read the words out loud as they appeared on the screen.

"Hello darlings" (she could say that, grouping them together) "I miss you both terribly. Ti does too. She's sitting beside me and chattering. Especially, of course, she sends her love to On." ("I do too. I do too," said On.) "We have been for lots of long walks by the seashore and Uncle John visits us quite often. Alex, I have some rather sad news." (Christ, what?) "Poor Pagey did not like the Youth Retraining Centre—I believe the other inmates were rather cruel to him—and he escaped. He did manage to evade the police for eleven days—it's now known he lived down the sewers . . . well, you will understand, Alex." ("What, uncle?" Alex patted her hand and swallowed hard.) Finally they cornered him on a roof-top, and he fell to his death. Alex, I cried. He wasn't a bad boy. Just a stem. I still get emotional when I think about it. Some good did come out of it. They set the other two free.

"My last letter described the end of the long summer and how a really harsh winter attacked the Angles—almost as if it was punishing us for interrupting the usual weather cycle. The summer that followed was normal enough—and now we're back into winter again. Life goes on, quietly. I miss you both. When can we see you? What am I saying—we can't, can we?" (Ever? That's ridiculous.)

"Sorry, I didn't mean to get tearful" (she did, otherwise she would have erased) "but we get awfully lonely, Ti and I. Oh yes, the others are here too, but it's not the same. Give my regards to Nadine. And little Lucy. I love you both. Oh, by the way, Lila called. She's divorced you. And guess what! She married that man—the one that followed her around like a little puppy. You remember, the nuisance fellow. The private nuisance. You'll probably get the official notice at the same time as this letter. I can hear you saying 'At last'. I'm happy for you, Alex. We're both lone wolves now. Love again. Nicole."

"Mummy misses us."

"Yes, On, but don't worry. We'll see her. She gets upset."

"I want to see her soon."

"And Ti, we'll see her too."

The little girl's eyes regarded him.

"I don't mind so much about Ti, because I can feel some things with her. I can't feel mummy. Can you?"

Alex pulled her head close to his shoulder.

"No, sweetheart. I wish I could. You and Ti are special. Not many of us can share another person's feelings. Is Ti sad or happy at the moment?"

"She's ... happy, I think. A little bit. Like I am when I play with my toys."

He smiled. "Okay, fine. And you're happy?"

"Like Ti."

"Good." They would not be there for ever, of course. Other twins would be trained now that Strecker had shown the way. One day they would be relieved. A year? Two years? Three?

He sighed. "We'll see them soon," he lied. "Now you find Nadine and give her this letter. She likes to read about home. Then we'll go to the bar and you can have a fizzy drink ..."

"In a big glass?"

"In a big glass."

The little girl jumped off the bunk, grabbed the stud and left him alone in the cabin.

So he was free now. Lila had opened the cage door and let him out. No, *kicked* him out. *She* had divorced *him*. He felt piqued and wanted to know more. The nuisance? They had been getting rather close. Why, why did he feel jealous about it? He should be happy, singing. Instead he felt ... lonely. Nicole was not for him. She knew it and so did he. Nicole was an unmarried woman by choice. A perfectionist. Any liaison would be temporary. Any marriage would last until his faults drove her insane.

So having rejected Nicole, in his own mind, and having lost Lila (he had never really found her anyway), he was back seven years. To those empty late teens and early twenties. Twenty-eight? He felt twelve. And was he really trapped on New Carthage? Hardly. He could leave any time he wanted. Nadine could manage without him. Nadine could manage *very well* without him. The truth was, he didn't really want to go home. Not yet, anyway.

On came tumbling into the cabin and he quickly lifted her up on to his shoulders. Best get into company, even if Harry formed part of it. Alex had to find himself wanted somewhere.

"Let's go, let's go!" cried On. "Fizzy drinks in big glasses. Let's go." She prodded him with her heels and he dutifully trotted down the Burma Road making whinnying noises.

15 **Lost**

The raft was side-slipping to avoid the mountain range cruising towards it.

These mobile peaks lay directly behind the steep foothills which contained Harry's sun rock. Alex, lying in his bunk, could no more discern the relatively fast side-winding motion of the craft than he could the normally slow forward movement. Only the bumping, rocking movement produced by a high wind, when one of the stabilizers was malfunctioning, gave the occupants of the raft any cause to believe they were not upon solid ground. It had happened only twice since Alex had arrived, and both times he had been overcome by sickness to the point of death.

This morning he felt quite well.

Harry had left the cabin early, to follow either his natural or his artistic instincts. He would be on board somewhere: the Captain did not allow people to go outside while the raft side-slipped. It was easy to get left behind.

Suddenly the door slid open and Nadine stood there looking dishevelled. Her face was pale and she was obviously distraught. She opened her mouth, but before she could speak, alarms began hooting throughout the raft.

Irrationally, Alex immediately thought of Harry. What was it? Had he finally broken an inflexible rule?

"What's he done?" he cried above the din, not without a certain underlying satisfaction.

The alarm had reduced Nadine to tears.

"Who? What's who done? Oh Alex, On Lo has gone."

"Gone? Gone where?" He could not quite grasp the situation and Nadine was not helping him at all.

"She's outside. I think she's trying to find Nicole."

"But Nicole's ... on Earth." Now he had it. On Lo. The letter. The little girl was missing and Nadine suspected she had gone looking for her mother.

Alex jumped out of his bunk and struggled into some slacks. Nadine watched him, crying quietly to herself.

"I found a note on the visiscreen in the classroom. It said, 'Mummy wants me. I have to walk home. Love On.'"

"How in hell did she get out?" shouted Alex. The alarms ceased abruptly and left him yelling in mid-sentence.

"She's watched people go through the airlock, I suppose. It isn't difficult to operate. We keep her coop ... cooped up all the time. We tell her this is a different world, but ... but what does that mean to a little girl? She thinks her mother is out there ... somewhere."

Jameson appeared behind Nadine. He was wearing a life-support suit.

"The kid's lost. C'mon, let's go. You'll need a suit."

Alex pushed past the sobbing Nadine.

"Why?"

"Because she may go too far sunside. There's drones and wheelers out there, looking for her—or will be in a few seconds. We'll be better on foot in the high ground."

"Why should we go that way?"

"Alex, the gin are that way. If she sees one, which she's bound to do, she'll be terrified. Haven't you told me she's been indoctrinated to fear them?"

"Christ, yes."

"The old man is going berserk. The *Dido II* may be on its way already, chock-full of arms and troops."

"God," groaned Alex. He did not want to see the Captain. He went straight to the locker room and donned a life-support suit. Then he and Jameson left the craft to join the search parties. The only difference between the suited figures was colour. Commissioned officers had red suits, non-commissioned officers blue, and civilians white suits. There was no one of lower rank than a sergeant on New Carthage. Visors were mainly in the raised position, so that the wavebands could remain clear for transmissions to the Raft Control Room.

"You look nice in your bright red suit," said Alex.

"Thanks," replied Jameson, ignoring the sarcasm. "What time do you estimate On Lo left the raft? Nadine found the message at 0730 hours."

"Hell, how do I know? She was always a light sleeper—On, I mean. At Manston she and her sister would be up at two o'clock some mornings, playing with their toys."

They stopped walking and each took a whiff of oxygen by lowering the visor for a few seconds. There was a force-seven wind blowing which took their breath away and made it difficult to keep a straight course.

"Now look," said Jameson afterwards, "just where do you think she's gone? She was looking for her foster-mother, right?"

"Exactly right."

"So, where would she expect to find her? I mean, does the area look anything like this Manston place?"

"No, except ... the lake," said Alex. They could see the edges of the water shimmering in the far distance. "Manston is a house on an island. She may be attracted by the water."

Jameson lowered his visor, said something to Control, and then lifted it again.

"Let's go," he said.

They passed some gin on the way, who looked at them curiously. A vehicle sped past them. Another came up behind and picked them up, dropping them by the shore of the lake.

"So you think the high ground is out," confirmed Jameson. "That's where the drones are at the moment."

"Definitely," said Alex. "The Angles were flatter than a launching pad."

The lake was a long one, starting from somewhere in the night and disappearing into its own steam at the edge of day.

Some way before the steam it was simmering. Beneath the steam it bubbled. The winds took the vapour high and out, into the dayside. Near the edge of day, patches of thick, swirling water vapour obscured the vision.

"How are we going to find her in that?" said Alex.

"We'll have to do our best, that's all. At least it's not consistent." He pointed to a drone that was moving slowly but confidently through the mist above their heads. "The rescue drones don't need visual aids—they're chock-full of detection devices ..."

This was true enough and areas cleared as fast as they filled with the swirling mists. The winds were freakish and unpredictable, their artistic creations temporal. They adopted transient shapes, and then cleared themselves instantly, like occulting spirits. Alex was reminded that Harry liked plenty of space in his paintings.

"If nature abhors a vacuum," Harry was fond of saying, "what the hell is all that stuff out there keeping the stars apart?"

Alex was aware of Jameson gabbling something at him.

"... you take the bank leading sunside, I'll go towards the hills."

Alex nodded. He felt superfluous. There were dozens of suited Earth people searching the lakeside. Reds and blues, mostly. They were continually vanishing and reappearing from the steam. Everyone was glistening with water droplets as vapour condensed upon their suits. Phantoms. Like running gin—now you see them, now you don't. Those gin could really move. There were two of them now, down on all fours, racing towards the high ground.

He began to walk along the lakeside, searching the dust-laden, steam-thick atmosphere for his missing charge. He winced as he thought of what Nicole would have to say. She would, of course, blame Alex for the incident. Why not? He blamed himself. Perhaps On Lo had already been found and was back at the raft? That was something to hope for. Moving behind some wind-shaped rocks to cut down the external noise, he pulled his photosensitive visor down and listened to the broadcasts. Nothing of any significance was being passed and he continued towards the day, hardly noticing, from within his thermosuit, that he was alone. As the day grew hotter the suit compensated, keeping the internal temperature constant. Intent on his search, Alex walked an Earth-time morning away. The wind behind him, he moved ahead like a sail.

"Red Seven to Control. Section E, foothills, no trace. Moving to Section F. Out."

"Control. Okay, Seven. Make contact with Blue Fourteen, already covering Section F. Out."

No trace. She had not been found yet. For the first time, Alex experienced real anxiety. Previously he had thought she would be found fairly quickly. His main concern had been that she might meet the gin. That was almost certainly a fact now—the gin were all around the lakeside. What worried Alex now was the thought that On Lo might be injured, or dead. He quickened his pace, hoping to circumnavigate the lake and walk along the far shore.

Although the steam was obscuring the sun, the water beside him bubbled and hissed. He looked at the line of fire parallel to the lake's end. Burning bushes. Moses, you wouldn't have known which way to turn for glory, he thought.

Suddenly, there was a gin, coming out of the steam. It had its head down and was trimmed for top speed: neck straight out, ears rolled and flat against its skull. Obviously it had waited too long, probably at a oneroot hole, and was racing back to the night. Its fur was steaming and it faltered now and then on its run.

Alex wiped the condensation from his wrist thermometer. Christ! Nearly ninety centigrade. It was hot outside the suit. The refrigeration unit was heavy too. The gin must have some sort of natural insulation for withstanding great heat for a short period. What about the water? It was already boiling. Pressure! Although the other gases in the atmosphere of New Carthage compensated for the lack of oxygen, the surface pressure was less than that of Earth at sea level.

A woman spoke excitedly in his ear.

"Blue Five to Control. We've found her. She was huddled in the mouth of a small cave . . . just a minute."

"Control. Well done, Blue Five. Captain Alexander here . . ." Ponderous tones, but Alex could feel nothing but relief. A noise, like wind cutting across an open pipe-end, filled his visor.

"Blue Five, here's On Lo. I'm putting my visor on her head, now . . ."

The sound of snuffled breathing, then a small voice: "Don't like those bogey men."

More rustling.

"Blue Five again. Okay, Control, we're heading back now. There's a vehicle in sight half a kilom below. Out."

"Control to Mass . . ." Not the Captain's voice. Everyone was to report back to the raft. So much for that. A bit of excitement, but not the sort Alex enjoyed. This time it was a little close to home.

As he turned to go back, the oneroot hole from which the gin had recently sprung caught his eye. Better to make sure that no more of the creatures were trapped inside it.

Walking towards it, he saw why the gin had been reluctant to leave. It was a large hole with several metres of root-tube exposed. Deep too. Must have been some find. It was not often the root travelled so close to the surface at a point where it branched off in several directions.

Alex turned to leave just as the perimeter of the hole began crumbling beneath his left heel.

To his credit, Alex kept his balance right up until the point of falling, which meant he went down feet first. However, his right foot hit the root intersection square on, jammed, and spun his whole body upside-down. His head hit the bottom of the hole, which was soft soil. That did not stop it hurting him— he felt as if someone had hit him with a rubber sledgehammer —but it did keep his visor from fracturing. When the pain had gone away, he assessed his position. Until now he had been reasonably calm, having had little time in which to become alarmed.

His right foot felt numb. It was either broken or dislocated. It stuck out at an odd angle.

Alex tried clawing his way up the sides of the hole, only to slip back down each time he made a few centimetres. The pain made itself known with the first attempt and increased with each subsequent effort at pulling himself up towards the lip. He had to get help. Stuck down a hole he would have a problem with signal strength, but they might be able to receive something. He pushed the slide on his wristbox to maximum power. The transceiver was equipped with a bouncing carrier wave that would ricochet around the rocks until it found a way out. It was just the power. Had he got enough power?

"Help!" he yelled. "This is ..." He had forgotten his number. "This is white ... this is Alex Craven. I've had an accident."

The voice sounded strangely flat inside his helmet. He checked his wrist, swaying painfully. The transmission switch was on but the meter was registered zero.

"Yah!" he shouted frantically, trying to force an indication from the meter that the equipment was live.

Nothing.

The meter did not move.

"Dead and in the water," he said softly, using the communicator's slang for unserviceability. Maybe it was just the meter itself? Perhaps the transmitter was working even though the meter had ceased to function.

It was a slim hope, especially since there was no background noise.

He felt around the top of his helmet for the omnidirectional aerial. The stud felt intact but inside his gloves his hands lacked sensitivity. Wait a minute! The power pack! He felt over the jagged edges, careful not to pierce his gloves.

The power pack had been shattered.

He was going to die.

Just like that? Snap? No, he was going to die *slowly*.

Either he would starve or die of thirst, or the cooler unit would stop functioning and the temperature would soar inside the suit.

Wait a minute. Power from the cooler unit. It worked on batteries, didn't it?

He fumbled around for a while and then realized how hopeless it was. The batteries were inside the suit. To reach them he would have to open the life-support and he felt sure the heat would kill him before he could manage to achieve anything useful.

With a great deal of determination, he pulled himself up to

the root to inspect his predicament. The foot felt like some-one else's. What was more, there were two ugly-looking creatures crawling down his legs. They were crab-like and hairy, with bulbous bodies. With a feeling of loathing, he swotted them away from him.

Inside his boot his foot had swollen. He felt a certain relief to find that no bone was sticking through the flesh. He doubted he could have stayed conscious were that the case.

Pulling himself on to his good foot, he realized something else was wrong. The oxygen was hissing from his life-support. A tear! There was a rip in the suit! Grabbing the area tightly in his fingers, he frantically twisted the fabric until the gas was no longer escaping.

Now what?

He had to climb out, that's what. With one fist plugging his punctured suit and the other nursing a damaged limb, he had to climb out. He limped pathetically for a pace and then real-ized he would have to repair his suit first. If only he had a piece of cord.

There was a way. The stones out in the direct sunlight above would be hot. He took hold of a piece of the tattered oneroot and, standing on his toes, reached up to the lip. Using the oneroot as an extra glove he pulled a stone from the soil, and, falling backwards, pressed it to the bunched synthetic material around the tear. Smoke rose and a foul smell filled the inside of the suit. The suit bubbled beneath the stone, forming a coagulated knot with the stone as the centrepiece. Gingerly, he let it go and carefully moved his leg inside the suit. It held and there was no escape of oxygen.

Gradually, Alex heaved himself out of the hole using the root as a climbing rope. One or two creatures spilled out of the end but he was no longer concerned by them. He grasped the lip and hauled himself out, standing on one leg.

He took a small step, using the bad leg, and almost passed out with the pain.

This was hopeless. He couldn't hop all the way. If only he had a stick or something. But there weren't any. It was going to have to be done by hopping and then falling carefully on to three limbs to rest.

Not only was it painful, he felt it was a most ignoble way to travel.

The world was made of a gelatinous substance that trembled before Alex's eyes as he crawled forward. It stuck to his body in lumps and hampered his forward movement. Inside his helmet there were birds, thousands of them, all singing in discordant voices. He stopped, sat up and raised his visor to let them escape. Obviously they had entered his suit by way of the gaping, tattered hole in his leg.

"Out, out, out!" he yelled.

Most of them did not want to go. It appeared they enjoyed his company. It was, Alex soon realized, much more fun to perch in his ears, eyebrows, hair and teeth, than fly. Flying was probably hard work—singing was relaxation.

"Out, damn birds, I say!" he yelled, and then collapsed in a fit of laughter which culminated in another coughing bout. He lay prostrate for a few moments and a flicker of sanity began trickling through the haze in his head.

What am I doing? Why do I feel so strange, so bad? Topsy! Harry's been feeding me topsy. I'm drugged up to the eyeballs, the bastard. He's always wanted to get me on dope. Can't bear to see a straight guy, that Harry. Got to warp everyone, bend them into more Harrys so that he's not alone in his erratic scumhead world.

"Harry, you scumhead. I don't wanna be like you! I'm *me*."

The birds were fouling his mouth now, trying to stop him from screaming at Harry. Guano filled his throat and he swallowed, filling his lungs.

"Gaaah! Harry, stop them."

They began beating their wings then, in front of his eyes, to prevent him from attracting Harry's attention. Harry was several metres away, watching him intently. Around the distant figure snakes writhed and squirmed, protecting him from the approach of Alex.

"Harry?"

The figure began moving closer. It was Harry all right; Alex could see through the flimsy disguise. Trying to masquerade as a gin. Did he think he could fool people that easily?

"Say something, Harry," Alex croaked. "I'm dying. You pushed too much topsy in me. I couldn't take it all. It's blocking my throat—I can hardly speak to you, Harry ... Harry, say something you bastard scumhead. I hate your guts. Why don't you say something, damn you?"

Harry just stood there, looking like a gin. Then he did a funny thing. He dropped on to all fours, like a monkey, and knuckled around the edge of Alex's vision, circling him.

"What're you doing, Harry? Are you going to kill me? I can't help hating you ..." Tears began streaming down Alex's face and he lapped at them with his tongue. "I can't help it. You're just a gross human being. You invite hate. Look at you, man. Pretending to be a gin so that I won't hate you ..."

Harry continued circling, moving inwards all the time. Another thing, he had no mouth. Perhaps that's why he was giving all the topsy to Alex? Because he couldn't swallow it himself? Must be terrible to have no mouth. Hard to breathe without a mouth. Likely to get a cold and gag to death on mucus.

"Look, Harry, I'm going to die. I can feel it. My life's hissing through holes in my body, like gas getting out. My soul's like gas, Harry, and it's escaping from me. Can't live without a soul. I want ..."

He swallowed hard, taking down his thick, swollen tongue. Before he could speak again, he had to cough it back out, which was difficult because it was dry and adhesive. "I want you ... to ... kill ... me."

There, it was said and done. Harry would kill him now. Get it over with. Thirsty, so damn thirsty. Harry would stop that. Kill him, and get him to a place where water didn't matter any more.

But Harry just stared at him questioningly.

"Look, what else?" wailed Alex. "I'm offering you my life. What else do you want? Nicole? You can have her. Just kill me, please please kill me," he sobbed.

Harry remained still.

Finally Alex began picking up stones and hurling them at his room-mate. They were wild throws and had no power behind them. Most of them missed, falling in the dust some few metres away. Alex began to see rainbows, jagged ones, which came crashing out of the sky and into his field of vision. They shattered before him, their coloured glass splinters piercing his eyeballs. The pain was excrutiating and, mercifully, a single fragment went in deeply, penetrating his brain and causing blackness.

Ooma was bewildered. What was this thing that flapped and croaked on the edge of the day? Surely it knew that if it stayed where it was eventually the day would swallow it whole, and it would not be able to continue its unusual dance? Gota would eat it. Certainly, it looked like one of the newcomers, but it was covered in hot mud from the edge of the drying lake. Difficult to be sure that it was a newcomer.

Now it was picking up the *nnin* creatures and tossing them towards Ooma. Was this an offering? A gift? Everyone knew that the *nnin*—fist-sized lava-like stones that were in fact a form of life—had no goodness in them. They were too dry, too brittle. The only creature that stayed on the surface when the world swung sunwards, the *nnin* could withstand the temperatures of the day by falling into a dormant state until they reached the night again. Internally, the *nnin* had little body flesh, being composed mainly of calcium and silicon. In its night state, the *nnin* had to be fast-moving, scuttling like a swift crab from place to place, in order to avoid its one enemy, the *rerr*, which hid in rock fissures and, wrapping itself around a *nnin*, would crack it open to feed on the juices.

Ooma had no use for the *nnin*, which had moved into their dormant state prior to going out into the sun. The rock creatures were more trouble than they were worth to break open.

The ears heard something in the wind. There were others passing by to night*ward*. Newcomers. It did not occur to Ooma that the newcomers should be fetched to help their comrade. If this one was wounded beyond help, what was the point in returning it to its *vilpa*? To live one had to be able to move. A permanent cripple should be put out of its misery. That was the thing to do, the law. Ooma could do that without their help. It revived memories of the *manaha*, which was shortly to arrive.

The creature was still now. Ooma went across to it and the six-fingered foregrips, with padded running knuckles, turned it on to its back. Ooma stretched the creature's limbs into the shape of a star: it should not be denied last rites simply because *manaha* was not yet here. Gota of the shining sky would take this one to its stomach; would dry the flesh to powder; would sniff the body-dust into the great cavernous nostrils on the burning face. The newcomer was going to a good place, to the gut of God. What more could it ask of Ooma, who did this thing for love of all life's creatures? Gota *asked* that all creatures should become a whole—Gota of the black-white face.

Turning round, Ooma selected the largest rock he could lift and carried it towards the newcomer. There were shouts behind Ooma but the ears did not hear while the brain was turned to the ritual of death. Standing above the creature, Ooma lifted the rock high and brought it down hard.

16 Broken Wing

While, according to the gospels of Dresnig, nature might not abhor a vacuum, it did love an octagon. Captain Alexander was watching Harry copy an octagonal spider's web which had cellophane wrapping joining its ribs. The wind was a shambling, desultory beast kicking up a few tufts of dust here and there, but seemingly without much interest in life. Many of the raft's inhabitants were taking advantage of the relative calm.

The web was, in fact, one of the few surface animals on New Carthage. "Animal" was perhaps too strong a word for it. It seemed more of a plant than an animal, but the Captain had been told it was formed of tiny creatures similar to coelenterates—coral polypi. There was great beauty in these webs—or "mmaa", as the natives called them. Measuring about twenty-five centimetres in diameter they spread themselves like hundreds of transparent sea-birds' feet over large areas of the dawn country. Moisture condensed on their undersides and formed glistening droplets of water which each creature ingested along with minute organisms. One might find several hundred webs over a piece of flat ground.

When the raft had first arrived on New Carthage, the Captain had been fond of cataloguing the native life forms. It was seven years (during which scientists classified and prepared a two-way immunization programme, the gin receiving their treatment unwittingly via a convenient water supply) before the Captain could walk out without a life-support and he caught one of his men "experimenting" on a mmaa with a lighted cigarette: studying the creature's withdrawals. The man almost went back to Earth *without* the next ship.

"What about the kid? Did this telemetry thing work?" asked Harry, not looking up from his work. It was a light-emission plate—not his favourite medium, the Captain knew. Harry preferred traditional techniques.

The Captain reluctantly took his attention away from the charm of the webs. He enjoyed being outside with Harry Dresnig; it was the one place where the artist dropped his sullen attitude and became an animated, interesting person. Dresnig was most relaxed when he was working and most tense when he was relaxing.

"We shan't know for some time, but the child didn't seem too distressed. Just kept saying she didn't like bogey men. I understand they indoctrinated the twins with the idea that the gin are ghouls that eat children alive, or something like that. Nursery-room tales ..."

"Doesn't sound like nursery stuff to me—sounds horrific. Human instruments for measuring levels of terror."

The Captain sat down in the dust. He felt close to nature when he was outside, which was trite but he could think of no other way of putting it. The responsibilities of running the raft fell away from him and he lost his aggressive domineering attitude. Harry was a good medium through which to view nature; a window through which Captain Alexander could sense the new world, and he was a sensitive man although his appearance, his bulky engine-room muscles, seemed to belie that fact. Outside, he could be the small boy again who felt no shame in admiring a frog or even a flower. This scene before him would not be witnessed live by many poets. Yes, *poets*. The word was extremely delicate resting on his frame and he only used it to describe himself in his most private thoughts. He knew that even his favourite officers would be amused if he confided that he, Captain Miro Alexander, thought of himself as a poet.

"Well, what d'you say?" asked Harry, almost irritably.

Alexander brought himself back to the present.

"Sorry, was it a question?"

"Yeah. I said it sounds horrific. The kid's indoctrination."

"Depends. Most literature for children at nursery level is an indoctrination against known dangers. Hansel and Gretel, for instance, or Red Riding Hood—don't speak to strangers. Then there's Struwwelpeter with stories of children burning themselves to death—don't play with fire. It's all macabre, Harry. The whole process of growing up is a grisly affair."

Harry grinned. "Didn't know you were a child psychologist, Cap. Read Piaget have you?"

"Don't call me 'Cap'. I'm Captain Alexander to civilians and servicemen alike."

He was annoyed because he had not heard of Piaget.

"Take it easy, Captain. It was a joke. You're too serious for words. I thought you came out here to relax. Let the labours fall away ..."

"Yes, you're right. But it's difficult. Getting back to the child—I feel almost sure there was no traumatic experience. I don't think we'll see the troops."

Harry was hardly listening any more. He was back into his "painting". The Captain watched him work, envious of the casual, almost lazy way in which Harry Dresnig recreated the webs. A reflection in a mirror that was Harry's own mind. Each picture was individual, yet Captain Alexander could see that Harry captured all the salient points of beauty in his work. It wasn't brilliant, but it was very, very good.

"I don't know how you do that," he said admiringly.

"We all have our talents, Captain. Yours is a genius for making men quake with fear when you roar out an order. You have a delicately balanced talent for destroying a man's self-respect while he stands rigid and unable to reply; for extracting that last ounce of initiative and resource in the name of discipline; for reducing a man to an unprogrammed machine. There is sagacity in you, Captain. A wisdom which goes deeper than the soul of a ..."

"You're baiting me again," grumbled Captain Alexander. "I won't be drawn, Harry. You can chatter all you like. Ah, here comes Maya. Perhaps you would care to repeat your remarks to her?"

"No chance. She'd fell me with a single blow."

"I thought so. Well, I'll leave you two to talk."

"Don't do that," said Harry, in what appeared to be genuine panic. "I can't stand the woman."

"Suit yourself, but I can't stay for long. It doesn't look good for the Captain and his deputy to be missing at the same time.

Can you imagine what a field day the media would have back home if the raft caught fire now—and only we three lived? The artist, the Captain and his second-in-command were the only survivors. God!"

It was one of his nightmares, losing his ship and surviving to face the media.

"You'd rush back in there, in order to die like the Captain you are, Captain."

Alexander nodded. "You're right. I'm that much of a coward. Burning to death would be a far less painful death than being sent home in disgrace. Believe me."

"I believe, I do indeed."

Maya had reached them now.

"What do you believe in, Dresnig? I thought you were an atheist? One of those who spend their whole lives protesting to others about how much they don't believe in any kind of god or religion. It seems to me that all those atheists who claim to disbelieve waste an awful amount of time and words in defence of their non-belief. One might say," she added sweetly, "that they make a religion out of not believing in anything."

"Piss off," said Harry, without looking up.

Captain Alexander was shocked.

"Mr Dresnig, this is a commander you're speaking to. I won't have that sort of talk."

"Sorry," said Harry, "but she does it on purpose."

"I would have thought," continued Maya undeterred, "that not believing was, in itself, an end to the argument and thereafter the atheist need say no more. But he seems to do more preaching than the preachers—trying to convert others to his belief in non-belief."

"Commander Kleppel, will you stop attacking this man?" ordered the Captain. It was an order, though framed as a question.

She sighed. "Okay, Captain. It's just ..."

"Now that," said Harry, pointing his light-emitter at the Captain, "is what I call *talent*. I wish I could do that—man, how I wish I could shut them up like that."

Alexander repressed a sharp rebuke.

"Well, you just have to have a feel for it. Now, sort this out, you two. Why all the animosity? We're a small community here—we can't afford to have in-fighting. Especially between the sexes."

"Ahhhh!" Harry threw up his arms. "I'm trying to work, for Chrissakes—and just because I'm an atheist doesn't mean I can't blaspheme like everyone else . . ."

Maya pushed away a wisp of hair which the strong winds had worked loose and were using to whip her cheek. She shrugged.

"Okay." She nodded to the Captain. "I've just come from the sick bay. Craven seems to be a lot less feverish now. I asked the doc to give him a pain-killer but he'd already had one. When he comes round he's going to hurt."

"*Pain-killer*," said Harry, scornfully.

Alexander raised his eyebrows. "What's wrong with that?"

"Pain is a normal process. It's there for a reason. We shouldn't tamper with bodily mechanisms the way we do. Maybe we should all have a smack of pain sometimes—gives a man's soul some depth . . . and a woman's," he added after an insultingly long pause.

Maya shook her head and said in a spiteful voice, "You know, Harry, you talk the most god-awful shit—'scuse me, Captain—sometimes. You remind me of a chauvinist idiot I once knew. With a cigarette dangling eternally from his mouth, and his fist forever full of whisky, he berated doctors for pampering housewives by prescribing tranquillizers for their nerves. 'Stupid females should learn to do without their daily junk.' You remind me of him, Harry."

"I don't smoke or drink."

"No, but you take things for your pain, don't you, Harry? I don't mean physical pain—but your agonized spirit . . ."

Captain Alexander felt he was missing something important as he glanced from face to face. Harry Dresnig looked as though someone had hit him hard in the gut. He was white and trembling. Breathing hard. Commander Kleppel looked grim and her normally full lips were as taut as aerial wires. Something vital was passing between their eyes.

Harry turned and began packing away his equipment carefully. When the exercise was completed, he tucked the cases under his arms and strode away without another word. They watched him marching towards the raft.

Captain Alexander said, "Why in Heaven's name do you two insist on burying hooks in each other?"

"I think it's because of Alex Craven."

"What?"

"I think it's because of Alex. Harry doesn't like me spending my time with him."

The Captain was genuinely puzzled.

"Why should he mind that?"

"He thinks I'm out to ensnare Craven in a marital net."

"And are you?"

She smiled. "Excuse me, you may be Captain, Captain, but that's a personal question I don't care to answer."

The Captain stuck his meaty hands into his hip pockets. He was a little piqued since he himself had a fondness for Maya which he had carefully kept to himself.

"I can judge from your inference that it's not a million miles from the truth."

"Can you?"

"Anyway," he continued, ignoring the question, "what's that to Dresnig? Does he feel protective? Thinks his friend needs defending from the older woman?"

"I think so. Alex is nearly thirty but he's a little immature when it comes to women. By the way, he's single now in case you're worried about *me*. Divorced recently."

"I wasn't worried. You're a big girl, Commander," he laughed. "That sounds foolish, doesn't it?"

He was embarrassed by the conversation and he knew he should not be. He wondered if Maya thought *him* immature. Surely not a bald-headed gorilla like him? But he had the distinct impression that Maya equated immaturity with a disinclination to make a pass at her. If that was eternal adolescence, he was a pimply-faced non-starter. He changed the subject quickly.

"So Craven's on the mend? He's lucky. If his suit hadn't still been partially inflated that rock would have broken all his ribs. What made the gin do that? They're usually such passive creatures—non-violent. Why should it want to hurt an already crippeld human? Twenty-eight years we've been here and we still don't know how they think. We pick up little snippets of culture and believe the whole pattern is on the way."

He looked towards the north where the mountains were. The raft had slipped south around the horn of the crescent range. There was something happening to the gin—something stirring their nest. They were beginning to migrate to the central regions. The equatorial mountain range was drawing them to its many breasts. From even as far away as the poles they came, bringing with them their small differences in colour, stature and markings. Harry had painted one or two of the outsiders to contrast them with the local gin.

What was the big attraction? A pilgrimage perhaps? To what?

A campaign? Against whom?

A safari?

Wanderlust?

An all-night party?

One could only guess at the reasons, for the time being. Excursions north and south from the raft had indicated that as yet only a small number of gin were "on the road" but more were making preparations.

It's not the seasons, thought the Captain, because there aren't any. Nothing to warn them of approaching bad weather. The weather never changed. It was cooler at the poles but not cold. The mountains were not that high. It had to be the sign-posts.

"Penny for them?" said Maya.

Captain Alexander pulled himself back to present company.

"Sorry, I was just contemplating the gin. I find them ... mystifying."

"So you should—they're an alien race."

He nodded.

"You're right. But they have to have reasons for what they're doing, and, providing the reasons aren't completely insub-stantial, we should be able to gain an overall understanding. I mean, they eat because they're hungry. That's the important thing. *Because they're hungry*. There might be all sorts of meal-time rituals associated with the eating, high spiritual overtones which cloud the real issue, but underneath is a common or garden technique for staying alive."

Maya looked at the Captain with an intense expression.

"Maybe their racial thoughts are so different from ours we would regard them as insane. What about Alex Craven? Why would someone who thinks like a man strike an injured person with a rock? A person half out of his mind with delirium?"

"I don't know, but I can guess. Maybe the gin felt threatened? Craven did look a bit grotesque with that mud all over him."

"Maybe the gin was putting him out of his misery. The bird with the broken wing?"

The Captain did not like the way the conversation was going. Previously he had felt uncomfortable. Now *he* felt threatened. The search party that had found Craven believed that he and the gin had been fighting and the gin had got the better of him. It had been a natural assumption. They had had no reason to think that Craven had injured himself. Later, when Craven had explained, they let the gin go and the popular theory of "the bird with the broken wing" had passed quickly by word of mouth. Now, after twenty-eight Earth years, the colonists felt threatened. They could have understood a fight. They had the mental equipment to deal with that sort of situation. They had even been expecting it. It was difficult, however, to rationalize killing a man because he had an injury which put him outside the physical norm. Insecurity. Know thy enemy. But if the enemy is a friendly unpredictable killer with good intentions . . .

"What are you thinking of now?" she asked him.

"If you're right, we have to be on our guard against good intentions. There is nothing more deadly than those who know what's best for you—who might kill you for your own good. You see, they know what's good for you, when you yourself are least expecting it. We don't know if that was what the gin had in mind. This is all supposition and it could be that Craven aroused the creature's anger in some way. He wasn't exactly in his right mind himself. But we have to beware of assuming the aliens think like we do . . ."

Maya put her hands on her hips.

"Well, you . . ."

The Captain smiled.

"I know. I know. I've flip-flopped. That's *exactly* what you were saying and I was arguing with you. Well, I'm not arguing any more. I agree with you. How's that, Commander? I agree."

She stood looking at him with a puzzled expression and the Captain knew she was thinking of a way to contradict him and probably herself. Maya was like that. Once she had won a battle she wanted to start the fight over again, only on new ground.

The time of the *manaha* was coming.

Even now Ooma could feel the stirrings of excitement in the fluids of the body. The mind was only vague concerning the last *manaha*, a memory one worldly revolution old. Dimmed by time, only a faint trace of the rituals remained for Ooma to recollect. It *was* a time of great excitement, this much was sure.

The stones told of the coming.

Their surfaces patterned with the pictures of a star harnessed by the mountain-god Aruma, the stones' number language captured the blinding light of Gota's face. Such a time. Such a time.

Before the last meeting, Ooma had stood with another to pass between them the seed of young. Ooma had tried this twice previously in the lifetime, without success. All had to be correct with the world before conception could take place. The wind needed to be from the right quarter, and at a certain speed; the dust channels created by those winds at a certain angle in relation to dayward. Bodies needed to be in tune, not only with the individual mind, but with each other. A successful union depended upon so many things. Prior to the passing-between, Ooma had for some time eaten only the sweet juices of the *vrirr*—an animal which reproduced with great frequency —considered to be a potent fertility drug. Although Ooma had never managed to conceive, Ooma was aware of the body's own fertility, for one of the previous mates had given birth to a young one. That it had subsequently died was not of any great concern because at that time the *manaha* was but a quarter's distance from becoming an event. After the *manaha*, births would count for more, which was why Ooma was so pleased at having passed and received seed.

Unless, of course, Ooma became a victim of the *manaha*, which was unlikely. There should be another term at least to run, for the body was strong and able. It was not impossible, though, and spiritual preparations needed to begin soon. The inner self was to be controlled, calmed, made ready for death.

Death. Even the word was comforting. Ooma, spread like a star amongst the ancestors; sharing a common grave with the dust and chest shells of a thousand others. This was something to look forward to rather than fear.

That creature. The newcomer. It had obviously not prepared for death, which was a sad thing. Unless a being was in prime condition, there was no allowance for life to remain in the body. It was in breach of Gota's law to permit the lame or sick to remain among the living. Their term was over, otherwise the body would not have failed itself. Ooma had tried to do the correct thing but had been thwarted at the last moment. Ooma thought, there must be despair in the cave of the newcomers at this time, for Gota would surely not be baulked of one intended to leave this life. Gota would soon take steps to right such a wrong.

Maya took a long walk alone back to the raft. She had some questions to ask herself and wanted the solitude to be able to mull over them without interruption. Only outside the raft was that possible.

"Question," she said aloud. "Am I in love with Alex Craven?"

What the hell was love? What she *should* be asking herself was: did she want to live with Alex Craven and share his life? It did not bother her that she was older than Alex; what did concern her was that Alex was younger than her. Now what did that mean? she asked herself. Did she really believe him to be immature? Yes, it was true to say he was, in certain ways. Especially when it came to forming a relationship. Always he appeared to be reaching out towards her, and as soon as she began to reciprocate, he backed away quickly. It was almost as if he was afraid of forming anything more than a casual companionship with her. Yet she knew he wanted her, physically, almost as much as she needed him. *Want* and *need*. Could one equate them like that? They were totally different feelings, after all.

Was it important? The physical side of a relationship? She knew some women who would say no. She knew some men who would agree with those women. Yet few of those who preached spiritual togetherness practised sexual abstinence.

It was, Maya reflected, always reduced to individuals. She knew that she, personally, needed a physical side to her relationship with Alex. Nicole, on the other hand, from what Alex had told her, did not. She might *allow* it but she did not appear to need it.

Back in the raft, Maya visited Alex. He was still in the sick-bay, "strapped up, wrapped up but not shacked up" as Harry Dresnig had put it. Funny, she thought, much as she disliked Dresnig there was no doubting the influence of his personality. If Harry originated something, it was usually repeated many times. Often it became a catch-phrase.

"How are you feeling?" she said to the mummified creature in the bed.

The eyes turned to her.

"Pain's gone now, but it hurt earlier. Feel a bit dopey."

"I'm not surprised. Broken ribs, broken ankle, heat exhaustion, delirium—to name but a few. Next time, pick on a gin your own size."

"I didn't ..." he began, but she stopped his lips with her hand.

"I know," she said, smiling. "How are they treating you in here?" She nodded towards the NCO male nurse, who grinned.

Alex said, "Okay, I suppose. But I don't want to stay here much longer."

Just then On Lo came tumbling into the sick-bay, breathless from running.

"Hello, uncle. Nadine told me to come and say I was sorry." The eyes were full of innocence.

Maya laughed. "I'm sure she didn't ask you to say it that

way, you monkey. Have you got over seeing all those ghoulies yet?"

"Ghoulies?" questioned the child.

"Bogey men," explained Alex.

On Lo nodded hard. "Oh yes, I wasn't frightened anyway. Not *really*. They look much worse at Manston House. I'm *glad* I didn't see one of those kind because they creep up when you aren't looking, don't they, uncle? You remember."

"The suddenness of a hologram appearing," he explained to Maya. She nodded. It was that suddenness which produced the fear. It would frighten *her* to death, and *she* quite liked the gin.

Maya let On Lo chatter for a while, then took her hand.

"Come along, dear. We mustn't tire Uncle Alex." To Alex she said, "I'll come back later. I have some work to do, then I'll drop by."

His angular face turned towards her. There were shadows under the dark eyes and the corners of his mouth still bore the vestige of his recent pain.

"You don't have to," he said at last.

"I *want* to."

He nodded, head still on the pillow.

"That gin . . ." he began.

She interrupted him. "It didn't get away. Didn't *try* to. There was some talk of punishment but only amongst the party that found you—the Captain would not sanction any reprisal, and neither would I. Finally they let it go. The interpreter—such as she is—could not discover the underlying reasons, although she did find out . . ."

"Thing is," said Alex quickly, and On Lo gripped Maya's hand tightly at the sound of his voice.

"What?"

"Thing is, I had a funny idea it was trying to help me . . ."

"That's what it told the interpreter," said Maya. "About a dozen times."

17 Breaking Cover

The sick-bay is a comfortable womb. The longer an invalid remains within the security of the white plastimetal walls, guarded from unwanted intrusion by devout handmaidens and body servants, the more difficult is the leaving. In the sick-bay the patient is fed and watered regularly; is preened and petted; is treated firmly but with filial kindness. Sleep is unearned but seems all the more restful for so being. There are few things more miserable than spending hours working the body into a state of near exhaustion, only to lie awake, head buzzing with untamed thoughts, until morning.

Harry dispelled any doubts Alex had that life would be allowed to slide by in the tranquil fashion of the sick-bay once they let him—forced him—out into the open again.

"What are you saying, Harry?" asked Alex.

Harry Dresnig was sitting in the visitor's chair opposite Alex, who was perched on the bunk.

"I'm saying that we ought to go out and look. You're on the mend, aren't you? One more week will see you flying again."

Harry was being cryptic, as was his custom. There was an eager look to him, though, which reminded Alex of tales of dogs at harvesting, when rabbits were about to break for cover, across cornfields razed to stubble.

"Harry, you're about as explicit as a Greek oracle. What the hell are you trying to tell me? I'm not going to go off with you into the mountains without some sort of explanation. Why can't you tell the Captain?"

"Because I want to find out for myself. The sun rock—remember? I know what it is. I worked it out not long after we got back. I've been waiting to see what it meant."

"And what does it mean?"

A hand, full of tension, gripped Alex's arm.

"I can't tell you—yet. Later, when we get near."

"Near what, Harry? You're driving me mad. I don't even want to leave this *room* let alone go trudging off into the mountains without permission. I've already been through one helluva bad time and you're asking me to risk another—with a . . . I don't know what to call you. A bag full of half-cocked enthusiasms. Certainly not a methodical planner, a steady, reliable expedition leader I would trust with my life. Harry, believe it or not, there's no cure for death yet. Practically everything else, but not death."

Looking as though someone had just robbed him, Harry growled, "All right. I'll tell you. *Milestones*."

"Milestones?"

"Right."

Alex stared at the unshaven face of the artist with its two bright points of light above the high cheekbones.

"And I'm supposed to be satisfied with that? What does 'milestones' mean?"

"Not milestones—*milestones*. Get some feeling into it. It's an important word. Remember I asked you how many suns? The motif on the rock?"

Alex nodded, and Harry continued, "Five hundred. And I had a picture—a hologram—of the one before that. Four nine nine. Skip a couple, we missed them, then four hundred and ninety-six. You see the pattern?"

Alex grunted. "Don't treat me like an idiot."

"I'm not. I'm just telling you. *Milestones*. One every thirty-one kilometres. Each stone appearing six-point-two months apart, Earth time."

"*Mile*stones as a figure of speech. Okay, Harry, so the natives measure the progress of the rotation of New Carthage. What's the significance?"

Harry stood up suddenly.

"We're there—at the end. It takes two hundred and fifty-four Earth years for this planet to perform one revolution on its axis. The next milestone will read *one*."

Alex was well aware of what was occurring outside the raft. The gin were gathering in great numbers in the mountains. They had travelled from all over the dawn country to be there.

Something was about to happen and most people feared it would be an attack on the raft. They still had one child who might be capable of signalling any impending disaster to Earth, but few had faith in that system any more. Harry read his thoughts.

"Look, Alex, when the gin began their artistic fracturing of the obsidian surfaces of rock, we were over two hundred years from ever setting foot on this world. They didn't do all this for us, they did it—this signal for the gathering of the clans—for some reason which doesn't involve anyone but themselves. There's something very extraordinary going to happen. A religious festival of some kind. The crossing of the line. Something of that nature. And I want us to witness it."

After a long while Alex said, "You look like a fox to me."

"What?"

"You look like a fox."

"I scare you—that's what you mean. Look, there's nothing to be afraid of. We take an airwheeler, head for the mountains and witness something no other human has ever seen. A ceremony—that's all it'll be. This is no xenophobic race we're dealing with. We don't want to steal their land. There's nothing to be afraid of . . ."

"You said that. Okay, Harry, but we should tell someone where we're going."

Exasperation flowed through Harry's features and Alex knew that, shortly, his room-mate was going to storm out of the sick-bay in a temper. Just exactly what was it that frightened him? He didn't know. He didn't know. The only thing he understood was that they were dealing with strange creatures and there was no way of even guessing what sort of reception the pair of them might receive.

"Get out of here, Harry. Let me sleep. Come and see me later. They're going to throw me back in the cabin tonight."

The artist grinned at him, then turned and left. Alex began thinking about Pagey, the stem youth who had died. He wished he had given Nicole more understanding now that the tragedy had occurred. If Alex had been a sympathetic listener, had observed the warning signs, Nicole would never have run to the stems for help, and Pagey would be alive. Possibly.

More than likely. But he was dead, and all because Alex could not read people very well. People very close to him.

Now Harry Dresnig needed him and this time he had to do the right thing. Give Harry some rope and, in the meantime, find some way of stopping the man before he got himself—and maybe others—into serious trouble. He had time. A week.

Alex lay back in his chair and contemplated existence on New Carthage. It was not so much New Carthage that formed a life-style for him but Stingray, the hovering city. Stingray was his world. A floating world. Where had he heard that before? At university? Yes, that foundation course he did on art appreciation. The ancient Japanese printers. There was a school once called the *ukiyo*: "the floating world", derived from *Ukiyo-e* or "pictures of the floating world". Harry probably knew them. Wood-block engravers of the highest order producing prints not only of high quality, but full of life and vigour. Hokusai's thirty-six views of Mount Fuji. Utamaro's courtesan, "Hinatsura". Most of Utamaro's girls were willowy creatures with solid lower jaws. They had been beautiful in their time, but beauty changes with each new decade, let alone over hundreds of years. Ageing men see beauty in every young woman, while young men have a narrow field of vision. Is it that youth can afford to choose, or that its critical eye is sharper?

Art appreciation is far more satisfying than producing the work. There is no competition, no fierce working pace with which to contend. The older man can lie back, observe and enjoy. He sees more. Moreover, he is *willing* to see more. Is willing to concede a point in favour of a solid lower jaw at the same time as noticing that the right breast has slipped clear of the robe, as in Utamaro's *bijin-e* print, "The Wanton Type". Older men are more ready to generalize in favour of beauty. Young men tend to be specific.

"I think her eyes are her most beautiful feature," says the young man.

"Her features are most beautiful to my eyes," agrees the older man.

Alex wanted to ask Harry if the story of how the Japanese prints came to the notice of Europeans was true. It was said that when Japan first began exporting goods to other nations, wrapping paper was used upon which was printed pictures of bridges, sailboats, water, cliffs and strangely clad figures. These prints came to the notice of European artists who recognized behind them an exceptional talent. The artists began collecting the wrappings and questioning their exact origin. Their enquiries led them to *Ukiyo-e*, *ehon* and the eroticism of *shunga*—the sexual explicitness of *shunga*. It was a romantic story and Alex liked it. Perhaps it were better he did not ask, and risk having his dreams flattened.

Later, on leaving the sick-bay, Alex went directly to Maya's single cabin. She was lying on her bunk, reading. Her hair was loose and hung down over her face, and she wore a clinging robe.

"How are you?" he asked.

"I'm fine. And you?"

"Okay now." He wondered whether to bring up the subject of Harry's expedition but decided it could wait. The "second-in-command" in her might outweigh friendship and send her to the Captain.

"Shall we go for a walk? Keep pace with the raft?" she asked. "You haven't been outside for some time. The exercise might do you some good."

Was her breast going to slip out of her robe like that of Utamaro's wanton girl? He thought not.

"Walk?" he repeated.

She nodded, taking his arm. The raft moved forward at only seven metres an hour and once outside they were soon well out in front, it being tiresome to make circuitous routeings of their home.

Under the stars, with the wind blowing their hair straight out behind them, he took her hand. He did not feel the same quickening of the pulse that occurred when he used to touch Nicole, but perhaps that was because Nicole was virtually inaccessible and any contact with her was an achievement beyond reasonable hope. Nevertheless, with Maya there was a certain controlled excitement.

Under the cover of the darkness, probably to lessen the impact of any rejection, she asked him to stay with her that night.

He said he would. Their hands gripped each other more tightly then, the bond having been formed. Secrets could flow between them now.

Mountains shuffle together: by nature they have the herd instinct. They seem to need the close society of their kind. Already formidable, each supports the other to make a block-shouldered, often impossible rank of dumb giants.

Alex stared at the mountains through field-viewers and his awe of them increased with the sudden nearness of their tall sides.

Mathew Tse had said, "God is his own neighbour." Somehow the mountains gave those words more meaning. Ever concerned with agoraphobia, Tse manufactured a finite universe by introducing it as the home of a domesticated God. It is difficult to imagine a house as having no boundaries—homes have walls. And if His dwelling is enclosed, thought Alex, those high black peaks, with their elbows on each other's shoulders, were surely the walls.

Alex was out walking with On Lo, the little girl being no longer terrified of the gin. Afraid, perhaps, of approaching them too closely, for though the spell had not been broken, it had diminished considerably in strength. She gave the distant figures wary, sidelong glances occasionally but, apart from that, and clinging to Alex's hand, she seemed at ease.

Alex himself was entirely well again. It was seven days since his talk with Harry and he hoped the artist had forgotten his passion with the sun rocks. They had not seen very much of each other over the last week, principally because Alex spent so much time with Maya. He was in love with her, he thought, or why would they spend so much time together? Alex and Maya, Maya and Alex. It flowed, metrically, but was that love? When two names were iambically suited? Hardly, he thought drily.

"When are we going home?" demanded On Lo, kicking up some dust with her outwear boots.

"Home? Which one?"

"Home to Ti. I want to see my sister now."

The wind was beginning to increase in intensity and Alex

looked up at the sky. He did not want them to be caught in a full-blooded windstorm, especially in an oven of sand.

"When?" she asked again.

"Very soon, I think," Alex said at last. "Perhaps the next starship. Do you want to go by yourself? You can you know." He wondered what excuse he could find in order to remain on New Carthage once On Lo had returned to Earth.

"No. I want you to come, uncle. Mummy wants to see you. She said so. In that letter."

"Maybe she's changed her mind. She may have met somebody else," he said, hopefully.

"What do you mean, somebody else?"

"Nothing. Forget it. I'm just thinking out loud. If you want me to come with you of course I shall. We came together and we'll go home that way."

"What's that?" On Lo was pointing to a tall cloud of dust billowing higher than the current wind force would take it.

Alex squinted.

"Looks like an airwheeler. Maybe Maya is coming to give us a ride back to the raft?" He was rather relieved since they had taken no tanks with them and had walked further than he had intended. If a storm was coming, they would need to run and that was hard work without a supply of oxygen.

They watched the wall of dust draw nearer and finally the vehicle itself became visible. It slowed to a stop beside them. Alex opened the hatch immediately and dropped On Lo gently inside before climbing in himself. Pulling the hatch shut he turned and said, "Hi, I was . . . oh?"

"What's the matter?" A poker-faced Harry Dresnig had restarted the motors.

"Nothing. I thought you would be someone else, that's all. I was expecting . . . it doesn't matter. What are you doing out here?"

"Came to give you a lift. Control said you were out for circular walk."

Alex stared at Harry Dresnig thoughtfully.

"What's wrong, Harry?"

Harry looked over at him.

"Something wrong?"

Alex tried to see if Harry's pupils were dilated. Had the man been taking topsy? Then something else began to bother him.

"Harry, where are we going? This isn't the way to the raft. What are you doing?"

The other man immediately began increasing the vehicle's speed.

"Where are we going?" shouted Alex, causing On Lo to jump.

Harry gave him a peculiar smile.

"To the mountains. I told you. We have to go there."

"I have a child here. We have a little girl here with us."

"Too bad. I'm not going to hurt her, so long as you sit tight. You'll soon change your mind about this trip, once we reach the mountains. You wait. Something really big out there."

Inside the vehicle were deep bucket seats separated by a tall transmission tunnel. To reach Harry and force him to slow down to prevent an accident would take Alex too long. Besides, he had On Lo sitting on his lap. She was looking from one man to the other with a worried expression on her face.

"Don't worry, Tiger," he said, using the nickname she liked. "Harry will take us home soon."

"Is he going to make us crash?"

"No. I'm not going to do that," replied Harry in softer tones.

Alex stroked her hair and soon she began looking out at the whirling dust once more. What the hell was the matter with Harry? He looked excited, feverish. The man had some problems, that was certain. Mental problems.

Suddenly Alex blurted out, "For Christ sakes, you're *kidnapping* us. What is this? Are you high, or what?"

"High on expectations, that's all. Don't be so dramatic—and stop looking at the comm. panel. I've pulled the plug."

"Look at all those bogey men!" exclaimed On Lo. "They're going the same way as us. I don't want to talk to them. We don't *have* to, do we?"

Alex peered through the dust clouds and saw the child was right: they were weaving through the scattered ranks of gin on their way to the mountains. All at once Alex was as interested as Harry, in spite of the danger in which they were placing the child.

"You don't have to, Tiger. If any talking needs to be done, Harry or I will do it."

"Like hell," retaliated Harry. "Neither of us speak gin."

"Take it easy. The girl . . ."

"He keeps shouting," said On Lo.

She was annoyed. Alex could feel her small body go rigid. Harry took no notice, his attention obviously having been captured by the army of gin outside the vehicle.

Finally they came to a place where the gin crowds were so thick they had to stop the airwheeler. Alex could have made his move then. The problem was, it was too late. He was as fascinated by the scene as his room-mate. The only member of the party who seemed unhappy about staying was On Lo.

"I want to go home."

"Don't worry. You stay in here. It's safe. Harry and I just want to see what's outside."

Harry nodded eagerly and the two men climbed out of the hatch. The wind was crashing around the side of the mountain, clattering amongst the scree on the slopes and tearing up handfuls of sand to fling in the direction of the two men. Beyond the ridge it looked as if it would be comparatively calm. It reminded Alex of the days when he had witnessed storms over the sea on the Angles coast: wild, crazy days, when the rearing waves had teeth, and ripped and bit each other with a savageness that frightened him beyond measure.

"Let's get behind that ridge!" he yelled. They closed the hatch carefully behind them but their caution seemed totally unnecessary. The gin were quite uninterested in the craft. They had eyes only for a spur of rock not far ahead and it appeared that nothing would turn them from their path. Alex had never seen so many of the creatures in one place. Not a sound came from their vocal flaps. They moved in a silent, determined flood towards that bright spur.

Bright? Yes, behind it was a powerful light of some kind, *coming from the direction of the night.*

"What is it, Harry?" asked Alex in a whisper. He almost

took the other man's hand in his own for reassurance. Harry appeared not to notice.

"I don't know. This is what I came to find out."

The pair of them joined the flow and as they rounded the spur they were temporarily blinded. A dazzling spiked star had settled on the peak of the tallest mountain and its white fire illuminated the thousands of gin that lay, face-forward, in the lanes of its light.

"Harry . . ."

"I know. I know."

"But look."

"I can see them."

Harry turned and ran back to the vehicle, leaving Alex with an irrational fear that now he was alone the gin would turn and attack him. There seemed to be so many, all still, as if mesmerized by the light. They seemed to be bathing in it, their eyes transfixed. Alex turned to follow Harry but they almost collided as Harry returned at a run.

There were purple and green patches before Alex's eyes and he had difficulty in adjusting his vision to the objects in Harry's hand. Glasses. Dark glasses. They would be able to see the light source.

Near the peak of the tall, fang-like mountain was a large concave section high enough to be caught directly by the sun. Within this irregularly shaped bowl was a crystal bed unlike any Alex had ever seen or heard about. The crystals themselves must have been huge and multifaceted, for they reflected the rays of the sun with such intensity that the valley was a channel of brightness cutting across the dawn country. There was colour, too, around the reflector, where the crystals had a prismatic effect.

"It is a natural?" Alex asked.

The question was misunderstood. "Who knows? I mean the supernature . . ."

"No, no. Has it been deliberately cut that way? Or is it something that just happened—a rock fracture or something?"

The answer was merely a shrug. It was uncanny, the silence coupled with this incandescent hypnotic light. Over the floor of the valley the gin lay in rows. The overall effect was like the peaceful aftermath of some terrible massacre: bodies arranged neatly for the mourners to pass by. At the far end of the valley were two narrow tracks, which appeared to circumnavigate the fiery mountain. Gin passed along them, joining their fellows. Alex watched as each one rounded the spur to be stricken into immobility on contact with the imbedded star. Slowly, eyes still on the light source, their faces bathed in serenity, they found a place amongst the bodies and sank to the ground. This was their symbol, their rock motif. Not the sun, as Harry had thought, but a reflection of its rays in a star form. Everything bathing in white light. The brain saturated with colour.

How could one convey this experience back to the raft? They could take pictures, though Harry did not seem to have brought a camera of any kind, or they could describe the scene and the effect upon themselves, but there was no way of putting across the emotion. By the time they got back to the raft that part would have gone.

"I'm going to paint such a picture. Am I going to paint!" said Harry fervently. "This is unique, absolutely unique. I told you, Alex. I *knew* it would be something like this. The milestones weren't there for show—and we're the first. The very first. The Old Man won't be able to take this away from us."

Alex was about to answer when something caught the corner of his eye. A small figure had stepped out into the streams of light and stopped, her eyes upon his face.

"On Lo!" His voice sounded unnaturally loud in the valley's silence, away from the noise of the winds.

She smiled and turned to look directly into the reflector. Suddenly she stiffened, her small arms rigid. She reached out then, with her hands towards the sparkling mountain peak. Both Alex and Harry let out some sort of sound, completely unintelligible, as her hair stood on end and crackled with visible static. Her lips moved in a face that began shining with an internal unnatural energy. Alex remembered then: the trigger which had created the trinity on Earth. A shock to the vision centre of the brain had produced the original effect. What now?

"On Lo?"

"She's back, uncle." On Lo smiled. Then the light on her face seemed to arc upwards from where she stood, curving out over their heads towards the horizon on the edge of the day. Such was its intensity that Alex was blinded, even though he was still wearing his dark glasses. When his sight returned, she was gone. He screamed in fright. No trace of her remained upon the spot where she had been standing.

"What happened?" he heard Harry asking. "Where?" The questions belonged to a child. They were both children, at that second, incomprehension draining their minds of any mature thought processes. Distress welled up in Alex's throat. He could not speak for a moment. Had he done so, he might have choked upon his heart.

"She's gone," he said at last.

"Where? Where?"

The words had no meaning. There was no answer. The balloon of reality had been pierced by two small children. Alex fought to retain a grip upon sanity. A tourniquet was being applied to his mind, stemming the flow of reason. He had no answer. There was no answer. "Where" was a place, and On Lo was in another dimension.

18 A Killing

Probably because there was no breeze in the valley to carry it away, the multitude of reverent gin produced an odour Alex recalled from his days on the farm. It was the smell of cabbages rotting in the silo. Alex tried to concentrate on the smell, tried to build within himself a revulsion for the gin. That stink was a body odour: sweat or faeces or something like that. He wanted to hate the gin in order that he could believe they were responsible for On Lo's death.

Was she dead, though? Or was she something else? Something incomprehensible to a normal man. He would have liked to have thought of it as a spiritual ascension, but her body had gone too. In its place was a familiar sensation. Besides, it was difficult to think of little On Lo as being divine. She was just a small girl—lovable and sweet, and a little out of the ordinary, but not an omniscient, omnipotent God that dealt in universal justice.

The smell made him feel sick but he could not blame the gin for On Lo. That was his fault: his and Harry's.

"What're we going to do?" asked Harry in a dull voice. "We can't go back without her. We'll have to search for a bit ... I know she's gone, but they won't understand back at the raft. We'll *have* to make the effort at least. You and I saw her disappear, but they didn't. They'll think we hallucinated. Something caused by the light. You know they'll never believe us," he concluded.

Alex's mind was buzzing. It was as though someone had taken the world and tilted it on its edge: he was about to slide from the surface and fall spinning through empty space. Through this uncanny vertigo came Harry's words and Alex knew that his companion cared nothing about the loss of the child. Harry was still indulging. He wanted an excuse to see more of the gin ritual. The creatures were still pouring into the valley. Somewhere at the head they were filing off into the mountains.

"Harry," he began, hopelessly. He knew he was wasting his breath. The artist was obsessed with the moment. Even the apparent death of a child was not going to deter him from following the experience through to its conclusion.

Alex realized that Harry was no longer in control of himself. Something had taken hold inside and was manipulating the puppet body, influencing the malleable artistic brain. His companion was beyond persuasion.

Yet On Lo was gone, and in her place was a faint atmospheric disturbance resembling static electricity. Was that a replacement for flesh, blood and bone? Perhaps the mind or the spirit or the soul was still present, still existing in this worldly state, the body a superfluous carrier, no longer needed and therefore reduced to dust?

On the edge of reason, and sick with the effort involved in trying to understand the incomprehensible, Alex fell to his knees. Somewhere in the back of his mind there registered the thought that Harry was wandering amongst the gin—an Alice in Wonderland.

The giant fell. A sun dropped from its place in the sky and hurtled spinning into the shaft of space, over and down, until the rose-to-ashen spot was not part of the vault of the sky. Yet suns do not fall—they collapse or they explode, but they do not suddenly let go of their holds on the firmament and disappear from sight.

Why not? thought Alex. Why don't they vanish down the throat of the universe, as small Chinese girls do? Surely if there is one scintilla of magic, then all is magic? One shade of supernatural, then shadows abound? If, say, a single man can remove the most insignificant of the laws of scientific fact for one split moment in time, then nothing is ordered and chaos rules. There are no fractions in thaumaturgy: a rock becomes a bird that flies, a sun falls, a child disappears and leaves a trace of something indefinable in the air. Anything can happen at any time.

Such thoughts were birds picking at the threads of sanity

and Alex vomited words into the dust in an effort to cleanse his mind and pull himself back to his former state of belief in the cosmos. For a while he was still, adjusting to the thought that perhaps he had witnessed a phenomena which *was* within the laws of physics, yet new to mankind? If he could accept this he could help himself. A change had taken place—a change of state not previously experienced, not yet *recorded*. The latent energy released as a result of the metamorphosis was an accidental gift. The collective wish would provide the human and gin destinies. Just so long, Alex thought, as the gin did not have the death wish as a racial neurosis.

After a time, he regained full consciousness and, shading his eyes, he sought Harry Dresnig amongst the prostrate gin. His tall shape was there, about a kilometre away, moving towards the mountains, one of several bodies. The rest were gin. Light flooded into Alex through his eyes. His body absorbed it, like a sponge filling with water. Sometimes it was an angry, slashing brightness cutting with laser keenness the nerves behind his eyes; at other times a winding river of white in which his whole being was immersed and bleached into purity.

Alex called the artist's name but the shout and its subsequent echoes in the windless valley either went unheard or they were ignored.

Climbing to his feet, Alex followed in Harry's footsteps. Neither of them had oxygen tanks and therefore the going was slow and laboured.

Somehow Alex had lost his dark glasses and the light was vicious, blinding him as he stumbled amongst the bodies. Occasionally he stepped on a limb but there was no sound of protest from the injured party. The nearer he came to the head of the valley the more gin fell in with him. The light seared his retinae, giving him a dazed, drunken walk and a brain awash with organic colours. Harry was ahead of him somewhere, following his own inarticulate path to an unknown destination. Where were they going? Or more accurately, thought Alex, where was Harry going? He himself was just stepping in the footsteps of an artist whose personality ran on airwheels. A feverish man, looking for a way to satisfy his craving for new themes, new artistic dimensions. Alex wanted to shout, "It's in the man, Harry, not the place!" but it would have been foolish. Besides, he was out of breath and his chest was heavy.

They began climbing, up into the darkness of the mountains below the crystal mirror. Soon Alex began having difficulty in keeping his footing. Gin jostled him, but apparently by accident. They too must have been tired and the path was narrow. Once, he paused to look back, and through the swimming amoeba-like shapes of colour saw that the valley below was dotted with natives, stationary save for the occasional figure. It was an eerie sight. Far in the distance, sunward but still within the dawn, were some patches of surface water, shining like splashes of cooled solder. They shimmered in the blinding light rays, burning their paths through his brain.

Suddenly Alex thought he caught sight of Harry's tall thin form rounding a curve on the path ahead. Had it been Harry? Or one of the gins, the originals, the Carthaginians, taller than his fellows and walking on his hind limbs? It was impossible to tell, for in this light they were only shadows. Hazy silhouettes against a backdrop of violent brightness.

The mountains were malevolent hunched shapes that crowded the walkers into a narrow pass. Alex sensed an oppressive atmosphere ahead and he began to jump the queue of gin that were filing through the narrow gap, hoping to reach Harry before Harry reached ... what?

Once through the pass, an acrid smell met Alex's nostrils. It was the stink of smouldering root. Torches had been lit to show the path from the pass to a cave entrance—and beyond. The atmosphere was foul with their burning and Alex began a fit of coughing which he fought to control, stooping lower to try to find oxygen more substantial than he was already getting.

The cave was a tall narrow fissure in the wall of the mountain, wide enough for a single person to enter.

Oxygen must have been filtering through from the outside. The dimly lit passage snaked into the rock face and Alex followed the figure ahead, now aware of a new fear—confined spaces. Between claustrophobia and agoraphobia was the comfortable area taken up by an Earth city. How Alex yearned to be in one at that precise moment. London, New York,

Bombay, Singapore—any of them. Instead, he was light-years from comfort and many kilometres from safety.

A terrible thought occurred to Alex as he shuffled deeper into the side of a mountain, an active member of an inescapable native ritual about which he knew nothing at all. *Perhaps Harry had come to his senses and had doubled back, leaving Alex to take part in whatever it was that was happening at the end of the line?* Blood pounded in Alex's temples and he almost panicked. Had he been able to turn without disturbing the gin, he might have attempted to claw his way back, over the natives, to the entrance. As it was, they were packed so tightly he could not even twist his body. Misery clutched at his heart and soon he fell into a state of dispassionate belief in the inevitable. What was coming was coming, be it the gas chambers or Eldorado.

They came out into an open chamber of sorts, a cavern on the side of the mountain just below the reflector. The bottom lip of the crystal had curved down and under, filling the chamber with light. Inside were tiers of stone seats, sweeping upwards to form an amphitheatre which appeared to be almost full. Alex was ushered to a seat in the upper tiers and he sat down before searching the audience for Harry. Finally he saw the artist's pinched face, white with anticipation, sitting just three rows up from the stage area. Harry's eyes were fixed on a small dais in front of him. Clearly this was to be the culmination of the ritual and Harry was not going to miss a single event. Beyond the stage the edge fell away, a sheer drop to the valley below. Although the cavern exit was oblique to the sun's rays it was unbearably hot. The beams of light followed a zigzag course, from crystal to crystal, to finally strike the back of the stage area.

Perspiration ran from Alex as he tried to attract Harry's attention without making a noise. The artist took no notice of the gestures and Alex slumped back before shouting, "*Harry!*"

The sound echoed loudly throughout the amphitheatre and a thousand heads turned towards the source of the disturbance. Some gin near Alex made certain sounds. He interpreted them as notes of disapproval. Harry looked up but had regained his former position almost immediately. Finally a deep silence descended.

Two gin stepped from the shadows at the side of the cavern. Both were carrying crude clubs—rocks with holes through which were threaded fibre ropes. Maces? They stood well away from the dais and waited. Guards? Security? The gin on the end of the front row left its seat, padded across to the dais and stood on it, facing the audience. A deep silence had descended on the hall.

Nothing happened. The gin on the dais merely stood, stone-still, while all heads craned forward. Alex could see the ears of the audience turned towards the solitary figure. There was a strange, intense atmosphere within the cavern. Alex felt as if his body was overheating; he could feel the blood pulsing behind his eyes. The figure on the dais waited.

Something had happened to Alex's power of perception. It had been sharpened. He could see ... could see ... could *perceive* the internal workings of the gin's anatomy. Alex felt heavily drugged but not sleepy. He was alert, his senses acute. He was aware of emotions that were not originated by him. The feelings of others mingled with his own. When Alex concentrated deeply, the gin's bodily juices flowed noisily within its frame.

The gin left the dais and regained its seat. Its neighbour took the stand. Alex could hear its breath hissing through its nostrils. The acoustics were superb. Even its heartbeat was audible. The design of the theatre produced, either by natural causes or for a purpose, the exact conditions for the transmission of base audio frequencies. But Alex could *see* too: he was aware of a dozen pulses or more, palpitating, beating.

Several more gin took their turns on the dais before the first one was attacked. There was a sudden buzz from the audience and the club-wielding "security" gin swiftly felled the unfortunate creature with a single blow. Alex could not catch his breath for a moment. He felt a stab of anxiety mixed with sadness. His respiratory system was ahead of his conscious thought and the action was so swift it took several seconds for the incident to register. Then they dragged the crushed corpse away and the next gin in line took his place on the dais as if nothing had happened.

Well, what the hell *had* happened? Alex couldn't understand what the creature had done to deserve such punishment. Nothing that the previous participants had not done. Why, then?

The ears listened intently. Alex observed. Soon another gin was beaten: broken in two. Their skeletons seemed so fragile. But Alex had it now. He had caught the difference in the rhythm. This one, probably like the other, though he hadn't really noticed at that time, had an irregular heartbeat.

They were listening to each other's hearts.

The whole exercise was a body scan, for respiratory complaints, heart problems. It was not just a matter of listening to the equivalent of blood rushing through arteries and witnessing organs carrying out their multitudinous and complex tasks: it was an inspection of every inhabitant of New Carthage, for malfunctioning body parts.

Alex looked about him. Harry still seemed fascinated in the grisly scenes being enacted before him. They had to get out. Alex tried to move along the row but was firmly pushed back into his seat by his neighbours. The commotion he caused turned a few heads below and he could see Harry giving him a look of annoyance. *The artist was still wearing his dark glasses.*

Harry, thought Alex, don't you know what's happening here? He wanted to scream it. Perhaps if he did become angry, shouting and laying about with his fists they might scatter? *Or* they might cast him over the lip of the cavern, into the stillness of the valley.

It was too late. He saw Harry assisted to his feet. They motioned him towards the dais. Funny thing was, Harry looked pleased with himself. Was he so stupid? No, once on the dais his face took on a worried frown and he tried to step down. The two gin with the clubs indicated that he should go back. Harry looked uncertain, and then put his foot back on to the dais.

They listened.
They studied.

"No!" shouted Alex, terrified now. He could hear Harry's heart beating, pounding out its irregular pattern. The murmur. The heart murmur. They could all hear it. They could all see it. Alex, the audience, the executioners.

The clubs struck several times. Alex turned away and was violently sick. He sat, white-faced, awaiting his turn. He was quiet now, resigned to whatever was in store for him. Once on the dais he felt his heart racing, the result of a mixture of different kinds of fears, some he could not even identify. To his amazement he passed the test, his heart's rhythm being even and strong, his respiratory organs functioning smoothly.

Once the audience had, to a member, undergone the test, the gin carried the bodies of the dead reverently on their shoulders through an exit on the far side of the amphitheatre.

Behind the mountain a second valley was littered with burning torches between which were displayed the bodies of the freshly dead. The corpses were arranged with the arms and legs outstretched to form the shape of a star. Every limb touched a partner's extremity. Harry's now cold hands touched the paws of his two immediate neighbours. They lay on their backs. *Spread-eagled, face-upwards towards the pit of the sky,* thought Alex.

Poor Harry had not deserved such an end. Now he was to hold hands with his alien killers for the rest of eternity. What did it matter? Harry was either nothing or somewhere else, like On Lo. The only difference in her case was that there were no remains, merely an additive to the atmosphere. He could feel it gently coursing through his veins and bones as he stared out over the gin graveyard. He was happy to think of her in terms of immortality—Harry too, who had left part of himself behind in his paintings.

Later, Alex was to discover that the Captain and other members of the raft had not been prepared to ignore the gin pilgrimage but had sent crew members to investigate. It was, after all, a basic function of the colony that they were there to observe the native culture. Alex met the expedition party on returning to the valley of prayers. It was led by Maya Kleppel.

Commander Maya Kleppel found Alexander Craven wandering amongst the rock formations at the head of the valley. He looked gaunt and shaken, and was mouthing obscenities under his breath. He had obviously been through a bad time so she did not question him too closely at that particular point, beyond establishing that the artist, Harold Dresnig, was dead—killed by the gin—and that the child, On Lo, was apparently dead. (A subsequent detailed search revealed no trace of the child's whereabouts and the official verdict was "missing, presumed dead".)

On learning of the ceremony in the cavern, Commander Kleppel despatched three of the personnel under her command to the cavern. They forced an entry through the waiting gin and left the amphitheatre by the exit passages, encountering the minimum of resistance. None of the party, two of which were women without exceptional physical strength, was carrying weapons. Captain Alexander, in his final summing up of the situation, concluded that Dresnig and Craven were to some degree responsible for at least the death of the former in that they had apparently taken part in a native ceremony willingly and without sensible regard to the consequences. Their state of mind, the report conceded, was possibly influenced by the hypnotic effect of a powerful native beacon. The rescue party had been wearing dark visors. Dresnig had been exposed briefly to the unfiltered light. It was clear that both men acted with extreme irresponsibility.

The final verdict was recorded as "death by misadventure". The report added that though Craven could not be exonerated from all blame for the events which occurred immediately prior to Dresnig's death, he had apparently acted in a more responsible manner than his companion. Although both men, like all human residents of Stingray Raft, were under martial law, no disciplinary action was recommended. Alexander Craven would *not* be informed of the contents of the report.

Commander Kleppel had helped compose a separate report on the child, On Lo. While, in essence, it dealt with the facts of the girl's disappearance, the concluding paragraph attempted to explore the possible known scientific causes of the incident. There had been, for example, several cases of

223

spontaneous combustion throughout history on Earth—people who had caught fire without any cause being apparent.

In 1938 there had been the case of a twenty-two-year-old girl named Phyllis Newcombe who was dancing with her boyfriend when she combusted before a room full of people. There were several other cases but such incidents were so uncommon they received little scientific attention. It was possible that people had dematerialized before, without witnesses. Perhaps On Lo's case was just the first to be reported. It was strange, but no more supernatural than spontaneous combustion.

Commander Kleppel was prepared to accept, as fact, a change of state from flesh, blood and bone to pure energy. Captain Alexander was less inclined but, nonetheless, endorsed the report.

19 A Crisis Passed

Captain Miro Alexander was at the helm of his raft, guiding her gently over the undulations of New Carthage. A crisis had passed and two young people had been lost. The Captain stared out at the gin. Their ceremony was over and the post-culling migration was in progress. Immortality was still a dream. They did not live forever but, like certain other creatures, thinned their own ranks of the halt and sick amongst them. Sad, but perhaps necessary to them. There was no place in a nomadic race for the lame.

Their religious doctrine, however it was communicated, obviously preached a care of the sick *up to a certain point*. At that point, ritual euthanasia took place and the dead held hands in a communal grave. Together their spirits were safe. In company they moved out into the sun and eternity. The mesmerizing effect of the crystal bank would possibly ensure the absence of pain. The weak removed, the fit walked on, a race without encumbrances.

He shuddered. It was not a policy he would advocate for the human race but he was forbidden to interfere with the gin culture. Perhaps that would change now?

He locked his hands behind his back, emphasizing the barrel chest. A well-fed Caesar, he thought. His image and his role. Harry—well, Harry was the sort of man the Captain would like to have been: carefree, insolent, openly contemptuous of authority. There had been some superiors in Miro Alexander's life whom he could have willingly destroyed with his tongue. But he wasn't made that way. Pity. Harry was, but then Harry was many things. One thing he wasn't was a Captain with responsibilities.

He had loved Harry because he was Harry—no other reason. I can love a bird, a deer, a leopard—I don't need to justify each affection, he thought. This man was a wild creature that stayed by my side, not because he had any fondness for me, but because he could use me: staid, rooted, dependable me. The rock to which the bird always returns to roost. Immovable. Instead Harry had relied upon a man who was near to himself. Not as eccentric, of course, but still a man with a mind full of feathers. Craven.

Then there was the child. The less he pondered that problem the better. He was too old for such ideas. The child had disappeared. Period.

Just then a gin climbed on to one of the stabilizing fins on the port-leaning edge. It lay on the warm metal and appeared to be resting. It was a youngster. They were bolder, this new generation. Soon they would be hammering on the airlocks requesting admission. Familiarity and all that, he sighed. He pressed a switch which retracted the stabilizer and dumped the young gin by the wayside. There was a flicker of annoyance on its face as it picked itself up, but it didn't appear to be hurt. Good thing. The Captain had pressed the switch on impulse, forgetting the grave consequences of injuring a gin. He did not want any more deaths on his hands. One—two—were enough for any man.

Ooma had watched the incident with a certain amount of satisfaction. The one that had fallen in the dust was an enemy, a trespasser of oneroot holes. It had no respect for ownership, that one, and transgressed at every opportunity. Perhaps now it would be less eager to claim what others had found. Ooma had the right to punish wrongdoers. On a third cycle, Ooma was now a member of the oligarchal *vilpa* which was the top stratum of a complex clan hierarchy. In the culling Ooma had wielded a *nirna*—the mother-stone.

Having survived the *manaha* had given Ooma back some of the confidence that had been slipping away of late. There had been that argument at the oneroot hole, and the second incident with the injured newcomer. Both times Ooma had taken backward steps. That was bad. Backward steps mean Gota was displeased with Ooma and was calling before the time. But the *manaha* had gone well. Ooma was fit and strong and need to have no fear. Next time ... well, that was a long way in the future. Many steps forward. And stepping *forward* to death was good.

Something else had occurred which was, for once, to the advantage of the *vilpa*. The breeding cycle of the drinkbulbs had accelerated. Now they increased rapidly in number and food was plentiful.

Life was beginning to mellow.

Familiarity with foxes bred, if not contempt, then possibly a
control of fear and doubt. That time he had met his fox, face
to face in the grass, he had conquered much of his fear of the
animal. Now he had come face to face with another animal—
death. Had he conquered his fear of death? Perhaps, but then
he doubted he was still sane as a result.

He switched on Nicole's letter. Perhaps she could help him
forget?

"Hello, Alex, it's Nicole. I expect you were wondering when you
were going to hear from me again. Thank you for your tape ex-
plaining the circumstances surrounding On's leaving—we both
know she has not *disappeared*, so *now*, I think, we can afford to be
less emotional than the situation might otherwise warrant. You
must have received my previous communication to you and
Captain Alexander regarding the simultaneous—although we
didn't know it at the time—leaving of Ti.

"Obviously I was frantic, apart from receiving a shock which
stunned me—as you know, I was holding Ti's hand at the time of
the transformation. Can I call it that? I think so. For three weeks
I just walked and walked, hoping to come across her, perhaps
standing on the beach, or riding that old mare.

"Gradually I came to accept the fact that she had gone forever.
I still get a lump in my throat—I can't help it—talking . . . never
mind. Then your letter arrived. Well, you probably went through
the same sort of terrible time I did myself. I know you were very
fond of both of them.

Jacey keeps asking me—oh, Jacey's a girlfriend by the way. You
never met her but we talk about you. Jacey wonders whether the
twins are now *holy*—you know we talked about it, quite often,
when they first produced the field. But I think if the twins have
created *God*, or the *Holy Ghost*, then mankind has made God and
not God, Man. You see what I mean? It can't be true . . ."

Alex stopped the tape to consider her words. Was this a new
God? He thought not. A new shining firstness of a unique

power, perhaps, but Alex was not prepared to accept that as a definition of God.

"Nothing has happened yet, here on Earth, that convinces anybody of the presence in the universe of our twins—you remember we had the long summer in the Angles. Nothing like that has happened yet, and this time the power must be a thousand times more potent. I keep expecting something to happen, don't you?"

He did, but then again, he was not sure they would recognize the change. The energy field must span the gulf between the two worlds, Earth and New Carthage—and possibly radiated beyond. Alex gathered together his thoughts on the twins and their godhead. *The metamorphosis of the twins had polarized the planets of New Carthage and Earth: between these two worlds was now an invisible field of energy having benign powers.* At Manston the catalytic shock to On Lo, on being confronted by her bogey man, had resulted in a manifestation of the closeness factor that bound the twins together. They themselves had acted as the poles for their creation on Earth. This minor nexus had been severed by distance. Worlds apart, the energy needed to link their empathic oneness was so powerful the transformation had reached its apex. The twins themselves had been drawn into their own creation to become part of it: a wholeness, a single entity. The mana had overpowered its carriers. This affected at least two races alien to one another in thought and culture. Perhaps there were others out there, that fell within the field's influence? In which case a *collective wish*, encompassing all individual minds, might be so subtle in physical form as to escape immediate recognition. Possibly one day they might look at each other and say, "Yes of course! Why didn't we see it before?" But now they were sitting on top of it with no clues to guide them and their only aids inadequate senses.

"Jacey is very good with me, Alex. You know how difficult I can be. I am a cold person by nature—Jacey has managed to draw me out, produce warmth I never knew I had . . ."

What was this leading to? Alex could detect a note of forewarning in Nicole's voice which made him anxious to finish the letter.

"We now live in the City—yes, I *finally* moved back—in a nice little apartment on the West Side. It's not luxurious but we have all we need, which is mostly each other. I'm sure you understand, Alex, and won't be too upset. It was you, after all, who introduced me to Lila and allowed me to find out just who I am. I don't *blame* you for that—I'm glad. I like being me. And I shall always be fond of you, you know that, don't you? *Never* be afraid to come and see us when you get home. You will always have a kind reception—you are part of my life after all, a nice part . . ."

Lila! Why was he always so stupid? With Lila, it would have been a game—something new—but, of course, Nicole took everything so seriously . . .

"One of these days you *will* be home, I know, and I look forward to that time. So does Jacey—who is a kind, sweet person, Alex, as I'm sure you'll confirm . . ."

Confirm? Did she need his confirmation? His endorsement of her choice? Nicole was her own person and whatever she wanted for her life, Alex wanted for her too. He hadn't always felt that way but he did now.

"She's obviously dying to meet you. Well, it's autumn here at the moment—or rather, out there, in the Angles. I still think of poor Pagey and his tragic death but perhaps he and the twins . . . no, that's silly, I know, because the twins aren't dead.
"Oh, you'll be pleased to hear that the suggestion you made concerning quick-growing trees, and turning the Angles into a plantation, is going ahead. The stems are suspicious of it at the moment but I've spoken to a number of them and they're beginning to see the benefits of the scheme. It's possible they may even be able to purchase the land providing they turn most of it to forest. The Government is now training Forestry Commission Officers—perhaps we're crawling out of our holes at last?
"I am back working for John Strecker by the way. He is still the busy man, never stopping. I can't tell you about the project because it's classified and you *know* what a blabbermouth you are, ha ha. John is very bald now but doesn't care even though Jacey makes fun of him when she meets us for lunch. All he worries about is work. No change, you see.
"I was sorry to hear about your friend, Harry Dresnig. Were you very close? He sounds a nice person."

Now where the hell did she get that idea from? Harry might have been a lot of things but he was never "a nice person". Certainly Alex would not have given that impression, even

accidentally, in his letters. He guessed she had invented it because Harry had been killed. Entering the kingdom of the
dead automatically made one "a nice person".

He did not bother to listen to the rest of the letter. It would
be small talk, and he had learned the lesson she had wanted to
teach. There was no point in returning to Earth—not for the
sake of Nicole, anyway.

So that left him with New Carthage—if he was allowed to
stay, and no one was chasing him home at the moment—and
Maya. He had been sleeping with Maya for some time. She
had "nursed" him through the shock of Harry's death with
affection and—yes, hell yes—with love. But did he love her?
When he thought about it, he did. Then why not tell her?
Why not? But not so soon after the arrival of Nicole's letter.
That would not be fair to himself or Maya.

Maya had joined a cable-break team on a difficult exercise.
The very tip of the tail, the segment peppered with solar cells,
had become detached. Since this segment hovered above the
ground *and* contained the power, it swam away into the day
like a blind wayward snake. About a third of a kilometre in
length and very light, it was subject to the whims of turbulent
winds. Maya and her team chased it with instruments but it
had a head start and was fickle in its choice of direction at any
one time.

Finally they caught up with it, harnessed it and hauled it
back to be spliced to the main segment.

When she got back to the raft she found Alex missing. He
had checked out at Control: "Gone for a walk," they told her.
Since she had something important to tell him, she did like-
wise and was soon searching the faces of the evening strollers
around the raft for the chiselled features of her lover.

A question Maya had asked herself at the time of On Lo's
disappearance was: did she really believe in Alex's version of
the disappearance of On Lo? The most logical answer lay in
the state of Alex's mind at the time of the incident, coupled
with some natural disaster which had swallowed the child's
body whole. There were numerous such mantraps: earth-
quakes, volcanoes, quicksand, deep water, the Carthaginian

day . . . It would have been easy to tell herself that one of these agents had removed On Lo from sight and the shock had resulted in Alex being temporarily deranged. But then there was that indefinable presence in the atmosphere which the Captain could not bring himself to officially acknowledge but which all the raft's occupants could sense . . . or even *feel*.

Yes, she had believed him, crazy as the story was. She could believe all the more easily because she loved him, although that alone would not sway her. Maya was too level-headed for that. She knew he was telling the truth because . . . because she *knew*. That was part of it, part of the new wave of sensitivity which the spirit of the children had produced. Nicole Toupe's letter had, of course, verified Alex's version and one or two people had to either hide their faces or apologize.

Alex had told her to watch for changes in their circumstances, not necessarily for the good, because they might not know what was good for them. The world might slow to a halt on its axis. That might be what the community desired—the gin and the humans—but would it be to its advantage?

There had been no change after eight months—or, if there had been, it was too subtle to recognize. Except that perhaps she and others felt a stronger desire to remain on New Carthage. Even taking into account the cramped state in which they lived. Maya would not have been unhappy to spend the rest of her life there, despite her condition. She only hoped Alex would feel the same way when she told him. It had been Maya's influence that had allowed Alex to remain on the planet, even though there was no *real* work for him any more. She had argued that one more communications expert was always useful, although she had to admit he found it difficult to earn his keep.

Alex was only her second love, although she had known several men. The first had been Akoba, a dynamic young man from one of the central African cities. Akoba had been intelligent and gentle, and had been enthralled rather than amused by her stocky, peasant-girl's body. Alex could never replace Akoba, who died en route to the small colony on Uranus when his ship's power system had a sudden burn-out, filling its compartments with a toxic gas. But second love was no less potent for being so placid. Neither, she reminded herself, was a *second coming*.

What they really needed, though, if they were going to stay on New Carthage, was a *second contact*.

It had always concerned her that if there was a race of beings within reach, who matched or surpassed the technological achievements of humankind, they might be warlike. Earth's most rapid progress had been made in times of war. It was only during an emergency situation that the expense, time and effort could be justified. Perhaps, though, these desired aliens will have passed through that immature stage of moral growth, she thought. Maybe they'll be as high-minded as they are technically brilliant. She did not think it was too much to hope for. Earth required company. It had reached a point of stale thinking and desperately needed an injection of new philosophies, new ideas, new hopes for the future. Left as it was, its inhabitants, and those of its neighbouring colonies, would withdraw further into themselves and become isolated introverts dreading, not hoping for, new contacts.

Was this the purpose of On and Ti? To inform distant cousins of a willingness to join with them? There had to be a *reason* for the twins. Surely that was it? A peaceful union of equals, or near-equals. A signpost pointing to a neutral meeting place where races could approach each other without fear, because each had explored the other through the third entity. Each experienced the intentions of the other and knew the time was right, for the catalyst had appeared.

Catalyst. That was the purpose of the twins! Her heart raced. She knew it was the answer.

They *were* coming.

The granting of a collective wish was merely a side-effect of the Trinity. Its real work had only just begun.

Excited with her conclusions, she ceased her daydreaming and sought Alex in earnest. She found him a half a kilometre from the raft, leaning into the wind.

"Alex."

"Hello, Maya." He kissed her cheek affectionately.

"Alex, I think I have the answer ... the twins. I know *why*."

233

She looked into his eyes and was shocked for a moment. He knew. He *knew*.

"I've spoken to one or two people," he said. "Some feel it, some don't. It seems to hit us all at different times."

"Why didn't you tell me?" She was hurt.

"And spoil your revelation?" he smiled. "And anyway, although I was sure, I wanted to hear it from others. Especially, I wanted to hear it from you. So much has been happening to me, this past year, I'm no longer certain of myself. I suppose I lacked the confidence . . ."

"What I can't understand," said Maya, taking his hand, "is why Harry had to die."

"I've thought about that, too, and I've come to the conclusion that he didn't *have* to die. It was an accident—my fault, Harry's fault, but not the fault of the twins. It just happened. There'll always be accidents, Maya."

"Yes, I suppose so." She sighed. "I never liked him much but I wish he were here now. He would be *so* excited."

"Yeah." Alex's eyes took on a far-away look. "Still, he's not and that's that. He wasn't a good friend, in the true sense of the word, but, by God, he was volatile. Interesting. He made life colourful."

"Right. But stop brooding. Let's think about the future, not mope on the past."

He nodded. They appeared to become uncomfortable again.

"What's the matter, Alex?"

"Before we forget the past," he said, "I want to tell you something. Something about that day in the cave."

"Yes?" What was it now?

Alex gave a little laugh and then confessed. "Perhaps I could explain something. While we were there, Harry and I, participating in their game . . . okay, not a game . . . anyway, I thought my increased powers of perception were directed solely towards the functions, the mechanics of an organic body. I could hear the heartbeat, the respiratory movements, the bodily juices—in Harry's case, blood, enzymes, lymph—I could hear them coursing through their tubes, washing through the liver and the pancreas. I could see the network of veins in Harry's thin frame, observed his pulses throbbing, saw every movement of every muscle all at one time. It's difficult to explain."

He paused and she said gently, "Go on."

"Well, all this was a *whole*, you understand? Something I was part of and yet separately witnessing from a detached position. I was *aware* of everything at once. I examined all the cells that went into making Harry, as a person, and saw them each as a single entity ... But it wasn't just that. You see, fear is a physical thing as well as mental ..."

Oh God, no. What was he going to tell her?

"Jesus, Maya," he said, almost in tears, "I could feel Harry's fear. I could smell it, see it, hear it and *feel* it. Mostly I could feel it, and sometimes now I wake up ... It's in my nostrils, my *head* ..."

She felt her own tears coming now and pulled his face to hers, quickly, to smother the emotion.

"It's okay," said Alex after a while. "I'm okay."

She still clung to him.

"I died with Harry, Maya, and he was terrified. *I* was terrified. If you could experience violent death, as I did, you'd understand. It's difficult to forget such an experience. You know we decided that it was a drug—that reflecting device, I mean—a drug affecting the brain in the way ... Look, it's a good thing I shall be dead by the time it comes round again."

She could feel his trembling against her body.

"Why, Alex?"

"Because ... and this may sound weird. It *is* weird. Because, I should want to go back again. Maya, I would be compelled to go back and do it again. Am I mad?" The words were spoken so softly the wind almost took them away without her hearing them.

"No, darling, you're not insane." Please don't be insane, she thought. I love you.

He laughed again and, looking into his eyes, she saw they had cleared. "Anyway, it's not likely I'll live for two hundred and fifty years so I shan't *have* to go back. I'll be all right, don't worry." He pushed her away from him, but gently. "Imagine going through that again?" he continued, but it was a terminal sentence. The subject would not be raised again between them. Not unless Alex *wished* the subject to be resurrected, and she had a feeling he wanted it very much to be dead. Very, very dead.

They began to walk back to the raft and Maya felt it was time to tell him.

"Alex."

"Yes?"

She took hold of his hand.

"We're pregnant."

This news took a little time to wash away the previous thoughts.

"You mean you're having a . . ."

"Hey, this is a corporate affair. I just happen to be the first to know."

He grinned. "You're right. What's our schedule, apart from getting married tomorrow?"

She became serious.

"Look, Alex, you don't have to do that. I don't even believe in Mathew Tse."

"Neither do I. That was Nicole. I *want* to marry you Maya. I like security."

She smiled. "And what about Nicole?"

He shrugged. "I could have been happy with her—but she doesn't need me. Nicole doesn't need a man. She's . . . adaptable. And anyway, she's too intense for me."

"Say it."

"What?" He pretended to be confused.

"Say it, you bastard," she repeated fiercely.

"Okay, I . . . it sounds silly like this. Why don't you wait for it to come naturally?"

"It might never."

"Don't be silly. I'm bound to say 'I love you' sooner or later."

She hugged him hard.

"You just did. You *know* you did. You meant it too."

He hugged her and tried to lift her off her feet, but she was too heavy for him.

"I'll go on a diet," she said, purposely introducing panic into her voice.

236

He laughed. He seemed infected by her earlier happiness now.

"It's your bones. They won't get any slimmer. You have heavy bones. Jesus, Maya, I don't care . . ."

Epilogue

They came from all corners of the galaxy—not one, but several races—in response to the field of energy that flowed between and around the planets of Earth and New Carthage.

"I told you," said the Captain. "I had a feeling."

Alex and Maya exchanged significant glances and then looked back to the skies.

Through the transparent roof of the Control Room they could see the first of the craft descending from the mother ships high over the dawn country. Craft of strange designs and colours, falling slowly out of the sky like pieces of a shattered sun.

"See the way they do it?" said Alex. "Autumn leaves. They slip from side to side on the winds, just like a leaf. See?"

"I can see, I can see," said the Captain, quietly. The whole population of Stingray Raft was at the portholes, watching the arrival of the aliens. He added, "I knew those winds would be useful for something one day."

Alex wondered whether similar expeditions had been despatched to Earth, the other end of the rainbow: whether humans had produced the first meeting place for the galactic races. Perhaps some were from beyond . . . ? Here his imagination seized.

There were some powder-soft landings, and then a long, heart-timed wait. Finally, one of the flat, crinkle-edged modules seemed to split into two pieces suddenly, allowing the watchers a sighting of the craft's interior. It was a jungle of bright tubes.

"Perhaps they're not in them?" suggested a disappointed voice. "Maybe they've sent unmanned vehicles for a look around?"

"No," replied Captain Miro Alexander, confidently. "They're

in there. It's just a case of shyness on both sides." He tightened the belt of his dress uniform. "Well, let's get out there. We might as well be first."

Alex felt his life had reached the needle point of its purpose. Were they the shepherds or the kings?